*Sun Sand
and
Second Chances*

*by
J.B. Pettry*

Copyright © 2023 by J.B. Pettry
All rights reserved. No portion of this book may be reproduced in any form without permission from the publisher, except as permitted by US copyright law.
This is a work of fiction. Names, characters, businesses, places, events, locales, and incidents are either the products of the author's imagination or used in a fictitious manner. Any resemblance to actual persons, living or dead, or actual events is purely coincidental.

For Tucker and Colin
I love you forever.

Costa Mesa California

MONET

"I need your help." Monet's heart was pounding, and her whole body was trembling as she approached the bell desk inside the entrance of the trendy White Rainbow hotel. "Do you see that man?" she asked the young bellhop as she gave a slight nod in the direction behind her.

"The man in the red Ferrari?"

"Yeah." Monet casually glanced over her shoulder to see the car pulling away from the hotel's covered entrance and into the late afternoon sun. "He's coming back to pick me up in about thirty minutes, but I need you to tell him that I checked out." The quiver permeating her body touched her voice. "Can you guys do that for me—" Monet's eyes flashed to the nametag pinned to the white shirt the bellhop wore, "—Brady?"

His brow puckered, and the smile he'd greeted her with slipped away. "I'm guessing you're not really checking out?"

"Not within the next thirty minutes, no." She felt ill, like a rock had settled in the pit of her stomach. "I... I need to call my parents," she stammered, "and, um... change my flight."

The young employee studied her for a moment, and if it hadn't been for her state of distress, Monet would have been flustered under his gaze. She'd noticed him earlier that morning when she'd checked in—who wouldn't? His tall frame, emphasized by the way his shirt hugged his broad shoulders, revealed a muscular build that was enough to have you looking twice. But add in his defined cheekbones, strong angular jaw, and thick dark hair that fell in pieces across his bronzed forehead—he was rather breathtaking.

If it weren't obvious he was an employee of the hotel, Monet would have assumed he was there for the same reason she was—John Wessler's Modeling Agency.

The uncommonly handsome bellhop stepped out from behind the desk. "Come with me," he said, not adding anything else. He guided Monet through the swoopy abstract and organic shapes that adorned the interior of the lobby, leading her to the reservation counter, where, thankfully, there were no other guests at that moment.

"Hey, Ashley," he greeted a petite woman with a blonde pixie cut that was a mess of spiky waves. "Looks like Sleaze-essler is at it again."

Monet's forehead furrowed. *Sleaze-essler?*

The desk clerk, Ashley, must have noticed Monet's puzzled expression because she chuckled. "That's Brady's nickname for him, but his first name is really Scum, and his last name is Bag."

"Talking about Mr. Wessler again?" A sharply dressed gentleman wearing a perfectly tailored charcoal suit stepped up to stand beside Ashley behind the counter. "At it again, is he?"

The frantic pounding of her heart and her urgent need to escape overshadowed Monet's confusion over the conversation. "I don't have much time to explain," she blurted. "But that man—Mr. Wessler—is coming back to pick me up, but I can't go with him... I mean, I won't—" Brady's hand on her arm startled her, and Monet flinched as her eyes shot to him.

"It's okay." He smiled softly. "We get it."

Monet's desperation for the past three hours, coupled with the compassion behind the young man's striking green eyes, brought her emotions to the surface, and tears grew thick behind her eyelids.

"Will you help me?" Her words came out shaky. "Will you tell him I checked out?"

"Miss..." the older gentleman behind the counter drew her attention back to him.

"Everly," Monet said. "Monet Everly."

"We are, rather unfortunately, all too familiar with Mr. Wessler and know his," he drew one eyebrow up, "intentions."

Monet's face instantly heated, and she dropped a humiliated gaze to the smooth marble check-in desk.

"This is in no way your fault," the man continued. "On the contrary, the fact that you have come seeking our assistance in the matter speaks highly of your moral character, and it will be my pleasure to assist you."

He directed his next words to the bellhop as he handed him an envelope. "Brady, this arrived a short time ago for Mr. Parker in room 810. I'd appreciate you delivering it, and along the way, why don't you see that Miss Everly gets tucked away in her room, and I'll handle things down here when Mr. Wessler returns."

"But... what are you going to do... to say?" Monet's thoughts were in a frenzy, and her stomach was a mess of nervous knots. *How did I get myself into this?*

"Oh, not to worry," Brady said. "There's a reason Mr. Roberts was named Manager of the Year three years running for White Rainbow Resorts. He can handle *any* personality type thrown at him. It's quite impressive, too," he added with a nod.

The mounting tightness in Monet's chest had been almost unbearable since she'd discovered Mr. Wessler's plan to take her to his yacht for dinner that evening, but there was something about the easygoing bellhop that seemed to loosen her nerves, and she mustered a slight smile. "I suppose being the manager of a hotel would teach you that."

Brady chuckled. "Just last week, we had a guest come in and request his hotel suite be entirely rearranged because of the furniture's placement on his aura."

"Mr. Roberts didn't miss a beat," Ashley added. "He explained how most furniture is secured to the floor and can't be moved. However, in the next breath, he explained how a certain angle of the sun has a more powerful effect on one's aura and that there just happened to be a room available to position him at the precise angle for optimal sunlight."

Brady laughed—a deep masculine laugh, and the sound spread a calming warmth over Monet, giving her a slight reprieve from the constant quivering in her core.

"And it indeed did the trick," Mr. Roberts said with another arch to his greying eyebrows. "Now, off you go. I'll deal with Mr. Wessler."

"Alright," Monet muttered, "Thank you."

"I, for one, can't wait to see this..." Ashley was saying as Brady escorted Monet to the hotel elevators.

John Wessler's *The Look* modeling contest. Monet huffed a disgusted breath and silently cursed herself and her best friend, Lily, for being so naïve and gullible. She wasn't sure if the nausea swirling in her stomach came from fear or the humiliation over being so trusting and foolish. Monet suspected it was probably both.

It all started three months earlier when she and Lily saw an advertisement for the contest inside *Vurve*—one of their favorite fashion magazines—and impulsively decided to enter each other. Monet and Lily were both eighteen, so technically, they didn't need their parents' permission. It wasn't until Monet received a letter notifying her that she'd been chosen as a finalist that she even told her mom and dad about it.

Looking back, Monet understood why her parents had reacted the way they did—with suspicion and apprehension. At first, it frustrated her when they hadn't squealed and jumped up and down the way she and Lily had at the news, but she still lived under their roof, and Monet respected them, so she didn't complain when her dad started digging around to find out if the contest was legitimate. Which turned out it was.

"So, I'm guessing you're either a finalist or the winner," Brady said as they stepped into the waiting elevator.

Monet's eyes bulged a split second before her forehead creased, coaxing a chuckle from Brady. "Yeah, we're pretty familiar with the modeling contest here at the hotel." He motioned to the panel. "Which floor?"

"Eight." Monet's voice was soft and still a little shaky.

"Wessler's agency always has out-of-state girls stay here, and not just for the annual contest. He puts them up here when he's scouting for models too."

Monet nodded. "Yeah, when I flew in for the finalist photo shoot last month, this is where my brother and I stayed." Monet lived in Rollingwood, Utah. When Mr. Wessler's agency explained that all finalists would fly in for a photo shoot to help determine the winner, her parents insisted that her older brother, Evan, accompany her. Monet wished he were with her on this trip, too.

A dazzling smile brightened Brady's face. "Which means..." his head tipped, "if you're back, you must be the winner."

Monet's fingers went to the silver chain dangling around her neck, and she started fiddling with it. "Yeah," she mumbled, suddenly unable to meet his eyes.

From the moment Monet received the phone call telling her she'd won The Look contest, she'd existed in a state of utter disbelief—complete shock. It still boggled her mind that she'd been chosen over the other girls who'd made the finals; every one of them was statuesque goddesses—tall, high cheekbones, and exotic. Monet was tall, not as tall as they were, but above-average height. And as far as high cheekbones and exotic, she didn't see it—at all.

Even with the embarrassing fact that for the past two years, Monet had been compared to a younger version of Nikola Povondra (a brunette Czechoslovakian supermodel from the 90s) when Monet, as her Grandma Everly called it, "blossomed," Monet still didn't see it. She still saw the same scraggly young girl with bucked teeth and no fashion sense whatsoever whenever she looked in the mirror. Of course, Monet had gone through the awkward years of wearing braces, and her teeth no longer swallowed her bottom lip when she bit down, but Monet still felt like that girl, unsophisticated and silly. She still saw every flaw, every blemish, and cringed when she looked at pictures of herself.

But even through the haze of shock and bewilderment over being chosen the winner, Monet couldn't help feeling excited and even a little proud.

Until that moment.

It was taking all of her strength not to break down and let loose the sob trapped in the back of her throat, or to allow herself to collapse in a heap of humiliation. That's how she felt; she was humiliated—embarrassed, and her body weighed heavily with disappointment.

"I was the winner," Monet shook her head, "but not anymore. The price is too high." She heaved a heavy sigh. "I should have known better." She allowed her eyes to shift to him awkwardly, wondering what the kind—and very attractive—bellhop was thinking.

Brady was studying her with a soft smile curved to his lips. He opened his mouth to say something, but the ding from the elevator distracted him right before the doors slid open.

He gestured with one hand that she should go ahead of him, and Monet didn't hesitate. She wanted to get to her room quickly and call her parents.

"I've got to deliver this," Brady said, holding up the envelope the hotel manager had given him. "But then I want to get back downstairs." A glint of amusement lit his eyes. "No way I'm going to miss seeing Sleaze-essler taken down a notch." He paused; a look of awe settled over his face as his gaze fixed on her. "It's about time."

Monet's eyes softened. Brady was obviously trying to help her feel better, but she knew she wouldn't rest easy until she was back home. After her afternoon with John Wessler, it might take even longer before she'd entirely rid herself of the sickening sensation torturing her insides.

"I'm sure Mr. Roberts will let you know when the creep is gone," Brady said. "But if you need anything, be sure to let us know." He flashed her a charming grin, and her heavy heart lifted a bit. "You can reach me directly if you ring the bell desk, okay?"

Monet nodded, managing the most sincere smile she could. "I will. Thanks."

She turned and headed to her hotel room, while Brady's errand took him in the opposite direction down the hall. Monet's frenzied mind didn't allow her to linger on how Brady's smile made her feel. Instead, the second he was out of her sight, the reality of what she'd been through that afternoon and the terrifying fact that John Wessler would be coming back to find her checked out of the hotel in mere moments brought a new level of shakiness to her hands as fear struck her core.

Monet slid the hotel keycard from her jeans' back pocket, fumbling a bit as she tried to insert it into the digital key slot. It took a few tries before the button flashed green, allowing her to open the door.

Once inside, she quickly bolted the door before heading straight to her backpack, which she'd flung onto the king-sized bed earlier. She unzipped the side pouch, removed her cell phone and charger, and immediately plugged it in and set it on the nightstand.

Monet landed in California earlier that day, and having an older smartphone model, the battery didn't last as long. She'd used her phone to read on the flight, and by the time she arrived at the hotel, the battery was at 5%.

When Mr. Wessler surprised her in the lobby upon her arrival and invited her to lunch to discuss the events that would take place the next day regarding her winning the contest, Monet hadn't the time to charge her phone and instead left it at the hotel.

As the winner of *The Look*, she'd been offered a contract with the John Wessler modeling agency and would appear in a music video with the Dazed Mystics, a popular up-and-coming pop band. That was why Monet was in California; filming for the music video started the next day.

She experienced a brush of guilt, realizing she'd be letting everyone down by not showing up for the video shoot, but Monet was also smart enough to know she hadn't signed a contract with the agency yet, so she couldn't legally be held accountable—at least she hoped not.

She needed to talk to her dad.

Monet plopped down on the bed, grabbed her charging phone, and dialed her dad's number.

*

Ten minutes later, Monet ended the call on her cell phone. She felt somewhat relieved about her legal obligations but not any easier about her current predicament. The conversation with her father went pretty much how she'd expected. He was furious! Not with her but with John Wessler. Both her dad and her mom were ready to jump on an airplane and fly to California.

When Monet relayed the events that had taken place that afternoon—the disgusting and nauseating way Mr. Wessler tried to touch her and the raunchy innuendos he threw at her almost non-stop, she'd kept it vague—Monet's parents didn't need to know how bad it got; they just needed to know the gist.

The first red flag that tipped Monet off about Mr. Wessler's intentions came as they walked from his car into the restaurant where they were to have lunch. He'd put his hand on the small of her back and casually let it slide a little further south. When Monet gasped and pulled back, Mr. Wessler chuckled—a slimy, skin-crawling chuckle—before saying something that made Monet's heart drop. *"I keep forgetting; you're a sweet, wholesome girl from Utah—don't worry, you'll get used to me touching you soon enough."*

From there, it was more of the same. Monet spent the entire lunch avoiding his attempts at touching her and trying not to react to his vulgar comments. She was ashamed she hadn't fired back at him by slapping his face or dumping her tomato bisque over his head, but she'd been stifled by fear—her mind frantically searching for a way to get away from him without letting him see how scared she was.

After lunch, Mr. Wessler took her to the modeling agency to confirm the details for the video shoot the next day. It was there that he casually mentioned his plan to take her to his yacht for dinner that evening. *"Think of it as a date,*" he said. His words dropped like a weight in Monet's stomach. The audacity of his assumption sent a shock through her—this was not business; it was clearly something else, something more predatory. Wessler informed her that they'd leave straight from his office since it was about an hour's drive south. Even amidst her suffocating panic as he detailed his plan, Monet knew one thing: there was no way she was going anywhere with him that night—or ever again.

In a desperate attempt to get away, Monet pasted on a smile and explained how she'd like to stop by her hotel to change her clothes and check in with her parents since she'd promised she would and hadn't.

Thankfully, Mr. Wessler agreed and said he needed to run an errand and would do so while she changed and made her phone call.

That was about twenty-five minutes earlier. He'd be returning at any moment. The realization was almost more than Monet could bear. Her hands were sweaty and tingled from jittery nerves.

The sound of a text message chimed from her cell phone, causing a shot of panic to burn her insides.

Is it him?

Summoning her bravery, Monet glanced at the message. A wave of relief washed over her when she saw it was from her mom.

Mom: *"Don't leave your room. Mr. Wessler is at the hotel. He called the house—boiling mad! He's talking to Dad now."*

With unsteady hands, Monet quickly replied.
"He called you? Why? What's he saying? What's Dad saying? I'm totally freaking out!"
Her eyes stayed glued to the cell phone screen.

Mom: *"I'll call you in a second."*

Monet didn't respond. Instead, she stood and paced until the feeling of nausea crept into her throat, causing her to dash into the bathroom for fear of losing what little she had in her stomach. Thankfully, she didn't. Instead, she caught sight of herself in the mirror and noted how her typically ivory skin looked even more pallid and how her blue eyes looked a bit wild—scared.

Unable to wait any longer, she turned her barely charged cell phone over in her hand and pressed *call* on the name *Mom*. It rang once.

"Dad just hung up with him—or rather, hung up on him," her mom said by way of answering.

"What happened?" Monet's mouth felt dry, and she swallowed. "Is he gone?"

"I don't know, but don't go downstairs until you've talked to the manager to make sure he's not in the hotel."

"Why did he call you guys?"

"He wanted to know what had happened and why you'd checked out and left. Dad let him have it! Told the man he was disgusting and that his actions toward you were appalling."

Monet's heart was in her throat. "How'd he take that?"

"He couldn't care less. He was huffing and puffing about the whole thing being unprofessional, about how the band's manager was expecting you *to be in the video, and what was he supposed to do now? Blah-blah-blah."*

"Oh." Monet grimaced, unable to stop the guilt from creeping in.

"But Dad gave it back just as good— put that man in his place." Her mom paused. *"Aside from the disclosure you signed when you entered the contest, you haven't signed anything else—right?"*

Monet's mind swirled, but she was confident she hadn't. "No, Mom, I didn't."

"Even if you did, we'd handle it."

"I know. But don't worry, I didn't sign anything else."

"Are you doing okay, sweetheart?" The underlying tone of agitation in her mother's voice softened. *"I know how excited you were about this whole thing, and I'm sorry that man turned out to be such a creep—that you had to endure such vile behavior. You didn't deserve it. Nobody does."*

Hearing her mother's comforting words helped settle the wild pounding of her heart. "Thanks, Mom. I'm still pretty rattled, but I'll be fine once I get home."

"Dad's calling the airline to change your flight; I hope you can fly home tonight."

"Yeah," Monet said. "Me too."

"I want you to know how proud I am of you for staying true to yourself, Monet. What you did was brave and—good. Dad's proud of you too. I'm sure he wants to tell you himself. He'll call you once he's got your new flight info."

A small smile formed on her lips. Monet had always known her mom and dad were something special—that she'd won the lottery as far as parents go. They always supported her and were always there to catch her when she fell. Evidenced at that moment when, instead of scolding or lecturing her with "I told you so," they chose to tell her they were proud of her. The knowledge triggered an unexpected release of tension, and for the first time in hours, Monet exhaled.

*

Unfortunately, the earliest flight Monet's father could book for her wasn't until the following morning, meaning she wouldn't be able to completely relax until then. After her phone calls with her parents, Monet spoke with Mr. Roberts, who assured her that Mr. Wessler had believed she'd checked out, especially after the furious man called her parents and confirmed it. Once she knew he'd left the hotel, Monet spent the next hour talking to Lily. Her best friend had felt unnecessary guilt, seeing as it was Lily's idea to enter the contest in the first place. Monet did her best to allay those worries, but knowing Lily as she did, her tenderhearted friend would likely harbor a small amount of blame for a while.

As Monet sat, winding down from the chaos of the day, she found the events blending into one long, frantic blur. She hadn't even had the chance to open her suitcase due to Mr. Wessler's unexpected appearance at the hotel right as she'd checked in. At least it would save her the hassle of repacking before she left in the morning.

With nothing to do, Monet walked to the window inside her hotel room and stared out onto the busy city from her view eight stories up. The sun was gracefully sinking below the horizon, and the lights of Costa Mesa were beginning to illuminate the world below.

Monet's gaze stayed fixed on the glass as she let out a defeated sigh.

Things had certainly not turned out as she'd expected when she left home that morning. It was surreal, in a way, how quickly things could change.

Ten hours earlier, she'd walked onto an airplane with the vision of magazine covers and fashion shows in her future—but not anymore. That vision and those dreams evaporated the moment Mr. Wessler—no, *Sleaze-Essler* showed his true colors. The thought of the handsome bellhop's nickname for the slimy modeling agent coaxed a chuckle from Monet.

She wished she could think of an excuse to see Brady again and somehow take a picture of him to show Lily.

Monet was willing to bet her best friend had never seen a man that attractive in real life.

Monet's mind started concocting ways she could sneak down to the lobby and discreetly snap a picture without him noticing. Her best shot, she mused, would be to stroll downstairs to the hotel gift shop, then casually mosey into the lobby, positioning herself strategically near him while pretending to text someone, the whole time snapping away. Realizing it might come across as a bit stalkerish, Monet rolled her eyes at herself.

"Yep, unsophisticated and silly, that would be me."

*

As the night wore on, Monet found that her suppressed appetite was returning. Grabbing the room service menu, she quickly scanned the options and settled on a Black Angus beef burger and fries. She was no longer appearing in a music video the next day and wasn't overly surprised by the relief she felt that she could go back to eating whatever she wanted.

Monet reached for the handset to call room service but was startled when the phone rang beneath her palm.

Instantly, her body tensed. Who would be calling her on the hotel landline? A wave of tremors hit her insides at the thought of it being Mr. Wessler.

Monet carefully picked up the handset, held it to her ear, and waited.

"Miss Everly?" a rich, baritone voice came from the other end.

"Yes?" she answered with a hint of hesitation.

"This is Brady—the bellhop," he said, mistakenly assuming she'd need a reminder to remember him.

"Oh, hey," Monet managed to mutter as her heartbeat shifted from a fearful pounding to the kind that accompanied butterflies tickling her stomach.

"I was just calling to check in and make sure you're alright."

A wide smile spread across her face. "That's so nice. I'm feeling a lot better—not quite as nervous."

"Good. I'm relieved to hear it," he said. *"To be honest, I've been a little worried. You seemed pretty shaken up and were white as a ghost earlier... Understandably, of course."*

Monet's heart did a funny little flip at the knowledge he'd been thinking about her. "I know." She let out a shaky breath. "The whole thing shook me up quite a bit."

"Yeah, I'll bet," he said. *"But hey, I was talking to Mr. Roberts, and he suggested that since you'll be staying with us tonight, he'd like to offer you a complimentary dinner from one of the restaurants here at the hotel—just as a way to apologize for what happened today."*

"Wow." Monet was taken aback a bit. "That's incredibly generous and so kind... but Mr. Roberts had nothing to do with what happened today." Monet puffed in amusement. "If anything, I should be buying him dinner for fibbing to Mr. Wessler for me."

Brady chuckled. *"I think he just wants to do something nice for you. What you did wasn't easy, and he wants you to know he admires your courage—we all do."*

Warmth seeped through to Monet's core at Brady's praise. What would it hurt to allow the fancy chic hotel to comp her a meal? It wouldn't.

"Alright," she said, feeling lighter than she had all night. "If he's sure, that would be great. Thank you."

"He's sure." Monet heard a smile in his voice. *"But there is one condition,"* he teased.

"Oh, yeah?" Monet playfully responded. "What's that?"

"You have to wait for my shift to end and eat with me."

It took Monet's brain a few extra seconds to process what Brady said. Had the wildly handsome bellhop just asked her to eat dinner with him?

"But maybe after what you've been through today, you'd rather not—"

"No!" Monet cut in, realizing he'd misread her silence. "I mean, I'd love to eat dinner with you."

"Are you sure?"

Considering her experience with the vile modeling agent, one might expect her to feel uneasy about Brady's offer. On the contrary, Monet couldn't think of anything she'd rather do than have dinner with him.

"Definitely."

"Okay then," he said. *"I get off in about thirty-five minutes; can you wait that long to eat?"*

"Yep, that's perfect," she said as a new cluster of butterflies took flight in her belly.

"I was thinking maybe the Rainbow Café—it's got the best variety, and the atmosphere is super casual."

"Sounds good to me," Monet said. "What time should I meet you?"

"How about we say 7:45?"

"I'll be there. Thanks, Brady—and tell Mr. Roberts thank you too."

"Will do. I'll see you soon."

"Alright. See ya."

Monet hung up the phone and let out a small squeal. With the danger and anxiety concerning Mr. Wessler behind her, Monet's mind was free to acknowledge the extent of her attraction toward Brady. Monet was sure she hadn't seen him the previous month when she'd stayed at the hotel with her brother. There was no way she'd have forgotten a man that looked like that.

Moving to where her suitcase was still standing on end, she picked it up and tossed it on the bed before unzipping it and grabbing her toiletry bag. The day had been such a whirlwind that she hadn't had the chance to freshen up since she left home that morning.

Monet made her way into the brightly lit bathroom and set her bag on the vanity. She'd applied only minimal makeup when she'd gotten ready that morning, but what she had put on was worn and smeared. Realizing she needed a complete refresh, Monet removed a hair tie from her bag, piled her hair on top of her head, and began washing her face. The cool water was refreshing and gave her an added little boost.

As she dried and moisturized her face, Monet reflected on the rather drastic change of events. Not more than two hours prior, she'd been frightened, sickened to near nausea over one man's treatment and behavior toward her. And yet, in that very instant, another man had stirred quite the opposite type of frenzied emotions within Monet. A sort of breathlessness filled her chest—an excitement she hadn't felt since Tyler Peters asked her to the homecoming dance her freshmen year of high school.

She couldn't stop the silly grin that fixed itself across her lips, nor could she help the fluttering that grew within her stomach. With a final squeal of excitement, Monet reached into her makeup bag to finish freshening up before making her way down to meet the hotel's charming and utterly attractive bellhop for dinner.

Brady

"Niiice," Ashley drew out the word, nodding her approval as Brady replaced the telephone handset in the cradle. He stood across the check-in desk, facing his spunky co-worker. "I always figured you were smooth when it came to the ladies."

"Ha! I wasn't being smooth," Brady shrugged, "I just asked her to eat with me so she wouldn't have to be alone."

"Ah, that's right. The old soft spot for people eating alone in a restaurant." Ashley grinned.

It was true; Brady did have a soft spot for people eating alone in restaurants. It pulled on his heartstrings. Most of the time, he knew it was ridiculous to worry about someone being lonely during their meal, but he'd been that way for as long as he could remember.

"And I'm sure that's the only reason you invited her to dinner," Ashley teased.

Mr. Roberts, standing next to Ashley behind the check-in desk, chuckled.

"I have a hunch the reason Brady came to me with the idea to offer a complimentary meal to Miss Everly isn't only that she resembles a young Nikola Povondra—" He raised his eyebrows knowingly, and Brady nodded with a deep chuckle, while Ashley playfully rolled her eyes. "But also—and perhaps more importantly—the young woman intrigues him." Mr. Roberts turned his attention to Brady. "Am I right?"

One thing about Brady's boss was his uncanny ability to know a person's thoughts—sometimes even before they did. The gentleman had a gift for knowing what people needed—what they wanted.

"As always," Brady flashed a quick glance at his boss as he addressed Ashley, "Mr. Roberts knows me well."

"I see." Ashley's eyes held a teasing twinkle. "So, it's not just your chivalrous nature at play here?"

Brady tilted his head and clicked his tongue. "Afraid not. Someone like Miss Everly probably isn't short of dinner invites." He was thoughtful for a moment. "It's just that, from what I've seen—especially around here—lots of people know they're attractive and kind of ride that wave without much humility, you know? But Monet Everly... she comes across differently." He shot a glance at Mr. Roberts. "She's got me curious, that's for sure."

Brady looked back at Ashley with a mischievous grin as he reached across the countertop and took one of her hands in his. "Before she showed up, I was beginning to think you were the only down-to-earth beauty in this city." He winked.

Ashley pulled her hand back with an exaggerated huff, playfully scoffing. "Oh gosh, you are so full of it," she laughed. "And what about you, Mr. Adonis?"

Brady jerked his head back. "Pfft!" He hated it when people brought up his looks. It always made him uncomfortable—ever since he was in grade school.

It was in the third grade—Valentine's Day—when it all started. Back when all the holiday meant to Brady was an attempt to see who could make the most creative Valentine's box.

That year, his dad helped Brady design his box to look like a Pac-Man arcade game, and it was seriously the coolest thing—he'd walked into school that day with an extra spring in his step, excited to show off his creation.

As usual, everyone was instructed to bring one Valentine for each student in the class. Everyone followed that rule in the previous years—but not that year. Not only did the girls in his class give him far more than they were supposed to, but girls from the other third-grade classes also sneaked in and slipped goodies to him. Brady received so many heart-shaped love notes and pink treats that he couldn't fit them inside his Pac-Man Valentine box; the teacher had to give him a sack to carry everything home. His embarrassment had been brutal—to say the least.

From there, things just seemed to get worse. At first, the other boys in the class didn't care. The teasing wasn't too bad, but by the 5th grade, when hormones started to play a major role in their lives, jealousy reared its head, and the other boys—even one of his close friends—started resenting him. Middle school was more of the same. Thankfully, once high school came around, the guys began to mature, and there wasn't as much bitterness.

Unfortunately, those early years took their toll, and still, to that day, Brady felt uneasy anytime someone brought up his looks, not that he thought he was any great

Adonis by any stretch of the imagination. But he'd always been told he looked like his father, and his dad was a good-looking guy—always had been.

"Well, it doesn't matter if you think I'm okay to look at or the ugliest mutt you've ever come across," Brady said to his feisty co-worker. "I hope I've got a bit more humility in me than some people I've met."

An astonished huff flew from Ashley's mouth. "Brady, you are the epitome of humble and a tad bit better than *okay* to look at."

He threw his head side to side and let out a doubtful smirk.

"I'm not kidding!" She lightly smacked his arm. "And I'll tell you." Ashley hesitated as a flirtatious smile curved her lips. "If I weren't so blissfully in love with my fiancé, I'd have already claimed you for myself."

Brady squirmed. Ashley knew full well she was making him uncomfortable, and by the playful sparkle in her eyes, she was enjoying it.

"You both do realize I'm right here?" Mr. Roberts asked as he continued typing while his attention remained locked on the computer screen. "Flirting in the workplace..." He let the words hang in the air, but his tone was light. Everyone knew Brady's relationship with Ashley was all in fun.

"Hey, what time do you get off?" Brady asked Ashley as a way to change the subject.

"Same as you, I think. 7:30. Why?"

"It just occurred to me that after what happened with the Sleaze, it might help Monet feel more comfortable if another woman came to dinner with us—seeing as she doesn't know me and all."

Ashley's eyebrows squished together. "Really? Wouldn't that be sort of awkward?"

"I think Brady's right," Mr. Roberts spoke up. "I'm sure after whatever Miss Everly experienced today, she'd feel more at ease having you there—don't worry about the cost. I'll inform the café to send me the bill."

"Wow," Ashley said. "Okay, then... sure. Thanks, Mr. Roberts."

The polished hotel manager simply gestured in understanding before leaving the front desk to attend to whatever was currently in need of his attention.

"I'll meet you after I get off, but I can only stay for a bit. I'm heading to Cole's. On top of school and work, we've also been bogged down with wedding plans, so tonight, we promised to have a chill night at his place."

Brady nodded. "Cool, good for you guys. I'll see you in a bit then," he said as he turned and headed back to the bell desk to finish up his shift.

*

Brady's replacement arrived early for his shift, allowing Brady a few extra minutes to change and make his way to the hotel's open-air café, which was located off to one side of the stylish lobby.

He made small talk with the hostess and a few other restaurant employees while he waited. Brady had been working at the hotel for three years and was well acquainted with everyone. A few had even become like a second family to him while he was in California going to school.

Mr. Roberts had already called the café and given them the details. Brady was surprised to learn his boss was also covering his meal, causing a moment of internal conflict.

The truth was, Brady hadn't been able to get Monet Everly off his mind since the moment he'd left her at the elevator earlier and had been itching to see her again. His first thought had been to ask her to dinner, but he'd quickly shut down the idea after what she'd been through that day; he didn't want to seem too forward. That's when he'd come up with the idea for the hotel to offer her dinner instead. When Brady suggested the idea to Mr. Roberts, he'd never intended for himself to get a free meal out of it as well, but he was a college student—he wouldn't go as far as to say *struggling* college student, but he wasn't about to scoff at free food.

"Hey!" Brady turned to see Ashley bounce up to the hostess station where he was standing. "I'm starving! Where's little miss humble hottie?" she said, scanning the tables inside the café.

Brady glanced down at the time displayed on his cell phone. *7:41*

"I asked her to meet me at—" Brady's words trailed off as his eyes drifted behind Ashley to the restaurant entrance. Suddenly, his mouth went slack, and his words were lost as Monet appeared. He'd thought that seeing her again wouldn't be as overwhelming as the first two encounters of the day. He was wrong.

In his twenty-one years, Brady had never met a woman who could utterly paralyze him—both mind and body—the way she did.

He'd first seen her when she was checking into the hotel earlier that day. Brady arrived for his shift and nearly suffered whiplash with the double-take he'd done when he saw her standing at the front desk. In Brady's opinion, Mr. Robert's observation of Monet resembling Nikola Povondra in her prime modeling days was spot on, but Miss Everly blew the supermodel away. Her physical appearance was more than exotic; she held almost a mythical beauty. Monet seemed virtually flawless, from the enticing allure of her full, pink lips to her smooth, ivory skin and how her dark chestnut hair complemented the crystal blue color of her eyes. He wondered how her parents could ever dare to let her out of their sight. She was a rare beauty, one who would attract all types—as, no doubt, her awful experience with Mr. Wessler proved.

When Monet first approached him at the bell stand seeking escape from the slimy man, Brady's heart had all but stopped before jump-starting into overdrive. He'd instantly lost his train of thought, and his learned ability to remain cool in front of a beautiful woman evaporated.

It was when he'd seen the fear in her eyes and heard the quiver lacing her voice that he'd pulled out of his hot girl freeze-up. She'd been genuinely scared, and even though it was his first time speaking with the woman, his protective instincts flared, allowing him to calm the nervous quivers in his stomach over the sight of her.

As Monet approached where he and Ashley stood at the café hostess stand, Brady once again found himself grappling with a dry mouth as his thoughts scattered. Summoning the same strength he'd had when she'd been in distress earlier, Brady gave his head a slight shake and greeted her with a genuine smile stretched across his face.

"You made it," he said.

Her own smile was radiant, like sunshine, contrasting with the undoubtedly forced ones he'd seen from her earlier that day.

"I did," she said, a split second before the light in her eyes dimmed, and she shot a nervous glance through the open-air café toward the lobby. "Although, I didn't realize the café was out in the open." Her eyes slid back to Brady. "I guess I'm still a little jittery, nervous that Mr. Wessler will suddenly appear again."

Brady's heart sank. He hadn't thought of that—obviously, no one had. Of course she'd be on edge. "I—" he stumbled over the words in his head. "I am so sorry. I should have realized—"

"Oh, no," Monet said quickly. "It's fine. It never crossed my mind until I was stepping off the elevator." She smiled again with a slight toss of her head. "I'm sure he's not coming back."

"He won't be back, at least not tonight, anyway," Ashley spoke up from where she stood next to Brady. "I'm Ashley. We met earlier."

Monet's attention shifted to his co-worker, and she nodded timidly. "Yes, I remember." Her fingers went to the silver chain around her neck, and she began twisting it as she had during their shared elevator ride.

If Brady was anything, he was observant. His parents always said he may have been a quiet child, but they learned never to underestimate him. He noticed everything and knew way more than anyone realized, and Brady knew by the small action of fidgeting with her necklace that Monet was either embarrassed or nervous about something. He had a pretty good idea of which it was.

"Ashley's one of your new admirers too."

"Admirers?" Monet let out a nervous chuckle.

"You're the first person to ever put Mr. Wessler in his place." He glanced at Ashley. "It's pretty impressive."

Ashley was sharp-witted, and Brady knew she'd catch on. Monet needed reassurance that they didn't think any less of her for her association with John Wessler.

"Super impressive," Ashley piped in. "That took guts; you're officially my new hero."

Monet's eyebrows shot up. "Your hero?" She laughed, letting loose the chain she'd been nervously spinning. "Not quite."

"It's true," Ashley said, bending at the waist in a sweeping bow, "I bow to your awesomeness."

Monet's cheeks flushed at Ashley's antics. Wanting to spare the modest beauty any further embarrassment, Brady turned the conversation to dinner. "Ashley just got off work, so I invited her to eat with us."

He didn't miss the brief flash of surprise that jumped from Monet's eyes. "Oh. Okay." The same forced smile he'd seen earlier appeared.

Is she disappointed?

Monet's reaction gave him a boost of encouragement and caused an unexpected flutter in his heart.

"There's an open spot tucked away toward the back," Ashley said, gesturing toward the table. "Maybe you'd feel more comfortable if we sat there?"

"That would be great. Thanks," Monet said as Brady stepped aside and motioned for her to precede him. Her eyes sparkled up at him, and the sight momentarily stole his breath. *Maybe,* he thought, *I shouldn't have invited Ashley after all.*

Monet

The small round table Ashley led them to was typically meant for two people, so Ashley slid a chair over from a neighboring table, and the three of them fit cozily next to each other in a small circle. Ashley was to Monet's right, and Brady sat to her left.

Monet did her best to hide the disappointment she'd felt when Brady announced he'd invited Ashley to join them. She'd obviously misunderstood his intentions behind asking her to eat dinner with him. Even as Monet's mind fought the letdown, she struggled to think of any logical reason behind Brady's invitation to her other than he was simply a nice guy.

It didn't take long before the server appeared and took their food orders. Brady and Ashley made small talk with the young woman for a couple of minutes while Monet sat quietly listening and watching Brady.

His physical looks were striking; he was ridiculously masculine and delightfully animated in how he spoke. Monet's chest tightened over the thought of Brady and Ashley being a couple—an odd desperation to know if they indeed were pushed its way to the center of her thoughts.

Once their server left, Monet reached up and started fidgeting with the silverware lying on the table in front of her as she cleared her throat. "So," she said, focusing on the fork she was twiddling between her fingers. "Are you two a couple, then?" She forced a friendly smile and shifted her gaze to meet Brady's but caught Ashley flinch out of the corner of her eye.

"Brady and me?" Ashley's voice nearly shrieked. "Um, no."

Ashley's response caused Brady to snap his head toward her, furrowing his brow in drastic offense. "Hey! I thought you said you'd have me for yourself if you weren't engaged?"

Ashley laughed. "Yeah, I did say that." She directed her next words to Monet. "Can you blame me?" She winked. "I like to call him *Beautiful Brady* or *Brady the Beguiling*—"

"Okay!" Brady interrupted as he shot Ashley a warning look. "We don't need to go there."

Monet giggled, delighted in their friendly banter while breathing a soft sigh of relief as the knot in her belly loosened. At the same time, she inwardly scolded herself. Monet had no reason to be relieved that the two co-workers weren't an item. She was going home in the morning and would never see Brady again.

"So," Brady said as he shook his head and slid another irritated glance to Ashley. "Has the Sleaze tried to contact you since he left the hotel?" he asked Monet.

She shook her head. "No. Thank heaven. He did call my parents, though."

"That must have been who he called after Mr. Roberts told him you'd checked out," Ashley said.

"Whoever it was seemed to be giving Wessler as big an earful as he was dishing out."

Monet nodded. "Yep, that would be my dad. He was pretty upset when I told him what happened."

"Don't blame him," Brady huffed. "That guy riles me like no other."

Monet liked the fire that leapt from Brady's eyes when he talked about Mr. Wessler. She imagined for a moment that she was the reason for his strong distaste for the man, but that was her silly, wishful-thinking self. Brady didn't even know her.

Monet attempted to steer the conversation in a different direction instead of thinking about, let alone talking about, her humiliating experience that day.

"So, you're engaged?" she asked Ashley, who easily took the bait. The spunky woman's face lit up, and she eagerly launched into every romantic detail of her relationship and upcoming wedding plans.

Monet liked Ashley, and as she listened to the future bride gush over her fiancé, Monet's heart lifted. Ashley was a woman in love. Monet was only eighteen, but her feminine heart longed for that type of love one day.

During Ashley's excited ramblings, Monet let her gaze drift to Brady. She found him listening to Ashley with a smile playing on his lips, clearly entertained by his co-worker's enthusiasm.

"Now you see what we have to put up with every day," Brady said to Monet.

Ashley laughed. "I'm not that bad, am I?"

"Actually." Brady tipped his head with a pause. "Yes. You are that bad."

Ashley playfully swatted his arm, and he withdrew it quickly, chuckling. He shot Monet a flirty wink, igniting a flutter in her stomach. In the midst of trying to soothe the rapid flutter of her heart caused by Brady's innocent gesture, Monet made an effort to gracefully steer the conversation forward.

"Have you two worked together for long?"

Brady and Ashley looked at each other. "What has it been? A couple of years now?" Brady asked.

Ashley's head jerked back, and her face distorted. "A couple of years?" She turned to Monet while slowly shaking her head. "Is it all men, or just those I know who tend to be clueless?"

Monet bit her lip to stifle a giggle at Brady's offended "Hey!" and his utter look of confusion.

"Brady!" Ashley scolded. "I've only been working here for six months." She threw one hand up. "How did you get two years?"

Brady scowled. "You've only been working here for six months?"

Ashley's eyes were wide with irritation as she nodded.

"Huh." His brow was still furrowed. "It seems longer than that."

Their food arrived before Ashley could respond, mercifully saving Brady from further chiding. In truth, Monet found his cluelessness endearing.

They'd ordered a large barbeque chicken pizza to share, and the server placed it on a tall pizza rack in the center of the small table. As they all grabbed a slice, Ashley's cell phone rang. A smile lit her face as she glanced at the screen, and without hesitation, she answered.

It was Cole, her fiancé. The conversation was brief, and although she could only hear Ashley's responses, Monet got the impression Cole was missing his fiery bride-to-be.

Ashley ended the call and slid her phone back into her purse that was sitting on the floor under the table. "Would it be cool if I snagged a few pieces to go and bail on you guys?" She turned to Monet. "I was telling Brady earlier that tonight was supposed to be a chill night for Cole and me." She shrugged. "You know, a break from all the wedding stuff."

Monet plopped a slice of pizza on her plate. "Oh, of course," she said, wiping her hands on the napkin in her lap as her eyes moved to Brady. She was curious about what he would say. After all, he had been the one who'd invited Ashley.

He was holding his piece of pizza up to his mouth, about to take a bite. "Sure, take as much as you want," he said before his teeth sank into his slice.

"Besides," Ashley said, raising a teasing eyebrow at Monet but talking to Brady, "I don't think Monet will mind if I go."

Monet's eyes widened, and her face instantly heated. Was her attraction to Brady that obvious?

"Not when you tease her like that; she won't mind," Brady said.

Ashley laughed and placed a gentle hand on Monet's arm. "I only tease people I like," she said. "But seriously, Brady invited me to eat with you two because he thought you'd be more comfortable with another woman here after what you went through today."

At Ashley's confession, a tingle of warmth spread through Monet's limbs, and she turned her attention to Brady, who flashed her a bright smile and another heart-stopping wink in between bites.

"Thank you," she said as the extent of his considering her feelings soaked deeper into her heart. "That was incredibly thoughtful."

"That's Brady," Ashley said as she waved their server over. "I tease him a lot, but he's as genuine and kind as they come." She paused, and that mischievous glint entered her eyes. "Not to mention, he's a knockout, right?"

"Alright!" Brady grumbled through a mouth full of food. "Time for you to go." He glared at Ashley.

Monet giggled and was tickled when she spied a slight flush across his handsome cheeks.

*

Once the likable— and very entertaining—Ashley gathered her to-go box and left, Monet found she and Brady fell into easy conversation. Monet's worries over Mr. Wessler returning to the hotel vanished, and she felt comfortable and content. Brady, too, appeared to be enjoying her company. He laughed often, smiled near constantly, asked a lot of questions, and seemed genuinely interested in what Monet had to say.

"I find it hard to believe that you've never done any modeling before this," he said as he studied her across the table.

Monet's cheeks warmed, delighted over his implication that he found her somewhat attractive.

"Nope," she shook her head. "First—and last—experience with it. Don't get me wrong," she quickly added. "I'm sure there are plenty of legitimate agencies out there—ones that don't require extra 'benefits.'" She made quote marks in the air with her fingers. "But this experience put a terrible taste in my mouth, and I'm pretty sure the industry isn't for me."

"I don't think anyone would blame you," Brady said with a shake of his head. "But what are your plans now?" he asked. "You mentioned you graduated this past May. Are you going to college?"

Monet hadn't thought about what she'd be doing now that the modeling thing wouldn't happen. Admittedly, her head had been in the clouds since she'd received the news that she'd won the contest. Monet had mentally put her original plans on hold, wanting to see where the modeling thing went. Now she knew; it went someplace she wasn't willing to go.

"To be honest," she said, "I guess I'll go back to my pre-John Wessler plans."

"And what's that?" he asked.

"Interior design... Although, I'm also really interested in event planning."

Brady chuckled. "Maybe you could do both?"

"Maybe," Monet said. "I guess I'm still figuring it out."

"Nothing wrong with that," he said. "Sometimes it takes just going to college for a while to figure out what you want to do."

Monet nodded. "Yeah."

"Like me," he said. "All through high school, I wanted to be a dentist—"

Monet's eyebrows arched, and her head jerked back.

Brady chuckled. "Not what you pegged me for, I take it?"

Monet laughed too but shook her head adamantly. "No, no, no, it's not that." Actually, it kind of was. A dentist wasn't what she'd pictured Brady as. A male model, a hot firefighter, a super sexy construction worker—basically all of those stereotypical hot guy careers. The more she thought about it, Monet could totally go for a dentist who looked like Brady.

"Honestly, you'd make a good..." her eyebrows arched, "anything." Her eyes momentarily bugged out. *Did I say that out loud?*

A flirtatious smile curved one corner of his mouth. "Really?"

Yep, I did.

Monet shifted in her chair and tucked a strand of hair behind her ear. Her fingers found the silver chain around her neck, and she started twisting it. She always did that when she was nervous; it was a wonder the thing hadn't snapped in half.

"Um." She cleared her throat. "What I meant was, you seem strong... capable—"

Brady leaned back in his chair with a smug expression. "Capable?"

"Smart! I mean smart." Monet felt a scarlet flush race up her neck and cover her face. She reached out, picked up her glass of ice water, and took a very unladylike gulp.

Mercifully, Brady let her off the hook. "It's okay. I *think*," he said, narrowing one eye in a playful squint, "I know what you meant. And I appreciate the compliment."

A nervous laugh vibrated from Monet's throat, and her heart thudded hard against her chest. Good heavens, Brady unsettled her—and he wasn't even trying.

"Anyway," he chuckled. "Once I got into college, it didn't take me very long into my first year to know I didn't want to be a dentist."

"Oh?" Monet asked, still attempting to cool her embarrassed blush.

"Yeah. I had this very profound realization that I couldn't sit and look inside people's mouths all day."

His confession brought a giggle out of Monet. "I don't think I'd enjoy that either."

"I have a new appreciation for the profession, though."

"I'll bet." She smiled.

"I ended up going in a completely different direction," he explained, "and I'll have a bachelor's in architecture in another few months."

Monet's mouth dropped. "That is so cool," she said, genuinely awed. "Seriously. I've always been intrigued by architecture. All types, especially Romanesque and Gothic, like you see in Europe."

"Really?" he asked, his features softening with approval. "Have you been to Europe?"

"No." She shook her head. "Not yet, anyway."

"I haven't been either, but plan to as soon as I'm able," he said.

"Are you from Costa Mesa originally?" Monet asked. She wanted to know as much about Brady as she could. He intrigued her, not only with his unearthly good looks, but he was kind and unbelievably down to earth. In Monet's limited experience, most of the hot boys she'd known in school were cocky jerks. Not all, but many.

"No. Arizona boy, born and raised," he said, wearing a broad grin and holding his head high. "I moved here for school and have been at it for almost four years. My degree is one of the reasons I started working here." He glanced around the open-air café and out into the lobby. "My dream is to design these one day."

Monet followed his gaze, taking note of the luxuriousness of the chic hotel. Her eyes drifted upwards to the beautiful abstract chandelier cascading in colorful spirals from the ceiling above the hotel entrance. She wondered how she'd previously missed its unique allure. Her attention then shifted to the decor around the lobby, feeling the warmth emanating from the rich greens and browns that the designers had chosen. Eventually, her attention circled back to Brady, who was regarding her with his mesmerizing eyes.

"What an exciting dream," she said softly, caught in his intense stare.

Something about the young, aspiring architect stirred a potent attraction within Monet, the likes of which she had never felt before. Perhaps it was due to his age. From their conversation, she estimated that he was in his early twenties—not significantly older but more mature than the boys she'd previously dated.

"You know," he said as he leaned forward in his chair, placing his forearm on the table. "I—"

"Dude!"

The sound of a deep, booming, irritated voice cut Brady off, and they both turned to see a hefty-looking man stomping through the lobby. He wore a blue t-shirt with grey gym shorts and a rather severe scowl.

"Uh oh," Brady said, pushing his chair back and standing. "Excuse me for a minute."

"Don't you answer your phone?" the man asked as he walked between the empty tables until he stopped in front of Brady. "I've been outside for twenty minutes texting and calling."

"Tee, I'm sorry, man. I lost track of time." Brady slid his hand into the front pocket of his jeans and pulled out his phone, glancing at the screen. "And look." He held it up. "Dead battery."

The man let out a snort. "Whatever, dude, let's just go. You know I've got an early workout before class in the morning." Unexpectedly, he turned his frown on Monet. The intensity of it caused her heart to sink and her brain to contemplate slipping under the small dining table.

Just as she considered doing that very thing, the man's facial expression softened, and the downward curved corners of his mouth lifted into a lopsided grin.

He slid his gaze from Monet to Brady and back. "Ah-ha... so this is why you were staying late tonight?" He slapped Brady on the chest with the back of his hand before turning toward Monet and offering the same hand to her. "Theodore Jensen."

Monet tentatively placed her hand in his as she flashed a befuddled look at Brady. "Monet Everly," she said, returning her attention to the burly man.

"This here is my roommate, T.J.," Brady explained. "He's been my wheels for the past few days."

"That's right," T.J. said. "Your boy here's a sucker. Went lending his car to our roommate whose truck broke down and needed to get to Oakland this week."

Monet tipped her head. "I wouldn't say that makes him a sucker," she said playfully. "I think that makes him a nice guy."

"Nice guy—sucker, same thing," T.J. chuckled, slapping Brady on the chest again.

Brady exhaled with an irritated shake of his head. "See what I've got to live with?"

T.J. was a jokester. Monet had spent less than three minutes with the man, and she knew it. She had a hunch that had she not been sitting there, Brady probably would have dished it out as good as T.J. gave it. The thought made Monet smile.

"Okay," Brady said, taking the man by his broad shoulders and attempting to turn him in the direction he came from. "You head out to the car and let me say a proper goodbye to my new friend here. I'll be right out."

A deep chuckle erupted from Brady's roommate. "A proper goodbye, huh?" He waggled his eyebrows at Monet, and she couldn't help but laugh; at the same time, a nervous quiver tickled her stomach.

"Come on, man." Brady shook his head again. "Get out of here." He shoved his friend toward the lobby.

T.J. laughed. "It was nice to meet you, Monet." He shot her a friendly wink and turned to leave.

"Sorry about that," Brady said as Monet gathered her small purse from the back of her chair and stood.

"It's okay," she said with a giggle. "He's a character."

"I guess that's a nice way to say it."

Brady's smile was full of such genuine warmth that Monet found herself momentarily breathless. In the next instant, however, the reality of the moment caused her heart, which had been so light and content for the past two hours, to suddenly shrink.

She was saying goodbye. Goodbye to the most intriguing man she'd ever met. Monet was only eighteen and hadn't met that many men, but even in her youthful naivety, she knew she'd be hard-pressed to meet another man who stirred such interest as Brady.

"Well, I'll let you get going." Monet curved the corners of her mouth up and pulled her slumping shoulders back. "Thanks for having dinner with me... and for your help earlier."

Another smile tugged at Brady's lips. "Can I walk you to the elevator?"

The way his eyes studied her caused a fluster of nervous tickles to descend into her belly again. "Sure."

Brady guided her out of the café and the short distance to the set of elevators. Monet watched as Brady reached forward and pressed the up arrow on the panel before he turned to her.

"Listen." His tone took on a more serious vibe. "I wanted to tell you something... and it has to do with what happened to you today."

The bundle of nerves in her stomach suddenly spread through every part of Monet's body, but she forced a gentle smile. "Okay."

"Earlier, when I guessed at you being the winner of the contest, you said after what happened with Wessler, you weren't the winner anymore because you gave it up."

Monet nervously chewed on her bottom lip, and she nodded.

"Well." Brady's eyebrows rose. "I've been working here for three years, and I've watched that guy come in with these young women one after the other, holding his glass of champagne in one hand, while strolling to their room and not leaving until morning." He shook his head slowly. "Not once did I see a woman say no... until you." Brady took a step closer to Monet. "So, if you ask me, you are the real winner."

The unexpected compliment caused Monet's heart to swell, and a soothing warmth spread over her limbs, comforting the unsettled nerves pestering her.

"Thank you," Monet said, her voice rich with emotion. She didn't dare say more, fearing it would give away how deeply he'd affected her.

Monet inhaled sharply at the feel of Brady's hand taking hold of one of hers. "I mean it," he said softly. "You're a rare beauty, Monet Everly... inside and out."

With those words lingering in the air, he leaned in and pressed a soft kiss to her cheek. Monet's arms erupted in goosebumps, and her breathing entirely abandoned her at the feel of his lips on her skin. Brady pulled back, and with a mischievous, lopsided grin, he winked at her, making her already weakened legs wobble even more.

With one last squeeze of Monet's hand, Brady ushered her onto the waiting elevator before saying, "Goodnight."

Her brain had turned to mush, and her mouth had gone dry, but Monet managed to push out the word "goodnight."

And with that, Brady stepped back, and the elevator doors closed.

Monet stood unmoving inside the elevator, breathless, as the lingering effects of Brady's words and actions played harshly with her young, tender emotions. Brady, the bellhop, was entirely too charming, too handsome... and too unobtainable. She knew she'd never see him again. Those blissful hours spent in his company were a happy fluke—a blip in time. She'd return to Utah and whatever life had in store for her, and he'd live his dreams.

Monet exhaled a long sigh. "If only..."

Still, she resolved to look at the bright side. What started as a nightmare that afternoon—a harsh reality check on life's twisted and unfair parts—ended like a dream, where a handsome man gave her the time of day and made her feel worthwhile.

Monet wouldn't dwell on the fact that she'd never see Brady again. Instead, she would always cherish the time she spent with him. Because if there was one thing Monet knew, it was that no matter who came and went in her life, she would never forget the irresistible bellhop, Mr. Brady...

"Brady?" she questioned herself. "Brady what?"

Monet's shoulders dropped, and her body slumped against the elevator wall. "After all that," she sighed, shaking her head. "I don't even know his last name."

Five Years Later

Monet

"Are you ready to have your day made? No, wait!" Monet's friend quickly blurted, dramatically throwing her palms toward Monet. "Your entire month! No! Year—your entire year." Juliet's deep blue eyes shimmered with some barely restrained excitement.

Monet returned an amused glance to Josh Hafen, Juliet's adoring fiancé, sitting across the glossy white restaurant dining table. Juliet was adorable and always happy—her zest for life was contagious.

"Of course." Monet's smile was wide. "It must be pretty good if it's going to make my entire year."

"Oh, it is," Juliet said.

"Hey, Jewels." A young man with a white apron walked up to them. "I know you're on break, but I'm having trouble with the lava cake." He scrunched one side of his face. "Any chance you could take a look real quick?"

"You bet!" Juliet hopped up from where she'd been sitting next to Josh and pointed at Monet. "Don't go anywhere," she said before following the young chef into the kitchen.

Juliet Quinn was a recent culinary graduate and had landed a Sous Chef position at The Garden, a new upscale (yet casual) restaurant in the heart of Manhattan. Juliet had invited Monet to eat lunch with her and Josh on Juliet's lunch break that day; she'd told Monet she had something *huge* to tell her.

The two girlfriends had met four years earlier after Monet moved to New York to study interior design. Juliet was the gift Monet needed at the time: a beautiful woman who, in a sense, saved Monet.

"How does it feel to be an official college graduate?" Josh asked in between bites of his battered fish and chips.

Monet inhaled and blew it out. "Scary."

Josh chuckled with a nod. "Yeah, I hear ya—things get real pretty fast. When I got my bachelor's and made the decision to leave Colorado to move out here for law school, it caused me some pretty intense anxiety," he said. "Even though I never once second-guessed my decision to be closer to Juliet, it was still scary." He shrugged. "But that's to be expected with change, right?"

One side of Monet's mouth quirked up. "I suppose," she agreed.

Josh was right; change was hard for most people, but Monet knew her worry over what life had in store for her went much deeper. It was a fear that plagued her for five years, ever since John Wessler had entered her life.

"Juliet says you've been having trouble with your boss?" Josh asked.

"Yeah." Monet leaned forward and took a sip from her water glass. "She's back-peddling on the full-time position she offered me once I graduated." She set her glass down and slumped back in her chair. "It seems boyfriend of the month has a sister who just graduated in design too."

"Pfft." Josh shook his head. "Not cool."

Monet inhaled a deep breath. "Nope." She exhaled. "My boss said I could work for her partner, Charlie, but there's no way." His personality reminded Monet too much of someone else—someone who had almost ruined her life.

"Okay, I'm back." Juliet gracefully took her place next to Josh as her eager eyes locked on Monet. "Have you heard of Nash and Perkins—"

"The architect firm?" Monet cut in.

Juliet nodded slowly as her smile grew. "The very one."

"After the publicity they've gotten lately, I doubt anyone in the industry hasn't heard of them," Monet said. "What about them?"

A swirl of curiosity tickled the inside of Monet's stomach. Nash and Perkins was a highly successful architectural firm based in Phoenix. The company, though young, had managed to carve out a notable reputation in the mere span of three years since they'd been in business. They'd recently gained national attention for designing a very posh hotel for a well-known socialite, a wealthy widow named Velma Larsen.

Juliet leaned closer to the table as she quirked an eyebrow and grinned. "What if I were to tell you Nash and Perkins is overseeing the construction for a blow-your-mind luxury resort they designed... in Cancun?"

Monet's forehead crumpled. "I'd say... that's cool?" she questioned, wondering why Juliet was acting so giddy about an architectural firm working on a hotel resort in Mexico.

Josh chuckled. "She's gotta build it up; you know that."

Monet smiled, but the wrinkle on her brow only lessened a bit.

"And what if I told you," Juliet continued, her eyes still glowing with the excited anticipation of revealing some well-guarded secret, "that the assistant to the hospitality designer they are working with found out she's pregnant with her first child and decided she needed to be closer to home and couldn't continue living in Cancun for weeks on end, so... she quit! Leaving an opening for a new assistant!" Juliet squealed and bounced in her chair.

Monet understood instantly; Juliet thought Monet should apply. Her heart sank, knowing she was about to disappoint her friend.

"I know what you're thinking, Jewel." Monet huffed a sarcastic laugh. "But there is no way I could land a job like that this fresh out of school—especially since the job sounds like it's already started; they'd need someone seasoned. Besides, the designer probably has backups."

Juliet shook her head. "Uh-uh, nope."

"How do you know that?" Monet asked.

Juliet glanced at Josh with a smug grin before settling her attention on Monet. "My dad *might* just know a certain wealthy widow from Phoenix who owns the aforementioned future resort."

Monet's eyes bulged. "Your dad knows Velma Larsen?"

Josh chuckled as he wiped his hands on his napkin. "Of course he does." His fingers rubbed at his brow as he looked at Juliet. "I wonder if I'll ever get used to how affluent your family is."

"How affluent my parents and brother are, you mean." She smiled coyly, leaning in closer to him. "I'm just Juliet, a simple Sous Chef." She kissed him sweetly on the lips.

Josh cupped her chin with one hand. "I can assure you, Miss Juliet Quinn," his voice held a seductive tone, "there is nothing simple about you." Juliet sighed as he guided her lips to his once more.

Warmth radiated through Monet's chest at the familiar sight of the beautiful couple's affection for each other. She'd grown used to witnessing it, and she was genuinely happy for them.

Juliet was the daughter of Ronan and Camila Quinn. Ronan was an only child and inherited his wealth. Juliet's mother's money came from family as well. Camila's father founded the highly successful media company Royce Corporation, which was currently run by Juliet's uncle Nolan and her brother, Sawyer.

Juliet and Sawyer were as close as any siblings could be. Juliet had met Josh through Sawyer's wife, Violet. Violet and Josh were best friends.

Juliet broke the seal of their kiss and giggled. "Stop kissing me; you're too distracting."

"Me?" Josh blurted before turning to Monet. "Who kissed who first?" he asked.

Monet quirked a brow and looked at her friend. "I'm afraid he's right." She shrugged. "You made the first move that time."

"Do you blame me?" Juliet teased with a sly grin. "But!" She gave a shake of her head. "Back to what I was saying. Yes! My dad knows Velma Larsen; my grandma Quinn was one of her dearest friends, and my dad still checks in on her every once in a while."

"Is that the old friend you said your dad was having dinner with in Phoenix last night?" Josh asked.

"Um-hum." Juliet nodded. "He was a keynote speaker at a big charity event and stayed an extra night to catch up with Velma."

Monet smiled. When she and Juliet first became friends, she had been astonished by how completely different Juliet's life was from her own—the money, the glamorous social events, weekend sailing excursions, all of it—Monet didn't think she'd ever get used to it. Four years later, however, she had grown used to it but was not entirely comfortable with it.

"My dad asked Velma about her new hotel," Juliet explained. "She mentioned it was going well except that their hospitality designer was somewhat frantic looking for a new assistant." Her eyebrows arched. "They are, after all, only about six months out from completion, so to lose her assistant at a time like this is causing the designer a lot of additional stress." Juliet's eyes twinkled again. "That's why Velma stepped in to find a new assistant."

"And your dad—being the stud that he is," Josh said, "dropped our lovely Monet's name, I take it?"

"He did, and…" Juliet started drumming her fingers excitedly on the table. "He got you an interview with Velma!"

"What?" Monet's eyes widened as sparks of adrenaline lit her insides.

To land her first job working with a firm like Nash and Perkins would be beyond her wildest professional dreams—especially a job as high profile as the resort was sure to be.

Still, as she thought about the magnitude of the opportunity, doubt crept in. The excited swirls in Monet's stomach ceased, replaced by a heavy thud. Her chances were low—lower than low, no matter if Juliet's dad knew the wealthy widow or not. Monet set her fork down. Suddenly, the oversized Cobb salad she'd been enjoying didn't seem as appetizing.

"Stop it," Juliet scolded. "I know that look, Monet."

"What look?" Monet feigned ignorance.

"The one where your forehead gets all crumpled and you start chewing on your bottom lip."

Monet freed her lip and forced her brow to smooth, which caused Josh to chuckle.

"You're doubting yourself," Juliet said before her expression softened. "I get it too. I know what you went through, but you've come such a long way and worked so hard—both on yourself and in school." She reached across the table and squeezed Monet's hand. "You deserve a shot at this more than anyone."

Monet stared into the warm eyes of her darling friend. As always, they held only sincerity. Juliet had a way—a gift—of calming Monet's worries and easing her insecurities. Josh had won a genuine jewel when he snatched up Juliet, and he knew it too; that's how Monet knew he was the perfect man for her best friend.

Sucking in that familiar calming breath, Monet exhaled and nodded. "Okay. I'm in."

Juliet squealed again and hopped up. She bounced around the table and threw her arms around Monet's neck.

"It's only an interview, Jewel," Monet laughed. "I don't have the job yet."

"Oh, but you'll get it. I know you will," Juliet said as she released Monet.

Despite Juliet's optimism, Monet wasn't as confident. Still, she pushed her doubts away and mentally leaned on her best friend's belief in her.

"Yep," Juliet said as she took her seat across from Monet again. "This will be the beginning of an all-new chapter for you." She winked at Monet. "Just you wait."

Monet

Monet felt the vibration of her cell phone buzzing from its place tucked in the side pocket of her new sophisticated-looking, camel-colored workbag—a *good luck on your interview* gift from her mom and dad. Monet's parents weren't wealthy, but they lived a comfortable life and were happy. The gift of the high-fashion work tote went against their frugal nature, but they'd been so excited that they'd splurged when she'd flown home to Utah for a visit the previous weekend.

The fancy handbag sat on her lap, and she reached into the pocket and pulled her phone out. Glancing at the screen, it read *Juliet*. Flashing a quick look at the receptionist across the modern-style lobby, Monet slid *answer call* across the screen and brought the phone to her ear.

"Hey," she whispered as she eyed the woman manning the front desk, greeting a petite young woman who'd just walked in carrying a drink holder with four tall white cups and a brown paper bag.

"Have you met them yet?" Juliet asked.

"No. I'm just sitting here in the reception area feeling like I could throw up because I'm so nervous."

"Monet," Juliet sighed through the phone. *"You have nothing in the world to be nervous about. You've already won over Velma, and it will be the same with these people."*

Monet let out a nervous smirk.

"I'm serious, Monet. You're going to blow them away."

Monet hoped so but wasn't as confident as her optimistic friend. She'd arrived in Arizona three days before to interview with Velma Larsen about the newly vacated assistant designer job. Juliet was right; Monet hit things off with the wealthy widow from the first moment they'd met. Velma was in her seventies but had the spirit of a woman in her youth. Velma had hired her on the spot, which was why Monet was still in Phoenix and currently sitting in the brightly colored foyer of Nash and Perkins Architect Firm; she was about to meet the team she'd be working with on Velma's new hotel resort in Cancun, The Grand Jewel.

"This is so weird." Monet kept her voice low. "A woman is talking to the receptionist, and I swear I know her."

"Really?" Juliet asked. *"Do you know anyone who lives in Arizona?"*

"Not that I know of, but she looks so familiar." Monet studied the woman who was in friendly conversation with the receptionist—her spiky blonde hair, her animated facial expressions, and her... voice.

"Oh my gosh," Monet breathed into the phone. "I totally remember her." She searched her memories, trying to put a name to the bubbly woman's face.

"Who is she?"

Monet's face scrunched as she shook her head. "I don't remember her name, but I met her that night—the night I blew off Mr. Wessler."

"Oh, dear." Monet heard the frown in Juliet's voice. *"This isn't good."*

"No, no. It's fine," Monet assured her friend. "It's been so long ago; I'm over what happened, and besides," Monet hesitated with a smile, "this woman is part of a good memory."

"Are you sure?" Juliet didn't sound so convinced.

"Yes. She ate dinner with me and... Brady."

Juliet gasped. *"The most beautiful, wonderful, dreamiest man you've ever met?"* she teased in an airy voice.

"The very one." Monet stifled a giggle over Juliet mimicking Monet's repeated description of the young bellhop who'd nearly swept her off her feet five years prior. "The woman I'm staring at right this second was the front desk employee who ate with us."

"No way!"

"I'm positive it's her."

"Wow. What are the chances, huh?"

"I know." Monet was stunned. Seeing the woman she'd met that night all those years ago triggered a flood of memories. Not the bad ones Juliet was worried about, but the good ones.

"Speaking of dreamy men, have you seen a picture of Mr. Nash?" Juliet asked.

"I don't think so. His partner is the one who seems to deal with the media."

"Exactly. Velma says since their newfound fame, so to speak, Mr. Nash doesn't like the spotlight."

"I can understand that." Monet kept her voice low.

"I know you can; better than most." Juliet paused. *"Well, last night, the elusive Mr. Nash was photographed out to dinner with Bethany Hawk."*

"The social media influencer?"

"Um-hum, and I have a suspicion as to why the guy avoids the media."

"Why?"

"Oh, I'll let you see for yourself." Juliet laughed. *"But let's just say, now that his picture is out there, he'll probably have women chasing him night and day."*

Monet's stomach rolled at Juliet's implication that Mr. Nash might be an attractive womanizer. Could she work with a man like that? She'd avoided the Casanova type for so long—as a matter of fact, the only men in her life were family or platonic relationships that had zero chance of ever turning into more. Only since Juliet came into her life did Monet feel comfortable with unrelated members of the opposite sex.

Before moving to New York to attend college, Monet had tried to avoid men at all costs, which had been a fairly fruitless attempt given the impossibility of avoiding the male gender in daily life. Still, she'd given it her best effort, all because of one man—John Wessler.

Contrary to what her young, naïve brain had expected, the night Monet escaped the vile modeling agent wasn't the last she'd hear from him. No, his chauvinistic, larger-than-life ego wouldn't let go of the fact that he'd been told 'no' for once in his life.

The humiliation Monet had rained down on him went even deeper, though. When she didn't show up for the music video shoot, Monet made him look bad professionally, driving him to near madness.

It had been five years, and still, Monet's body trembled at the memory of the first time John Wessler showed up on the doorstep of her parents' home.

"Miss Everly," the receptionist called from the front desk.

"I gotta go. I'll call you later," Monet whispered in a rush.

"Ahhh! Good luck!" Juliet squealed through the phone.

Monet giggled. She quickly ended the call and stuffed her phone back into the side pocket of her bag before she stood and walked toward the desk. Despite the raw nerves rolling through her body, she held her chin high and tried to exude confidence in her high-waisted floral pencil skirt, blouse, and cream heels.

The fear and mental upheaval that Mr. Wessler had caused Monet in the first year after the modeling contest took an unhealthy toll on her. Monet spent years hiding behind baggy, colorless clothing and found no use for make-up or jewelry.

However, thanks to Juliet and a supportive family, those days were in the past, and Monet once again felt comfortable and confident in cute, stylish clothes with a dash of color on her face.

"I'm so sorry for the delay," the receptionist explained. "It seems their conference call is going longer than planned. It will be just a few more minutes."

"Oh, no problem at all," Monet said. "Thank you." She dared a glance at the spiky-haired woman she'd eaten dinner with so long ago and smiled. It was her alright; Monet wished she could remember her name.

"In the meantime," the receptionist said, drawing Monet's attention back to her. "This is Mrs.—"

"Wait!"

Monet was startled as the petite young woman cut the receptionist off.

"Miss Everly?"

Monet's heart jumped at the possibility of the woman recognizing her.

"Yes," Monet said.

"The humble hottie?"

What? Monet gasped as the tiny blonde woman rushed forward and, standing on tiptoes, threw her arms around Monet's neck.

"I can't believe it!" the woman said, pulling back from Monet. "It's me, Ashley, from the White Rainbow Hotel in Costa Mesa."

Monet chuckled at Ashley's enthusiasm and nodded. "Yes, of course I remember," she said. "I knew I recognized you."

Ashley glanced at the receptionist. "Trish, this is Monet—crazy story, but we met about... what was it? Four years ago?"

"Five," Monet said, delighted that Ashley remembered her name.

"Five!" Ashley blurted. "Has it really been five years?" Her eyes bulged before she exhaled and tossed her head. "I guess that's right. I've been married for four, and I was engaged when you and I met." Her smile grew wide again. "My goodness, time flies, doesn't it?"

The receptionist, Trish, winked at Monet as a friendly understanding passed between them. Ashley hadn't changed. She was still as talkative and spirited as five years prior.

The nervous knot plaguing Monet's stomach since arriving at the firm lessened. Ashley's cheerfulness seemed to rub off on Monet, and suddenly, meeting the newly acclaimed architects at Nash and Perkins didn't seem as daunting.

"I can't believe it," Monet said, shaking her head. "Not to be cliché, but it is such a small world."

"It's not cliché! It's the truth," Ashley laughed. "I've got to say it, though; I didn't think you could get any more beautiful, but wow!"

Monet inwardly cringed, fidgeting with the strap of her work bag slung over one shoulder. Although her self-esteem had somewhat returned—primarily thanks to Juliet—her palms still became moist whenever anyone complimented her physical appearance.

She swallowed before pushing out a weak "thank you," followed by a cordial smile. "And look at you!" Monet attempted to shift the conversation off of herself. "You're as lovely as I remember and as friendly and cheerful too."

"Aww," Ashley cooed, her face lighting up. "Aren't you just the sweetest thing?"

"So, what brings you here?" Monet asked, glancing around the reception area. "Are you working with the firm on a design?"

Trish and Ashley both chuckled as Ashley shook her head. "No."

"Oh, so you work here?" Monet asked.

"Not technically, but I work *with* the firm quite regularly," she said. "And that alone is hard enough. Some days I wonder how we get anything done." Ashley winked at Trish, who smiled.

Monet looked from one woman to the other, wondering what she was missing.

"Cole works here," Ashley said. "My husband."

Understanding dawned on Monet, and her chin dropped. "You're married to Cole Perkins?"

Ashley laughed at Monet's obvious surprise. "Yep, and I can't believe I didn't connect the dots when Velma mentioned your name. Which I hope means," she pressed her hands together as if in prayer, "you're my new assistant?"

Huh? Monet blinked a few times over Ashley's revelation. "You're the hospitality designer on the Grand Jewel?"

"I am."

Monet attempted to wrap her mind around the unexpected twist. "Then I guess that does make me your new assistant."

Ashley squealed—much the same way Juliet had just moments before—and threw her arms around Monet's neck again. "This is so perfect!" She drew back and took hold of Monet's hands. "To think, after the three of us met that night so long ago, fate would bring us all back together like this."

Monet couldn't believe it either; it was unbelievable—*but wait?* Her head tipped, and a frown furrowed her brow. "I didn't meet Cole that night."

Ashley's giddiness subsided slightly as her eyes narrowed. "You do know who Cole's partner is... don't you?"

It took about three seconds before the pieces fell together for Monet. It was as if someone had thrust a shot of adrenaline straight into her heart, causing her breath to catch.

Instantly, she was transported back to her conversation with the handsome bellhop from five years prior, and words flashed like big, bold blocks in her mind—*"Arizona boy, born and raised"* and *"bachelor's in architecture."*

"Monet?" The deep masculine voice that rose from behind her caused another sharp gasp to erupt from Monet's throat; at the same time, a delightful shiver skirted her arms. "Monet Everly?"

Monet's posture tensed as she stood in frozen disbelief, her eyes locked on Ashley, who muttered, "I take it you didn't know."

Summoning every ounce of courage she had, Monet turned and, for the first time in five years, came face to face with the young bellhop who had unknowingly captured her eighteen-year-old heart.

But he wasn't the same twenty-one-year-old she'd met when she was eighteen. Brady had grown—matured into the most magnificent man Monet had ever seen. He was tall, with the same muscular build, but instead of filling out a bellhop uniform, he filled out a white button-up dress shirt. The top two buttons were open just enough to give Monet a glimpse of his beautifully sun-bronzed skin.

In an attempt to suppress the sudden rush of warmth that spread through her, Monet's attention moved to his face—the handsome face she'd never forgotten. Only now, he looked more mature—more manly and entirely grown-up.

Monet wouldn't have thought it possible, but his face was more chiseled, his clean-shaven jaw more rugged, but his eyes—they were the same, and as he stared at her, their emerald beauty held her captive.

"Brady?" she managed to squeak out. "The bellhop?"

He laughed, and the sound took her back to when he'd laughed during their short time together; it was deep—powerful and somehow soothing.

"Yes," he said. "The bellhop." Brady studied her from head to toe and back again, wearing a wide grin. The way he appraised her caused Monet to stiffen, and a disappointing rock dropped to the pit of her stomach. It couldn't be true; the charming, considerate bellhop couldn't have turned into a womanizer.

A slight frown touched his face briefly before he shook his head and released an astonished huff. "I'm sorry. I don't mean any disrespect by gawking; I just can't believe you're standing here," he said.

The tension in Monet's limbs relaxed, and she smiled, silently scolding herself for jumping to an unfair conclusion. With Juliet's help, Monet had been better about not lumping all men into the *creep* category. Besides, hadn't she just head-to-toe appraised Brady as well?

"I know," Monet said, trying to appear calm. "So, you're Mr. Nash?"

"I am," he said, offering a slight smile. "I finally had the chance to read Velma's email about Ashley's new assistant a moment ago." Brady's eyes remained fixed on her as he gave his head a disbelieving shake. "When I read the name, I had to get out here and see for myself if it was the same Monet Everly I'd met in Costa Mesa five years ago."

Monet's eyebrows rose with a nod. "It is," she chuckled nervously and gestured behind her. "Ashley thinks it's fate."

"That's my girl!" a smiling, scruffy-faced man bellowed as he strode out of a nearby office. His eyes danced with mischief as he walked over and wrapped his massive arms around Ashley. Monet instantly recognized him from his media appearances. Cole Perkins was tall and burly and literally engulfed his wife's tiny frame.

"This girl believes in all that mystical stuff," he said a second before kissing her. It wasn't a simple kiss either; it was long and mildly passionate.

Monet bit her bottom lip to keep from giggling as her eyes locked with Brady's. "Welcome to my world," he groaned.

"Okay, guys," Brady said, "not in the workplace," and then he mumbled, under his breath, "for the millionth time."

He winked at Monet as one side of his enticing mouth slid up. A delicious shudder skirted Monet's body, triggering a moment of panic in wondering if her heels were strong enough to keep her now weakened legs upright.

As far as she could tell, older Brady was far too attractive and too affecting. Not only had one wink from him caused her knees to wobble, but she also had to place a hand on her stomach to calm the swarm of butterflies flapping around.

Brady was evoking feelings in Monet that were foreign to her. She had built an ironclad wall around her heart and her emotions—around every part of her that could feel. Those feelings had been locked up tightly for so long that the ease with which Brady breached that wall felt nearly overwhelming to her. Nervously, she moved her hand from her belly to tuck a long, wavy strand of hair behind her ear.

"You two go on in, and we'll be there in a few," Cole said, teasingly nuzzling his wife.

"Oh, wait," Ashley said, untangling herself from her overzealous husband. "I brought Brady something." She reached into the brown bag sitting on the receptionist's desk, took out a small pastry sack, and handed it to him.

Brady peeked inside. "Mmm! You're the best, Ash. Thanks."

"I wasn't sure what you'd like," Ashley said to Monet. "But I did grab an extra coffee just in case."

"Oh, no, it's fine. I already ate something."

"She can share mine," Brady said with another wink. Monet couldn't help but return his playful smile. Although, she did wonder how on earth she was going to work with him, especially if he kept winking at her.

"I'm Cole, by the way." Ashley's delightfully charming husband offered Monet his hand.

"It's nice to finally meet you." Monet slid her hand into his.

"*Finally,* huh?" he teased. "Does my reputation precede me then?"

Before Monet could respond, Ashley jumped in. "That's right! You don't know."

"Know what?" Cole asked.

"This is Monet Everly, the girl who stuck it to that slimy modeling agent after winning that contest five years ago." Ashley motioned between her and Brady. "You remember us telling you about that, right?"

Cole stared at Monet with wide eyes. "No way. Really?"

Monet pressed her lips together and gave a nod. "Um-hum." The mention of John Wessler always caused her to tense a bit.

"So this is the famous *Monet*," Cole stretched out her name, and his gaze drifted between her and Brady. Suddenly, he reached over and slapped Brady on the back. "Well, I can certainly see what all the fuss was about, and I can bet Brady will want to share more than his croissant with you."

Monet's eyes rounded, and she inwardly gasped. *What?*

Brady closed his eyes, exhaling an irritated breath while shaking his head.

"Now, you stop your teasing, Cole," Ashley playfully scolded her husband before stepping up and hugging Monet again. "I am so excited to work with you, Monet," she said before releasing her. "Velma certainly has a gift for pulling tricks out of her hat, doesn't she?"

Monet nodded with a shaky laugh. "It appears so."

"Ash, why don't you take a few minutes and get him in line." Brady shot a warning look to his partner before his eyes fixed on Monet. "Miss Everly and I have a bit of catching up to do."

The feel of Brady's hand at the small of her back, coupled with the sensation of his breath against her ear as he whispered, "Sorry about Cole, he can be a bit too... playful at times," sent Monet's heart hammering as he guided her to his office.

In truth, Cole's behavior was the last thing she was thinking about at that moment. Instead, just before Brady closed the office door behind them, the final thought that flitted through Monet's mind was: *Brady, the bellhop, Nash... Juliet is not going to believe this.*

Brady

It was all Brady could do to keep it together. He felt overheated—flustered, and in an instant, he was transported back to his awkward teenage years, grappling with a jarring and all-too-familiar loss of poise in the presence of an attractive woman.

Monet Everly. He couldn't believe the woman he'd met all those years ago—the same woman Brady had thought about almost obsessively for months after their meeting—was the new assistant Velma hired and who, at that moment, stood in his studio office.

Brady gestured toward the floor-to-ceiling window on one side of the room, where six different colored contemporary-style armchairs surrounded a long white planning table. "Please, have a seat."

Monet glanced at him with those glacial blue eyes, the same ones that had plagued his dreams for months—years if he were honest with himself. The impact of her gaze sent his mind into a mush of words.

If Brady hadn't witnessed it himself, he'd never have believed she could be any more beautiful than the last time he'd seen her—but she was. He knew that had she chosen the life of a fashion model, she'd have skyrocketed to the top of the industry with her unique beauty. And she'd definitely grown up. Her eyes were more sultry, her lips naturally fuller, and her cheeks more defined. She was stunning.

There was something that struck Brady, however. Aside from the physical maturity she'd gone through, he was surprised to see Monet still held a trace of fear in her behavior. Her nervous fidgeting and how she'd stiffened when he'd first studied her reminded him of how she'd behaved the afternoon they'd met—the day the slimy modeling agent tried to take advantage of her.

Brady's heart lurched at the thought of making her uncomfortable, but in his defense, he'd been so stunned by Monet standing there in real life that he'd wanted to visually drink her in.

Monet took a seat, and Brady joined her.

Monet looked around the office and out the glass window to the city ten stories below. Her eyes sparkled. "You've certainly come a long way since the night we met." Her hand swept the air. "Back when all of this was just a dream."

Brady's heart seemed to halt. "You remember that?"

Monet smiled. "Of course." She slid her work bag off her lap and set it on the floor. "You told me it was your dream to build hotels, and," she nodded slightly while grinning, "you've done it."

The awe in Monet's voice, coupled with the genuine admiration on her face, boosted Brady's confidence. He suddenly felt taller, stronger in a way. He was surprised by how much Monet's good opinion of him mattered. They'd only spent a couple of hours together five years ago; how could she possibly have such a strong effect on him? Not willing to overthink it, Brady pushed his inner questions aside.

He chuckled. "We have—or at least we're in the middle of doing it," he said. "We got lucky. And don't they say success is 1% hard work and 99% luck?"

Monet laughed, and the sound was delightful. "I think it's the other way around."

Brady cocked one eyebrow with a tilt of his head. "I see. How about we test that theory?"

Monet flashed him a look of daring as her mouth twitched with humor.

"When Cole and I first started on our own, we started designing a few smaller homes. One of those homes happened to be for Velma Larsen's personal assistant's uncle."

Monet nodded, her brows raising in an impressed manner.

"One day, Velma saw a glimpse of the house we designed when her assistant had it pulled up on her computer screen." He shrugged. "It caught Velma's eye, and she asked to tour the home. After that, we got a call and set up our first meeting with her."

"Wow," Monet breathed. "That's—"

"*Lucky*," Brady cut in with a chuckle.

"A little, but still."

"Okay, how about you?" he asked somewhat smugly. "How did you get an interview with Velma?"

An adorable blush colored her cheeks, and she shifted in her chair. "Well... through my best friend."

"And?" Brady prodded.

She released a defeated breath. "Fine." She playfully rolled her eyes. "Her dad knows Velma and got me the interview."

"See." He sat back in his chair and folded his arms across his chest. "It all starts with luck."

"Not always, and besides, luck will only take you so far." She adorably jutted her chin out but smiled.

"What about you?" Brady asked. "I see you've followed your dream of becoming an interior designer. How long have you been doing it?"

Monet's eyes dropped to her hands, which she began to wring in her lap. "Um. Full time?" She hesitated. "Not that long, actually."

Understanding dawned on Brady. "Are you a recent graduate then?" he asked, masking his surprise.

She looked up at him then. "Yes. I graduated last month."

The way her eyes darted in worry tugged at Brady's compassion. "That's great," he said, determined to ease her mind. "We can use a fresh perspective. Sometimes we get tunnel vision on this stuff, and it's always good to bring in new insights and ideas."

"I hope so." Her features softened. "I know I'm only an assistant, but regardless of my responsibilities, I want you all to know that I'm grateful for the opportunity, and I'll bring my best to the job."

Brady didn't doubt it. His thoughts shifted to Velma, curious as to what drove the wealthy developer to take chances on the likes of him and Cole and now Monet. Brady and his partner didn't have much experience under their belts when she'd hired them to design for her.

Whatever Velma's reasons were, Brady was grateful to the risk-taking woman—in more ways than one.

"You obviously know what I've been doing for the past five years." Brady gestured to his surroundings. "Tell me what you've been up to."

Monet chuckled. "Well, nothing as grand as you, but I've kept busy."

"Where did you end up going to college?" he asked.

She cleared her throat. "New York."

Brady's eyebrows rose. "What took you all the way back east?"

A glimmer of that familiar fear he'd often noticed in her eyes momentarily surfaced, only to be followed by a melancholic expression that pulled at the corners of her mouth.

"It's kind of a long story." She dropped her head and smoothed her skirt. "But." She brightened and looked back up at him. "It ended up being the best thing for me."

"And why's that?" he asked carefully.

Monet's shoulders relaxed, and her face softened. "Because I met Juliet."

"Juliet?"

A genuine smile lit up her face. "My best friend."

Brady visually traced Monet's features, still astonished that she sat in his office and wildly intrigued by her. His memories took him back to the day they'd met and how captivated he'd been by her. Brady wanted to know why someone who, by all outward appearances, should possess the self-esteem of someone like Bethany Hawk (yet not as vain) didn't. What kept the humble beauty jittery and lacking the confidence you'd expect from her?

"Would Juliet be the best friend whose dad helped you get the interview by any chance?" Brady asked.

"Yes." She grinned.

Brady pinned her with a direct gaze. "Then it would seem your moving to New York and meeting this *Juliet* was beneficial to you and to me as well."

He had to stifle a chuckle at the lightning-quick way her eyes widened and then softened before she dropped them to her hands. Brady watched for any sign he might have offended her with his implied comment but was encouraged when he saw her bite her lower lip as her mouth curved bashfully.

The rapid series of playful-sounding knocks echoed a split second before Brady's office door opened, and Cole strolled in, followed by Ashley.

"Did we give you two enough time to *catch up*?" Cole snickered, and Brady heaved an irritated sigh.

"No," Brady said dryly. While his mind searched for an excuse to send them away for another few minutes, he glanced at the decorative wall clock hanging on the wall. With an inward groan, he realized he needed to leave for the airport soon. "But I guess we should probably discuss the project and expectations."

Cole took a seat at the table. "What time is your flight?"

"1:00," Brady said. "So, unfortunately, I need to take off soon." His eyes rested on Monet. She sparked such a deep fascination within him. Not only was he physically attracted to her, but he also felt emotionally drawn to her. He'd felt the same pull the night they had dinner together five years earlier, and it was still there—a connection that was hard to ignore.

"We flew back in to meet a new high-profile client," Cole said in response to Monet's furrowed brow. "It just happened to coincide with meeting Ashley's new assistant." Cole flashed her a playful wink and a surge of jealousy caused Brady's muscles to tighten.

He shook his head. His reaction was absurd. First, Cole was obsessively in love with Ashley, who had just taken a seat next to her husband, and second, it was Cole's personality to be playful.

"High profile client?" Monet asked, looking between the three of them.

"Yeah, uh." Brady attempted to reel in his scattered thoughts. "Bethany Hawk... have you heard of her?"

"I have, yes." She nodded before her forehead creased. "Is that why you were at dinner with her last night?"

Monet must have read the confusion on his face because she quickly added, "Juliet—my friend," she clarified, "saw a picture of you two from last night."

Ashley laughed. "That was quick."

"Ugh," Brady groaned as he turned a wagging finger to Cole. "This is why I avoid the media, man." His focus shifted back to Monet. "I hate the attention."

Brady's stomach clenched. He'd known going out to dinner with the popular social media influencer was a bad idea—an open invitation for the media gossips to go wild. But it was also Ashley's birthday; she and Cole were his best friends. The least Brady could do was solo the meeting so they could celebrate.

"I don't like a lot of attention either," Monet said softly, as her expression softened into sympathy. "So I understand."

Brady clamped his mouth shut to keep from blurting, *"good luck with that!"* He caught Cole's baffled expression, and when Ashley opened her mouth to comment, Brady narrowed his eyes and gave his head a firm shake. Instinctively, he knew Monet wouldn't want to be called out on her remark.

Ashley shifted the conversation back on track with a slight nod. "Cole is going to stay in Phoenix for a few more days to finalize a timeline for Bethany's design. Meanwhile, you and I—" she smiled at Monet "—will spend time getting you up to speed on the resort and discussing the tasks you'll be handling."

"Okay," Monet answered. "How long do you expect I'll be in Arizona?" She exhaled a nervous chuckle. "To be honest, I wasn't expecting to be hired on the spot, so I didn't come prepared for a long stay."

"Oh, of course," Brady piped in. "I guess we're getting ahead of ourselves." He leaned back in his chair. "What's your current situation? And what did Velma tell you about the job?" Brady's throat tightened. What if Monet didn't know she was expected to live in Cancun for the next few months?

Monet straightened her posture. "The lease on my apartment in New York was up last week, so I've been staying with Juliet." One of her shoulders lifted in a shrug. "I wasn't sure what would happen with Velma, so I guess I was sort of in limbo waiting to see how that went."

"But of course, she hired you right there and then," Cole said with a grin.

"She did," Monet said. "And I understand that I'll be living in Mexico for six months—until the resort is completed."

Brady released a quiet breath, relieved Velma had been upfront about expectations. They all needed to be onsite during the entire construction process.

"Yes," Brady said. "Velma has a private beachfront villa where the three of us have been living on and off for the past year and a half."

Monet began chewing her bottom lip, an innocent act that was entirely too distracting. Brady would have easily lost his train of thought if it hadn't been for the way her forehead drew together in a tiny frown.

"Velma mentioned I'd be staying in her villa." Monet's eyes flickered nervously around the table. "I didn't realize I would be staying with all of you." Her voice cracked on the last word, prompting her to clear her throat.

Of course she'd be uneasy about it. She barely knew Brady and Ashley and had met Cole for the first time thirty minutes ago. The situation would make most women jittery, and Monet was modest, kind, and had high moral standards. Hadn't she proven that the day she walked away from John Wessler?

To soothe her worried brow, Brady softened his expression and spoke in what he hoped was a reassuring tone. "It's a big villa; sprawling, actually. It has two wings. Each has two bedrooms with its own bathroom." He chuckled reassuringly. "And each room has a lock."

Monet gasped. "Oh! It's…" she stammered. "It's not that. I just—"

"You barely know us, Monet," Brady said kindly. "It's okay to be uneasy about it." Her eyes softened, and she gifted him a grateful smile.

"So," Monet shifted her gaze back to Ashley, "when do you need me in Cancun?"

Ashley sighed. "As soon as you can make it there." She shook her head. "I shouldn't even be here now, but with my assistant quitting and the opportunity with Bethany coming up," she glanced at Cole and then Brady, "sometimes, you gotta do what you gotta do."

Monet mimicked Ashley's glances between the three friends. "It sounds like even though you're technically not part of the firm, you all work together quite a bit?" Monet asked Ashley.

"Pretty convenient, isn't it?" Cole affectionately covered one of Ashley's hands with his. "It just sort of worked out that way."

"I think it's wonderful," Monet said. "You've obviously been friends for years, so it must be a dream to all be working together."

Ashley nodded with a warm smile. "It really is." Brady and Cole both agreed.

Aware of the time, Brady knew he needed to leave, and he hated the fact. He couldn't remember the last time he'd wanted to stay in a woman's company as much as Monet's. He needed to get her to Cancun as soon as possible.

"How soon do you think you could tie things up and get to Cancun?" Brady asked. "We can't afford too many delays if we want to meet our deadline, and Ashley needs you there." Brady needed her there, too.

"When is the deadline?" Monet asked.

"Velma wants to do the grand opening the first week of December," Brady explained. "Just in time for peak season."

She nodded thoughtfully and turned to Ashley. "Well, after we wrap things up here, I'll need a few days to sort out some matters in New York." Monet reached into the side pocket of her work bag sitting on the floor and pulled out her phone. She tapped the screen and pulled up her calendar. "When are you planning to head back to Mexico?" she asked Ashley.

"Cole and I have a flight back Sunday."

"So that gives us four days here in Phoenix," Monet said.

"Yep," Ashley answered.

"Okay. I could plan to fly out to Cancun next Thursday or Friday the 10th or 11th?"

"Either works." Ashley smiled. "Just let Velma's assistant know, and she'll take care of your flights and any other arrangements you need."

Brady forced himself to stand; he needed to leave. "Alright," he began as he walked to his desk on the opposite side of the room. "Sounds like you've got things under control here." He started gathering a couple of folders and other documents he needed and slid them into his black work bag.

He silently kicked himself over insisting that Cole be the one to stay in Phoenix to draft a timeline for Bethany Hawk. Once again, Brady had been the nice guy and offered it up as a way for Cole and Ashley to have some alone time together. Sure, the villa was large enough to have your privacy, but it wasn't the same. They still shared a kitchen and living areas, and Brady knew the married couple would appreciate the break.

Yet, as his eyes settled on Monet, now engrossed in conversation with Ashley and Cole, his chest tightened with overall irritation over not being able to spend more time with her that week. In the next instant, however, the tension in his body loosened at the realization that they'd be living under the same roof in one week's time, and he would get to see her nearly every day for the next six months.

A wide grin spread across his face when he imagined the possibilities that lay ahead concerning the intriguing woman from all those years ago.

Brady retrieved his jacket from the back of his drafting chair and slid his arms in. "I gotta take off, but I'll see you all in a few days."

Monet stood, and Cole and Ashley followed suit. "It was really nice to see you again, Brady—and fun catching up a little." She walked toward him, and it was all he could do to stop his eyes from caressing her from head to toe again.

Monet reached out to shake his hand. "I guess I'll see you next week."

One corner of Brady's mouth twitched as he finished straightening the collar of his sports jacket. He held Monet's icy blue eyes with his own as he reached out and took her hand. The feel of her soft skin was invigorating, sending a thrilling chill up his arm.

Monet's lips parted as she drew in a quick breath. The knowledge that she was as affected by their touch as he was bolstered his confidence.

Brady leaned in closer. "Walk me out," he said softly while still holding her hand.

A flash of surprise crossed her face before she looked quickly over her shoulder at Cole and Ashley, who wore satisfied grins.

"O...okay," Monet stammered as she withdrew her hand from his. She smoothed her hands over her skirt and glanced nervously at his friends.

"She'll be right back," Brady chuckled.

"Mm-hmm," Ashley mumbled before looking at Cole with raised eyebrows.

Brady motioned for Monet to precede him and was relieved that she was already halfway out of the office when Cole threw him a thumbs up and mouthed *"right on"* with a dramatic nod to his head.

Brady guided Monet through the reception area, where he said goodbye to Trish and thanked her for keeping things in order while he and Cole were in Mexico. Once he'd wrapped up his short conversation with their Phoenix-based secretary, he and Monet walked to the elevator a short distance from where Trish sat.

Brady reached out and pressed the down button.

"I'm having a little déjà vu," Brady teased, hoping to lighten things up. It was obvious by Monet's lack of eye contact and fidgety hand movements that she was uncomfortable—obviously wondering why he'd asked her to walk him out. Thankfully, his reference to the last time they'd said goodbye five years prior made her laugh, and she visibly relaxed.

"Yep," she said, still chuckling. "Except I was the one getting on the elevator."

"I remember." Brady nodded as he studied her. "I'm really happy to see you again, Monet. Honestly, I couldn't get you off my mind for months after that night, and I've thought about you many times over the years."

Monet's breath hitched. Once more her eyes searched his in a moment of surprise, and a slight flush crept across her cheeks.

"I've thought about you as well." Her voice was soft, almost breathless, and her words somehow lightened his heart even more.

The elevator dinged, indicating it had arrived, and the door was about to open. "I do have a question," Brady asked as trepidation inched into the calm he'd felt. "Are you... seeing anyone?"

She shook her head with a faint smile. "No."

An impish grin spread across his face. "Good."

Monet rolled her lip between her teeth as her alluring blush deepened. "Um... What about you?" she adorably stammered. "Are you—"

"No."

Her eyes danced with a playful glow of their own. "Good."

Brady's mouth twitched, both delighted and somewhat surprised by her response. "See you soon, Monet," he said as he reluctantly stepped onto the elevator.

"See you soon, Brady."

And with that, the door slid closed, leaving Brady spellbound and brimming with anticipation over what the next six months would bring with the bewitching Monet Everly at his fingertips.

Monet

"I still can't believe I did it," Monet said as she secured a strip of packing tape across the small cardboard box. "You know me; I don't flirt... ever!"

Juliet sat perched on the edge of her guest bed and shook her head. "Okay, first, what you did was only a mild flirt, and second," she said as her eyes lit with mischief, "when you like a guy, you totally have to flirt. Otherwise, he won't know you're interested."

"But Juliet, it's not—"

"Nope!" Juliet halted Monet's words with an abrupt rise of her palm. "No talking yourself out of this, Monet," she insisted. "The fact that Brady was able to coax a little playful flirting out of you is huge; it means you *are* interested, but more importantly, you're finally moving on."

Monet paused in her packing and looked at Juliet. The flutter in her belly bounced between hope and fear. She was fearful of Brady's true intentions but hoped that Juliet was right, that Monet was on her way to feeling normal again.

"Maybe you're right." Monet set the tape dispenser on a nearby dresser and plopped down next to Juliet. "Maybe I am ready to entertain romantic feelings toward a man."

"If I'm not mistaken," Juliet said, "you've been entertaining romantic feelings toward a certain hot bellhop for five years."

Monet giggled. "It's true." She tossed her head with a huff. "Even with all that John Wessler put me through—the stalking and harassment, I could never stop thinking about that dinner with Brady." Monet's face scrunched. "Weird, isn't it?"

"Not at all." Juliet sighed with a dreamy smile playing on her lips. "And the fact that Brady admitted to thinking about you over the years makes it that much more romantic."

"As romantic as yours and Josh's story?" Monet teasingly asked. "Or better yet, Sawyer and Violet's?"

Juliet grinned. "I know, right? You'd think it would be impossible to top my brother and sister-in-law's love story—Violet flying from Colorado to New York for a blind date with my brother..."

Monet's mouth curved into a small smile. "I still remember you telling me all about that weekend," she said. "I was so happy for Sawyer—especially after I met Violet. Those two are relationship goals."

Juliet's eyes sparkled. "They are."

"But," Monet lifted a single eyebrow, "I gotta say, Josh could give your brother a good run for his money," Monet said. "Your fiancé is about the most romantic man I've ever met."

Juliet's expression beamed with a silly grin. "He is, isn't he?"

"And it's not just the big things, like moving from Colorado to New York for you, or the way he proposed... Although," she tilted her head as her eyes widened, "a waterfall proposal in the Rockies *is* pretty swoony."

"Ooh..." Juliet placed one delicate hand over her heart and exhaled. "It was."

"But it's more than that, Jewel," Monet said. "It's the small things too, the way he's always finding ways to touch you, the little compliments he gives you every day, and as far as your cooking, it's no secret to everyone that Josh is genuinely your biggest fan." Monet exhaled an appreciative sigh. "It's those romantic gestures I love, and it's why I'm so happy for you."

Juliet had a tender heart, and Monet watched as her friend's eyes shimmered as she took Monet's hands in her own. "Thank you, Monet," she said. "And you're right. I found my happily ever after with Josh, the same way Sawyer found his with Violet." She gently squeezed Monet's hands. "And you'll find yours too."

Monet's heart lifted. "I hope so." And she meant it. She wanted what Juliet and Josh had—what Juliet's brother and his wife had.

"Thanks again for letting me stay here the past couple of weeks," Monet said, gesturing to the moving box sitting next to them on the bed. "And thanks for shipping the rest of my stuff to my parents' house." She shrugged. "I'm not sure what will happen after this job or where I'll end up, but hopefully it opens a few doors."

"Oh, I'm certain it will," Juliet said, her eyes holding that familiar glimmer of optimism and encouragement. Monet's throat suddenly felt thick over the thought of being away from her best friend for so long.

"I'm going to miss you so much." Monet's posture slumped. "How will I ever make it six months without seeing you?"

Juliet bit her lip before a grin broke through. "About that..."

Monet's head tipped. She knew Juliet well and sensed the dark-haired beauty was up to something.

Juliet's smile grew even wider. "Josh and I have finally picked a date."

"What?" Monet grabbed Juliet's hands. "When?"

"When did we decide? Or when is the wedding?"

Monet giggled. "Both!"

"Don't worry," Juliet said with a laugh. "We haven't known for long—we picked the date while you were in Arizona."

"And?" Monet quickly asked.

"December fifteenth!"

Monet threw her arms around Juliet as they bounced on the edge of the bed where they sat.

"A winter wedding," Monet sighed as the two friends drew back from their embrace. "It's so romantic."

"It is, but it won't be your typical winter wedding." Juliet's smile didn't leave her face, but she nervously pushed a dark strand of hair behind one ear. "Now that you've got the job with Velma and you're going to Cancun, I can ask."

Monet's eyebrows raised. "Ask what?"

"Josh and I have already talked to Velma, and we've decided we want to have our wedding in Cancun—at the Grand Jewel."

Monet's eyes bulged. "What!" she gasped, "Juliet... that's so perfect!"

Juliet drew her shoulders up dramatically. "I know," her voice squeaked. "Ours will be the first wedding the resort will host."

Monet was breathless, her heart warmed by the evident joy in her best friend's eyes. "It will be magical, Jewel," Monet said. "Believe me, I've seen the design, and from the looks of the pictures so far—" she took a deep breath, exhaling in awe— "it will be the perfect destination wedding."

"And Monet?" Juliet nibbled her lip. "I wanted to ask... well, Josh and I," she stammered, "we're in full agreement on this—we want you to plan the wedding."

Monet's head jerked back as her forehead wrinkled and her eyes popped. "Huh?"

Juliet broke into a fit of laughter and pointed at Monet. "Your face!"

Monet did her best to relax her features but still tried to process what Juliet said. "You guys what?"

"It's perfect!" Juliet said, ignoring Monet's need for reiteration. "You'll already be there; you'll know the ins and outs of the resort and the area—"

"But I can't plan your wedding!" Monet interrupted. "I'm not an event planner and don't know the first thing about it."

"Pfft!" Juliet's eyes narrowed. "Yes, you do!"

"No, I don't," Monet shot back.

"You forget," Juliet said. "I know what your other choice of degree was." She raised a cocky brow. "Does Hospitality ring a bell?"

Monet shot her friend a deadpan look. "Yes, but in case you've forgotten, I received my degree in Interior Design—not Hospitality."

Juliet laughed and clutched Monet's hands. "I know," she said. "But event planning comes naturally to you."

Monet rolled her eyes. "Juliet, planning a few birthday parties and one culinary graduation celebration does not mean I can plan a luxury wedding for Juliet Quinn." Monet huffed. "Your mom would never allow it."

"Oh, please." Juliet mirrored Monet's huff. "You'd keep it tasteful, not like some showy ball my mom would plan," she tossed her head with a defeated sigh, "and all for the sake of appearances."

A dull pang struck Monet's chest. She knew it wasn't easy being the daughter of Camila Quinn. Monet often wondered how it was possible that Juliet was related to Camila. Juliet's mother was selfish, arrogant, controlling, and snubbed her nose at anyone who didn't come from wealth and affluence.

"I know, Jewel." Monet's voice softened. "But your mom already doesn't like me—she barely tolerates our friendship as it is."

Juliet shook her head. "I don't care—you know that."

Monet did know. Thankfully, Juliet and her brother Sawyer inherited more of their father's genes, not only his striking good looks but also his humility.

"Besides," Juliet went on. "After the stunt she pulled trying to come between Sawyer and Violet before they were married, my dad lowered the boom on her antics big time," Juliet said. "And even though she still tries to control me, she won't fight me on this." She smiled. "At least not too much." Juliet winked.

Monet breathed a reluctant chuckle and tried to ignore the nervous quiver in her belly.

"Please?" Juliet jutted her lower lip while she dramatically batted pleading puppy eyes. "You know what I like; you have exquisite taste, perfect judgment, and you'll keep it classy."

Monet studied her friend. "Ugh," she moaned. "You know I can't say no to you."

Juliet squealed and threw her arms around Monet's neck. "Thank you! Thank you! Thank you!"

Juliet's enthusiasm quickly rubbed off on Monet, and she laughed despite how her stomach rolled with nerves. Monet knew the Hafen wedding would be plastered across the media and social websites in much the same way Sawyer and Violet's had. After all, Juliet was a Quinn, and the Quinns were pretty close to social royalty.

"And don't worry," Juliet said once she'd settled down. "We just want a simple wedding."

"Simple?" Monet's voice screeched. "Where the guests fly to a new luxury resort in Mexico—do you mean simple on top of that?"

"Uh-huh. Easy, right?"

"Yeah, piece of cake, Jewel," Monet smirked. "Especially since I'm also assisting with the interior design of the aforementioned resort." She snapped her fingers sarcastically. "Easy... Not!"

Juliet leapt up from where she'd been sitting on the edge of the bed. "I need to grab my phone; I can't wait to tell Josh."

Monet watched her best friend dart out of the bedroom in search of her phone, and Monet puffed a long breath. She marveled at how drastically her life had changed over the course of a week and a half. Not only was she moving to Cancun for six months to work alongside Ashley and Brady—the man who'd captured her teenage heart five years prior, but now, Monet had agreed to plan Josh and Juliet's wedding. The realization was—overwhelming.

She brought a hand to her temple, inhaling deeply before exhaling. Digging deep mentally, Monet mustered the self-confidence she'd undoubtedly need to pull this off. But she would do it. For Juliet, she'd do anything.

"I sent him a text," Juliet said as she walked back into the room. "The attorney he's interning with is meeting with a new client today. Someone is trying to patent *another* type of abs contraption."

Monet laughed. "Seriously?"

"Um-hum." Juliet nodded. "But, hey," she smiled, "dreams make life exciting," she said. "And the way people snatch exercise equipment up, they'll probably sell a million of them."

Monet chuckled before she sucked in a breath and glanced around. "Well," she exhaled. "It looks like everything's ready to be shipped."

Juliet's cheerful demeanor shifted into a frown. "I can't believe you're leaving in the morning. I'm going to miss you."

Monet watched as Juliet's eyes filled with emotion, and it caused tears to well in her own. "Me too." Monet embraced her friend and truly wondered how she would manage life without Juliet's bubbly encouragement.

"We'll be in touch every day, right?" Juliet pulled back but didn't release Monet. "And—" Juliet's head tipped. "Seeing as our wedding is at the Grand Jewel, it only makes sense for Josh and me to make a trip down there, right?"

"At least one." Monet smiled as they ended their embrace.

"Seriously though," Juliet said. "Thank you for agreeing to plan the wedding for us. And don't worry, I'll help too—especially with the menu," she said.

"Oh, you bet you will!" Monet laughed. "That's where I draw the line. I'll do everything else, but no way would I dare plan the food for the wedding of a culinary genius such as yourself."

"Genius?" Juliet smirked. "Not quite."

Monet admired her friend in so many ways, but one of Juliet's most noble qualities was her humility. Monet's cherished friend had everything it took to be conceited and think she was better than everyone else, but on the contrary, Juliet had a pure heart of gold, and Monet was thankful every day that they'd found each other.

"You know," Monet said, "even though I'm a little nervous about it—well, actually, *a lot* nervous—planning your wedding is one small way I can pay you back."

Juliet's brow furrowed. "What do you possibly owe me for?"

Monet reached out and clasped Juliet's hand. "For helping me be brave—for teaching me how to live again."

"Oh, Monet," Juliet's tone was soft, "you've always been brave, and as far as teaching you to live again, you just needed a little nudging here and there."

A gentle smile crossed Monet's lips, and she nodded.

"But now," Juliet's voice sparkled, "seeing as I only have you for one more night, I'm taking you birthday shopping."

Monet giggled. "My birthday isn't until next month."

Juliet pulled on Monet's arm and led her from the guest bedroom and into the living area. "I know it isn't," Juliet said. "But you'll be in Cancun, so we're celebrating a little early."

Monet stopped dead in her tracks and frowned. "That is a totally depressing thought."

Juliet laughed. "What is? That we're celebrating early or that you'll be in Cancun?"

"That I'll be celebrating my birthday alone in Cancun this year."

"Alone?" Juliet's eyes bulged. "You're kidding, right? What about a certain dashing architect?"

"Oh, well, yeah," Monet said as her heart leapt at Juliet's mention of Brady. "He'll be there, along with Ashley and her husband, but I won't be celebrating with them..." Monet stared at Juliet. "Will I?"

Juliet arched her delicate eyebrows, her face beaming. "Let me put it this way," she said with a dreamy sigh. "I have a hunch this year will be a birthday you won't soon forget."

Monet

"Would you like a drink before takeoff, Miss?"

"Oh." Monet glanced up at the well-groomed flight attendant before looking around at the other first-class passengers who were sipping everything from water to cocktails. "Do I have time?"

The woman smiled. "Yes. We still have fifteen minutes before the doors close."

"Can I just get some water, please?"

"Certainly, I'll be right back." The courteous flight attendant turned and headed to the small galley in the front of the airplane.

When Monet arrived at the airport to check in for her flight from New York to Cancun, she was surprised to find Velma's assistant had booked her a first-class seat. Monet had flown many times throughout her life but never in first class. Admittedly, she'd felt a nervous quiver in her belly when she'd first stepped onto the airplane and took the three short steps to her first-class window seat. She'd sensed the other passengers around her were eyeing her—pegging her as a fraud and wondering how she could afford to sit there.

Once she'd settled in her seat, the unease lessened, and she realized it was her insecurities making an unwelcome appearance. In reality, nobody cared one whit who she was or what she was doing sitting in their section.

The flight attendant returned and handed Monet a small bottle of water.

"Once we are in flight, we'll be offering breakfast," the woman, whose name tag read Cheryl, said. "In the meantime, please let me know if you need anything else."

Monet nodded. "Thank you."

After several more minutes of passengers boarding, an older gentleman rushed onto the aircraft and took the empty aisle seat next to Monet.

"I wasn't sure I would make it," the man told her. Monet's body stiffened—her natural reaction to men, especially older ones around the same age as John Wessler. She silently scolded herself; she didn't want to be that woman anymore. Monet didn't want to live in fear of the opposite sex—she *wouldn't* live in fear of them. So, inhaling a deep breath of courage, Monet smiled.

"Just in the nick of time too." She nodded to where a male flight attendant was closing the door.

The man returned her smile, and for the next thirty minutes, Monet shared pleasant conversation with the stranger before he reclined his seat and dozed off.

Monet rested her head against the seat and turned her neck to watch as the airplane glided across the cloudless blue sky. The corners of her mouth curved up as a feeling of buoyancy spread through her limbs. Monet had let her guard down and kept up an entire conversation with a man who didn't once hit on her or mention her looks. The experience was refreshing and exactly what she'd needed.

Her thoughts turned to her best friend—Juliet would be proud of her.

With nothing much to do, Monet's mind began to wander, her thoughts bouncing from the past to the present and back again. She thought about the first time she'd flown to New York with her parents. It was a significant step for Monet to leave the small bubble in which she'd lived, but it didn't take long before everyone agreed moving away was the best thing for her—it led her to Juliet. Monet was momentarily transported back to the first time the two friends met at a small diner near the university she was attending. The memory brought a smile to her face and a familiar warmth to her heart.

It was roughly four years ago. Monet needed to get away from Utah; she'd needed a change, a fresh start. She'd spent the first year after high school living a nightmare. One that found her terrified to leave her house, fearful of what Mr. Wessler would do next or where he'd show up.

It had only been a week after she'd returned from California when the horrible man first appeared on her doorstep. Even as she thought back on it, she felt the same uneasy tremor that had caused her to stiffen and lose her breath when she opened the door and found him standing there moments after her parents left for work. He displayed a sickly triumphant grin as he stared at her.

"*Hello, Monet,*" he'd said in a cocky tone that made her skin crawl.

She'll never forget how, in the next instant, she watched the way Mr. Wessler's eyes narrowed and morphed into irritation at the voice that echoed behind her.

"*Who is it, Mo?*"

The vile man hadn't planned on Evan being home. Monet's older brother had recently returned home from college for the summer and hadn't started his summer job yet.

Evan was less than welcoming, and after a verbal battle that ended with John Wessler threatening both Evan and Monet, Evan slammed the door and immediately called the police. There wasn't much the authorities could do—at least at that point.

From there, things just got worse. The man made it clear on the day he'd shown up at her house that he blamed Monet for tarnishing his professional reputation, which she and her family couldn't quite fathom. Monet was *one* woman; it was *one* music video—how hard could it have been to replace her? Besides, how could one job ruin an entire agency—it couldn't. But when he started to cyberstalk Monet and send her non-stop gifts and flowers with disgusting threats written on the cards, it was clear Mr. Wessler wasn't mentally stable—at all.

After a few episodes of in-person stalking, Monet was finally able to seek a restraining order against him, which seemed to knock some sense into him because the harassment finally stopped. Unfortunately, the damage to Monet's self-esteem and mental state was already done.

Monet sighed as she thought of her best friend from high school, Lily. Lily felt such guilt over suggesting they enter each other in the contest that it drove a wedge between the two girlfriends. No matter how hard Monet tried to convince her otherwise, Lily couldn't deal with it. Driven by guilt, Lily moved to Seattle to attend college. One of Monet's greatest hopes was that one day, their friendship would heal.

After all of that—a year filled with heartache and fear—Monet made the move to New York. Although she had the support and love of her family back home, Monet was alone in a big city—and she felt it. There were several times when she almost threw in the towel and hightailed it back to Utah. She's certain she would have if it weren't for that crisp autumn afternoon when a stunning beauty with an infectious smile befriended her.

When Monet first started school in New York, she became a frequent customer of a quaint, family-owned diner. The main reason was the food. The dishes had that home-cooked flavor, and the ambiance was quiet and cozy. It turned out it was one of Juliet's favorite places, too. "A hidden gem," her friend often called it. Monet typically ate alone until one day, out of the blue, the kindhearted woman approached Monet's table and asked if she could join her. Juliet's bubbly personality was contagious, and the two hit it off instantly. Four years later, the two were still the closest of friends.

Monet always admired the way Juliet was able to look beyond Monet's insecure mask of baggy, colorless clothes, a makeup-free face, and drab hair, seeing a real person who was in need of a friend.

It didn't take much time for Monet to confide in Juliet about her journey with John Wessler. Guided by Juliet's compassionate support and unwavering encouragement, Monet embarked on a profound journey of self-discovery, ultimately finding herself again.

*

Monet stared out the small airplane window at the white sandy beaches bordered by the turquoise Caribbean Sea. A sudden surge of adrenaline pushed away the grogginess caused by the long flight as Monet imagined what the next six months would bring while she lived in the tropical paradise she was about to arrive at.

As the pilots continued the gradual descent into the Cancun airport, Monet scanned the beachfront resorts and residences from her view above.

Brady's down there somewhere, she thought.

Ever since she'd said goodbye to him that day in Arizona, thoughts of Brady Nash would continually sneak into her mind, even with the fact that Monet's life had been nothing less than a whirlwind.

Over the past week and a half, she'd undergone a crash course to get up to speed on the resort with Ashley and Cole, flown back to New York to tie up her loose ends, and squeezed in as much girl time as possible with Juliet, which included her generous friend's gift of a birthday shopping spree. But even amongst it all, Monet found her thoughts would always float back to the handsome architect. And as she gazed down on the touristy city below, her heart began to hammer against her chest, knowing Brady was there and that she'd be seeing him soon.

The airplane wheels hit the landing strip a short time later as the flight attendant's voice echoed over the speaker.

"Ladies and gentlemen, it is our pleasure to welcome you to Cancun. Local time is 1:24, and the current temperature is 86 degrees."

As the woman continued her post-landing instructions, Monet reached into her travel bag tucked under her seat and pulled out her cell phone. Once the plane had arrived at the gate, Monet turned off Airplane Mode, and within seconds, her screen started popping up missed text messages. *Juliet, Mom, Evan, Ashley,* and a phone number she didn't recognize.

She opened her messaging app and quickly scanned the message from the unknown phone number.

"Hey, Monet. It's Brady—

Monet inhaled a quick breath, and her heart jumped again.

"If I'm timing this message right, you should be on the plane heading to Cancun, and you'll get this when you land. Hopefully, my plan works out because I wanted to be the first one to officially welcome you to Cancun – Well, aside from the flight attendant." Monet breathed a soft giggle.

"I'll see you soon."

With a throbbing pulse and a wide grin, Monet re-read the message. The fact that Brady had taken the time to send her a welcome message thrilled her far more than it probably should have.

"Who's the lucky fella?" the gentleman sitting next to her asked.

Monet startled a bit and turned to look at him.

"I figure it must be some dashing Romeo to put a smile like that on your face."

Monet released a nervous laugh as her cheeks warmed. "He *is* dashing," she said, tucking her phone into her bag. "But he's not my Romeo—just someone I'm going to be working with, a... a friend, I guess."

The man raised an eyebrow, and his lips quirked into a teasing smile. "A friend, you guess?"

Monet fidgeted with the strap of her travel bag. "Yes."

"Um-hum." He winked. "Well, enjoy your time in Cancun, and good luck with the resort and," his grin widened, "with your friend."

Monet's face turned a deeper shade of red, but she laughed. Throughout the flight, she'd learned that the man was embarking on an "old geezer getaway," as he'd humorously put it. He and a former business associate (now friend) owned a timeshare in Playa Del Carmen, where they met up several times a year since retiring.

"Thank you, Mr. . ." She faltered, realizing they'd never exchanged names.

"Hamlin," he said.

Monet's forehead puckered as a prickling sensation brushed her scalp. The last name was familiar to her.

"Mr. Hamlin," she repeated, quickly brushing off the weird sensation she'd felt. "I'm Monet," she said. "You enjoy your boys' trip as well." She gathered her belongings and stood as Mr. Hamlin stepped from his seat into the aisle.

"I'm sure I will," he chuckled. "You take care."

"You too."

Monet decided to allow a few passengers to exit before her. She couldn't put her finger on it, but she wanted to put some distance between her and her first-class seat companion.

Once Mr. Hamlin disappeared from her view, she inched her way into the aisle and headed for the exit. Monet stepped from the plane into the jetway and was instantly hit by the thickness of the heat and humidity from the outside air. It was so powerful that her body instinctively sucked in a deeper breath.

It was the first time Monet had experienced such intense humidity, and it triggered a moment of negativity; she wondered how she'd be able to live in such a wet, sticky climate for six months. She quickly exhaled and shook the thought from her mind. Monet figured she'd get used to it—eventually.

She was grateful she'd listened to Juliet and worn a cotton summer dress. Cotton and linen. Juliet had made sure Monet packed plenty of the lightweight material in tops, skirts, and dresses—along with a couple of swimsuits (compliments of Juliet herself).

Monet emerged from the tunnel and stepped into the airport. "Ahh, air-conditioning," she mumbled before realizing she'd only walked sixty feet through a jetway. She wondered what the outside would feel like.

Monet squared her shoulders, determined to make her experience in Cancun a fresh beginning full of new experiences and positivity. *It's just a little humidity.*

Once Monet made her way through customs and found the correct carousel in baggage claim, she scanned the area, hoping to see Ashley. Aside from the basic phrases like *Hola, Buenos días, Gracias, De nada*, and *Mi nombre es* Monet—she didn't know a lick of Spanish. Ashley and Cole assured her that Cancun was a tourist destination and that almost everyone spoke enough English to get her through her stay. Even so, Monet was grateful when she'd received Ashley's text saying she'd meet her at the airport.

"Monet!"

Her eyes shifted to an energetic squeal coming from the entrance, and a smile spread across her face at the sight of her tiny co-worker fairly bouncing towards her. Ashley's short blonde hair was complimented perfectly by her off-the-shoulder baby blue ruffle dress. Even in the summer wedge shoes on Ashley's feet, Monet was two or three inches taller than her new friend.

"Ahh! You're here!" Ashley threw her arms around Monet, causing Monet's bag to slip from her hands.

"I am," Monet laughed. "My goodness," she said as Ashley released her. "You certainly know how to make a person feel welcome."

"Of course!" Ashley chirped. "I'm so happy you're finally here—we all are."

Monet stooped and retrieved her bag that had fallen during Ashley's exuberant greeting. "Thank you. I'm excited to be here too... well, a little nervous but also excited."

"Now, there's no reason to be nervous," Ashley soothed. "But I get it. New job, a new country—" her mouth twitched, "a new boyfriend." She playfully nudged Monet.

Monet's eyes bulged. "What?" Her voice cracked, and her cheeks heated.

Ashley giggled. "I'm just teasing you, sweetie." She linked her arm through Monet's as the two took a step toward the baggage carousel that had started to rotate with luggage. "But between you and me," she leaned in closer, "Brady hasn't stopped talking about you since Cole and I got back on Sunday."

A jolt of adrenaline burned under her skin, but Monet schooled her expression. "What do you mean?"

"I mean, the man can't seem to think about anything else," she said. *"Ashley, can you believe it? After five years... Monet Everly!"* she mimicked. "He's repeated that one about fifty times. Oh, and *I can't get over how beautiful she is*, or, *do you think she's excited to be working with us—tell me the truth, Ash, do you think she was happy to see me again?* And on and on and on."

"Really?" Monet puffed a small giggle as her heart fluttered. "Brady said those things?"

"Um-hum." Ashley nodded. "And then some."

Monet chewed her bottom lip; being on Brady's mind delighted her to her core.

"And I'll tell you," Ashley said. "It does my heart good to see it; Cole's too." She shook her head. "Too many shallow women out there, you know? Brady deserves better than what he's had."

Monet's fears and insecurities regarding men were brewing just below the surface, but Brady Nash was different. She knew he was; even though she'd spent no more than three hours with the man, Monet knew he'd never harm her—intentionally.

"Brady wanted to be the one to pick you up," Ashley said, breaking into Monet's thoughts. "But he and Cole got dragged into a last-minute meeting with the contractor."

Monet forced a smile but silently exhaled in relief. The thought of Brady picking her up from the airport drew an anxious quiver to her stomach. She needed to pull herself together before seeing him again—mentally and physically. After a long flight and how her skin felt moist from the humidity, Monet knew a few swipes of deodorant and a refreshing body mist would be in order before meeting Brady face to face again.

"Oh, this is me," Monet said as she stepped forward and lifted the first of three suitcases off the silver carousel. It wasn't long before her last bag appeared, and she and Ashley headed out of the airport terminal and into the tropical Mexican sun.

Brady

Brady sat semi-listening as Jesse—the all-work and no-play contractor rambled on inside the blessedly air-conditioned construction trailer that had been their office for the past several months. Despite all the lightweight material that made up Brady's Cancun wardrobe, the heat was relentless.

Unable to sit still, he reached forward to grab his cell phone from the small conference table in front of him. Glancing at the screen, his brow puckered.

Still no response.

Ever since he and Cole had been called into a last-minute meeting with Jesse, Brady had been distracted by the fact that Monet hadn't responded to his text message. He noted the time displayed on his phone, confirming that her flight should have landed thirty minutes earlier.

With his thoughts preoccupied with Monet's arrival, Brady was having a hard time keeping his mind on what their contractor was saying about the delivery delay for the freestanding bathtubs going in the five oceanfront honeymoon bungalows.

He glanced across the table to where Cole sat leisurely in his office chair. His burly friend seemed to read Brady's thoughts—or, more accurately, Brady's fidgety movements and lack of engagement in the meeting. One side of Cole's mouth quirked as he turned his attention to his cell phone and pressed a few buttons. A second later, Cole flashed the screen toward Brady.

His eyes landed on the image displayed on Cole's phone, and Brady's heart jumped before its beat quickened over the selfie of Ashley and Monet standing in front of the thatch-covered Air Margaritaville snack bar outside the Cancun airport.

In a "*she's here*" gesture, Cole raised his eyebrows, and Brady squelched the grin that immediately sprang to his lips. In an attempt to keep his budding interest in their new assistant designer from Jesse, Brady simply tossed Cole an appreciative nod.

"What am I missing here?" Jesse scowled as he gestured between Cole and Brady.

Ever since they'd started working with the rigid contractor eighteen months earlier, it often bothered Brady how Jesse could make him feel like he was back in high school being scolded by Mrs. Brabbs—the scariest woman to ever receive a teaching license.

Cole gestured to his phone. "It's nothing. Ashley was just letting me know she picked up Monet from the airport."

"The new assistant?" Jesse's frown remained etched on his face.

"Yep," Cole confirmed before turning back to Brady. "Ash says they're going to stop by the villa before heading to the site."

Velma's villa, where they'd been living on and off for the past year and a half, was roughly forty-five minutes south of the Cancun airport but only a few miles down the beach from the construction site. If he left soon, Brady could be there to welcome Monet to Cancun properly.

He stood. "I've got something to take care of."

Jesse's face tightened. "But we haven't addressed the delay issue."

"We'll just hold off on the flooring around the bathtubs," Brady said as he walked to his drafting table inside the large mobile construction trailer. "We've got the specs for the tubs; we'll just make sure the plumbing is done and ready for the install." He lifted his work backpack off the floor and stuffed his cell phone in the outside pocket. "Once the tubs are installed, we'll finish the flooring." He tossed the black bag over his shoulder. "Shouldn't be an issue."

Jesse crossed his arms and leaned back in his chair. "I guess that will work."

Brady forced a stiff smile and tried to tamp down the irritation he frequently battled where Jesse was concerned.

That was one thing about Velma Larsen; she always gave people a chance, and Jesse Nickels was no different. He was a thirty-something divorcee who decided he needed a change of career after his marriage of ten years ended. Jesse had only been working as a contractor for a few years; his resume wasn't extensive, and he still had a lot to learn—but honestly, who didn't?

The perpetually frowning man should have resolved the delivery delay on his own, but as had become a habit, Brady mustered patience for Jesse. He and Cole had both been green themselves, and he knew if Velma felt Jesse deserved a chance, then he probably did—even on a project as high profile as The Grand Jewel.

"You can reach me on my cell if something comes up," Brady said. "Otherwise, I'll be back later." He opened the door of the mobile trailer and stepped out.

"Hold up a second, Brady," Cole called out before turning to Jesse. "Give us a minute, Jess."

Cole strode out the door and followed Brady down the steps toward one of the two Jeep Wranglers Velma provided them during their stay in Cancun. "You're heading to the villa, aren't you?" Cole asked, not hiding the humor in his tone.

Brady chuckled and dropped his head with a shake. "Am I that obvious?"

Cole laughed, slapping Brady on the back. "Only because I know you."

"I don't know what it is, Cole," Brady said. "I can't get her out of my head... and it's not just physical; something about her draws me in."

A knowing smile spread across Cole's face, and his eyes danced. "It was the same for me when I first met Ashley." He gripped Brady's shoulder with one strong hand. "And I gotta say, it's good to see you like this—I've never seen a girl capture your attention—or better yet, unsettle you as much as this one does."

Brady huffed a chuckle. "It's true. I just hope I can keep my head in the right place with the project." He exhaled. "To be honest, I'd like nothing more than to bail on work and spend the rest of my day showing Monet around." Brady opened the door to the Jeep and slid behind the driver's seat before closing the door.

"Don't worry," Cole said, stepping back from the driver's side window. "There will be plenty of time for you to charm Monet. Six months, actually."

Brady's heart drummed against his chest at the reminder of spending the next six months with Monet. A half a year living under the same roof, there was no saying goodbye at the end of the day, simply goodnight.

Fresh energy filled Brady as he finally let loose the wide grin he'd stifled in front of Jesse. Cole was right. There was plenty of time for Brady and Monet to get to know each other—ample opportunities for Brady to "*charm*" her, as Cole put it. As a matter of fact, Brady decided, why wait? He'd start that very moment.

Before putting the Jeep in drive, Brady pulled up the maps app on his phone and searched local flower shops. Flowers might have been a bit old-fashioned and cliché, but Brady had a feeling that Monet would be touched by the simple gesture. Besides, this was only the beginning— there was plenty of time for more exotic, fresh ways to woo her.

He reached up, pressed the auto button for the sky power top, and waited as the Jeep's roof slid open. The light breeze from the nearby ocean found its way through the windows and the opening above him. It was refreshing against the brutal heat and humidity Brady had grown used to since first arriving in Cancun a year and a half prior.

As the smooth Latin-infused sound of Carlos Santana poured from the speakers, he slid on his dark sunglasses, shifted the Jeep into drive, and set off.

*

Brady pulled into the circular driveway in front of Velma's luxury villa, grateful that the other Jeep wasn't parked outside. It meant he'd beaten Ashley and Monet back.

After shutting off the engine, he gently gathered the colorful bouquet of dahlias and lilies he'd picked up along the way. He'd asked the florist for something native to the area and was pleased with the vibrant arrangement he'd walked away with.

Brady made his way into the postcard-perfect tropical residence of the wealthy widow. Nestled amongst the lush jungle and resting just steps away from a white sandy beach and the clear aqua-colored sea, the villa was the ultimate destination for anyone wanting to escape into paradise.

He strode through the wood-trimmed double glass doors and into the tranquilly decorated residence. The hues were deep and rich, drawn from the colors of the sea and the surrounding vegetation. The floors throughout were exotic bamboo hardwoods, which were contrasted beautifully by seagrass rugs and modern teak and rattan furniture. Rather than faux plants and flowers, Velma insisted on natural tropical foliage, which was nestled in containers made of wicker and bamboo and tended to weekly by the housekeeping service that kept the villa in tiptop condition.

Brady went directly to the small library they used as their office at the villa and retrieved a small notepad and pen from the glossy rosewood desk. He took a seat and hurriedly wrote:

Dinner? 8:00?

A smile tugged his mouth when he thought of the blush his invitation would bring to Monet's cheeks. Brady didn't know too much about her or what made her mysterious heart tick, but something he did know about Monet Everly was that she was modest, free from vanity, and he suspected his bold dinner invitation would rattle her—in a good way, he hoped.

The sound of wheels rolling over the gravel driveway caused Brady's heart to jump. He set the pen down, tucked the small note inside the flower arrangement, and left the library. He hurried down the hall to the bedroom intended for Monet and gently laid the bouquet against the soft white pillows on the canopy-covered bed before quickly making his way back into the foyer just as Ashley opened the front door.

"It's almost magical, isn't it?"

The sound of Monet's melodic voice caused Brady to halt, his heart taking an even greater leap than it had moments before.

"That's why they call it paradise," Ashley was saying as her eyes landed on Brady. "Oh!" she yelped. "Brady!" She placed her hand on her chest. "You scared me right outta my skin."

Brady couldn't help but laugh. "I'm sorry... didn't you see the Jeep?" He motioned out the open door, trying not to let his eyes linger on Monet.

"Well, yeah, but I didn't expect you to pop up right inside the front door," she scolded. "You startled me!"

"One thing you'll learn about our Ashley here," Brady said to Monet, "is that she's easily spooked."

Monet smiled before shifting her attention back to Ashley. "Is that so?"

"A little bit," she said. "But it doesn't help when Brady and Cole take full advantage of it." Ashley playfully swatted Brady's arm.

"Hey!" Brady threw his hands up. "I was just coming to greet you. I didn't do it on purpose."

Ashley tossed her head with an exaggerated sigh, and Brady couldn't help but chuckle. He adored Ashley; she had a gift for keeping life lighthearted. In that way, she and Cole were a perfect match.

Turning his gaze back to Monet, he took a step toward her. "Welcome to our little slice of heaven—our home away from home."

Monet's face pinked up before her eyes shifted to their surroundings. "It's beautiful," she said. "Like something straight out of one of those exotic vacation magazines."

Brady glanced around and smiled. "Yeah, it is."

"I still can't believe I'm here… it's so surreal," she said as she continued to take in the tropical ambiance.

Brady watched her for a moment. "I agree." His tone matched hers as he drank in the sight of the young woman he'd met so long ago. "Surreal."

Monet's attention landed back on him.

"It's good to see you again, Monet."

Her face flushed again, and she offered him a bashful smile before her eyes darted to Ashley and then back to him. "It's good to see you too," she said as her hand nervously fidgeted with the handle of her rolling suitcase.

The gesture drew him out of the dreamlike spell the sight of Monet was weaving over him, and he reached out. "Here, let me help you with that."

A wave of tingles erupted as their hands brushed, and Monet sucked in a breath, quickly letting go of the handle as she stepped back.

Brady heard Ashley chuckle. "There are two more in the Jeep."

"I can help with those," Monet said as she fled for the open door.

He'd unsettled her again. This was the second time his touch made Monet jittery, however brief it was. His mouth slid into a satisfied grin, and his chest swelled with confidence.

"It's okay," Brady said as he made his way to where Monet now stood. "I can get them. That way, Ashley can show you the villa."

"Are you sure?" she asked.

"Yep, take a look around, and I'll put your bags in your room."

"Come on." Ashley walked over and pulled on Monet's hand. "Let him put those beefy biceps to good use."

Brady laughed. "Beefy biceps?" His eyebrows shot up. "Hardly. And you better not let your husband hear you talking like that."

"Yeah, yeah." Ashley waved him off while Monet giggled.

Brady escaped out the front door before Ashley attempted to embarrass him further. He loved her, but she could sometimes be merciless with her comments about his looks.

Making his way to Ashley and Cole's Jeep, he heard Monet's laugh floating in the air around him. No doubt his spunky friend had said something else to coax the beautiful sound from Monet's lips. Unable to help himself, he turned and caught sight of the two women in animated conversation through the open door as they stood in the living area.

A smile stretched even further across his face as the reality of Monet being back in their lives—his life—settled over him.

With renewed determination to charm the humble beauty into returning his growing desire and interest in her, Brady returned to his task of retrieving her suitcases and mentally made plans to break through whatever barriers were needed to make his way into her heart.

Monet

Monet did her best to focus on what Ashley was saying, but it became increasingly difficult. It wasn't just that she hadn't gotten to freshen up after her long flight and brutal introduction to the Cancun humidity; it was that Brady rattled her—not in a bad way, but in a good way—a confusing way.

Monet had encountered her fair share of attractive men before; take Josh and also Juliet's brother, Sawyer, for example. They were both ridiculously handsome, but they didn't bring out the same reaction from her. Neither elicited the butterflies that currently danced in her stomach. With them, she never felt the need to catch her breath from a fleeting glance or experienced the shivers that Brady's voice sent cascading down her spine.

True, Josh and Sawyer had become more like brothers to Monet, but there had been other men in her life, and not once had any of them ignited the same potent mix of desire and curiosity as Brady.

". . . And this," Ashley said as they walked into the villa's main living area, "is the crowning glory, the reason you'll never want to leave."

The room converged with the colorfully decorated kitchen, or '*cocina*,' as Ashley called it, and Monet's eyes still lingered on the beautifully painted palm tree that adorned one wall between the kitchen cabinets. Monet sighed, content with how warm and inviting the kitchen was, and thought about how much Juliet would love such a tropical ambiance for cooking.

However, as Monet's attention was drawn to where Ashley stood, opening the wooden plantation-style shutter doors housed along the entire length of the large room, her sigh turned to a gasp.

Lying just beyond the now open-aired living room was a sight that took Monet's breath away.

Ashley's smile was wide. "I told you."

"It's... like a dream," Monet breathed as her senses heightened. The salty smell of fresh ocean air and the exotic flora surrounding the villa brought an unexpected calm to her body and mind.

Feeling as if she truly was living in some magical dream, Monet stepped onto the private patio that snaked around an exquisite, contoured swimming pool. An arched bridge over the center led to white sandy beaches that rested mere feet from where Monet stood and only steps away from the turquoise-colored ocean and the soothing rhythm of the breaking waves.

"You should see it at sunrise." Brady's voice sent a bolt of electricity straight into Monet's chest. She didn't dare turn to him, fearing he'd read how easily he unsettled her.

"I can imagine," she pushed the words from her mouth and continued to stare at the landscape. "You were not kidding, Ashley." She glanced at her friend. "How will I ever leave this place?"

"If you think this is amazing," Brady walked past her and stepped onto the small bridge stretched over the pool, "wait until you see the resort."

Monet couldn't help but look at him then. "Really?" she said. "Because this…" she released an awed huff, "is hard to top."

"I agree." He grinned before meeting Ashley's delighted gaze. "But we've done it, haven't we?"

"Oh yeah," Ashley agreed with a firm nod. "Speaking of which, let's show you your room, Monet, so you can freshen up a bit, and then we'll head over to the site so you can see for yourself."

Monet followed Ashley back into the villa while Brady slipped into the library to take a call that had come in on his cell phone. He'd been right when he called the villa sprawling. Two wide hallways branched out on either side of the spacious living area. One led to the bedroom where Ashley and Cole stayed, with Brady's room next door. Ashley led Monet down the other hallway on the opposite side of the shared living room.

Monet was giddy to learn that all of the bedrooms in the villa were oceanfront with glass sliding doors and a private terrace that took you directly to the swimming pool and beach.

"There are two bedrooms down this hallway, too," Ashley explained. "Brady thought you'd prefer this room," she said as she turned the knob on the door and pushed it open. "But you can choose whichever one you like best."

"Hey, Ash!" Brady hollered from the library. "Can you come here a sec?"

"Be right there!"

Monet stepped into the room and instantly loved it. Although she would have chosen it just because it was Brady's preferred choice, she knew it was the room she wanted.

"The other room is next door, so feel free to look around." Ashley turned to leave. "When you're ready, we'll head over to the site."

"I'll just be a few minutes," Monet said.

Once Ashley disappeared out the door, Monet soaked up the gorgeous room—although *suite* was a more appropriate description. Unlike the rest of the villa, which was decorated in rich, vibrant colors, this bedroom boasted deep, smoky blues that radiated relaxation and romance. The atmosphere further soothed and calmed her. It seemed the entire villa would prove a healing balm to her recovering soul.

Monet's excitement flamed even more at the sight of the en suite jacuzzi tub. However, it was the sheer white canopy-covered king-size bed that truly sparked her giddiness. She envisioned waking up blissfully under the down-filled comforter to the view of the breathtaking blue waters outside her floor-to-ceiling glass sliding door. Monet once again questioned her strength to leave when the time came.

As her gaze swept across the lovely bedroom, it settled on a colorful bouquet resting elegantly against one of the snow-white pillows on the bed.

Monet walked over and gently lifted the flowers, raising them to her nose to inhale their sweet fragrance. The rate of her pulse increased when she noticed a small note tucked inside. She reached in, withdrew the folded paper, and opened it.

Dinner? 8:00?

For the briefest of seconds, Monet's thoughts scattered.

Are these for Ashley? Perhaps Cole left them for her? She quickly shook the idea from her head; he obviously knew which bedroom was theirs.

As she tried to puzzle out the mystery of the flower bouquet and dinner invitation, her attention was drawn to her three suitcases sitting near the dark wooden armoire that stood elegantly against one wall.

She glanced back at the note still in her hand. *Could it be...* "Brady?"

"Yes?"

Monet sucked in a quick breath and spun around to find the subject of her thoughts leaning against the doorframe.

"You startled me," she said, trying—and failing—to slow her heart that was currently pounding inside her chest.

Not only had Brady's voice caught her by surprise, but the sight of him casually standing there, looking entirely too appealing in his sand-colored slacks and white linen shirt, had the opposite effect, and her pulse continued to throb.

Brady pushed off from the doorframe, chuckling. "It looks like Cole and I have another victim," he said as he walked into the room. "You seem to spook as easily as Ashley."

His words struck deeper than he realized. For years, Monet had jumped at the sight of her own shadow, for good reason, given what she'd been through, but she'd worked hard to put those ghosts behind her and rebuild her confidence.

"I used to," she said, trying not to show how flustered she was, "but not so much anymore. She gestured in the direction of the doorway. "*That* was one hundred percent a legitimate startle."

"You're right, and I'm sorry. I should have let you know I was there." He stood before her then. "I just couldn't help myself." His voice was rich and low. "I guess the reality that you're here—that it's you after all these years—is still sinking in."

The intenseness of Brady's gaze caused Monet to swallow, moistening her throat that seemed to block any words from coming out.

His eyes shifted to the bouquet in her hands and then back to her. A smile tugged at one corner of his mouth. "A secret admirer?"

Brady's question shook Monet out of her stupor. "Oh," she said as she casually took a step back. She needed her distance if she expected to carry on any semblance of a conversation with him.

"No..." An unexpected spike of fear tore through her, causing her forehead to crease into a somewhat agonized frown. "I—I don't think so."

Brady's face instantly shifted from carefree teasing to one of concern.

"Well, they are from an admirer, but not a secret one." His features softened. "They're from me."

Relief washed away the tension that Brady's innocent question had brought on, and Monet mentally groaned, disappointed by the automatic anxiety that still gripped her. It had been years since the stalking and harassment and months since she'd experienced any real fear.

Enough!

It was in that moment, under Brady's charming gaze, that Monet made a decision: no more fear, no more hesitations regarding romance in her life. She would try— she wanted to try, and although Monet knew very little about him, it was because of Brady that triggered her resolve. She knew he was interested; he'd dropped more than one hint since they'd reconnected in Arizona, and she was brave enough to admit that she most definitely reciprocated that interest.

Monet's heart thumped harder. Just being in Brady's presence always left her feeling energized, but a new wave of adrenaline surged through her body due to her newfound determination.

"So, what do you think?" He broke through her striking epiphany.

Monet blinked, fully aware she'd been staring at him wide-eyed and mute.

Brady glanced at the bouquet in her hands. "Dinner?"

Monet quickly regained her inner composure. A welcome feeling of weightlessness consumed her, and she smiled.

"Dinner would be lovely."

The corners of his mouth slowly slid up, and his eyes softened with relief.

"Good." He continued to stare at her, and Monet fought the natural urge to drop her eyes. Something about the way Brady looked at her left her a bit vulnerable—like he could read her mind.

"Do you like the room?" Brady asked, finally taking his eyes off her as he walked toward the sliding glass door.

"Oh, Brady, I so much more than like it—I'm in love with it," she gushed as her eyes swept over the furniture and décor.

Brady chuckled as he slid the door open. "Lucky room."

Huh? Monet casually laid her flowers on the bed, making a conscious effort to remain calm. Had she heard him correctly?

"Come take a look," he said.

Delighted more than anxious over Brady's flirtatious remark, Monet made her way onto her private terrace.

The scene was much like the one she'd experienced only moments earlier when she'd first stepped out of the open-aired living area. The only difference was the small stone walkway that led to the pool, which sat off to the left. The beauty of the tropical ocean and surrounding vegetation again stirred excitement in her belly.

"This is my first time to Cancun—Mexico actually—and from what I've seen so far, it truly is a paradise, isn't it?"

Brady nodded slowly. "Most of it is—the parts we see," he said. "But it's like everywhere. You have the nice areas," he made a sweeping motion with his hands, "and the not-so-nice areas."

"True," Monet said.

"I guess that's one thing about being an architect, though," he said. "It's easier to see beauty everywhere, in structures and landscapes, that others might not."

Monet agreed. "Yeah, I'll bet you do."

"Since we've been here, Cole and I have started a little side project," he laughed as he shook his head. "We don't really have time for it but it's something that brings us both a lot of satisfaction—helps keep us grounded."

"Oh?" Monet's eyebrows lifted.

"Okay, you two," Ashley interrupted as she walked through Monet's bedroom and joined them outside. "I just got off the phone with Cole, and here's the deal."

Brady flashed a grin at Monet as a mutual understanding passed between them. They'd continue their conversation later. Ashley had a way of commanding attention—not in an arrogant way; on the contrary, her new friend was fun and had a gift of helping you feel carefree—happy.

She turned to Monet. "We're going to head over to the site for a couple of hours just to get your toes wet—literally, in the ocean if you'd like—and to show you the resort and give you a quick download on where we stand, timeline-wise."

"Okay," Monet said. "Sounds good to me."

"And then," Ashley said, pointing at Brady, "you and Cole are going to head to the store."

Brady's eyebrows knit together. "Okay. . ." The word held a questioning tone.

"Because you and Cole are making us dinner tonight." Ashley sidled up to Monet and linked her arm through Monet's.

"Ah, I see," Brady said. "Well, I hate to spoil your scheming for a *Brady Enchilada*." He looked pointedly at Ashley. "But I've already invited Monet to have dinner with me tonight."

"Pff!" Ashley waved him off. "You two have plenty of time for romantic dinner for twos." Her comment caused a tingle to sweep the back of Monet's neck and across her face, and she had to swallow an embarrassing squeak.

"It's Monet's first night in Cancun," Ashley said. "Not to mention she's been traveling all morning. Cole and I think a relaxing night in would be nice." She pulled Monet even more snugly into her side. "Besides, it will give us the chance to catch up."

Monet glanced at Ashley and couldn't help but return her friendly smile.

"And just wait until you taste Brady's enchiladas," Ashley whispered loudly enough for Brady to hear. "He's perfected them since we've been here. Mmm!"

At that, Brady dropped his head, swinging it from side to side with a defeated laugh.

"Alright, you win," he said, pointing a stern finger at Ashley. "But tomorrow night, she's all mine." He instantly seemed to regret his choice of words, for he turned an apologetic expression to Monet.

"If that's alright with you."

Monet struggled to steady her rushed breathing and rapid heartbeat, triggered by the playful tussle between the two friends for her attention. But when she caught sight of the doubt in Brady's emerald-colored eyes, she wanted nothing more than to reassure him. Mustering every ounce of her courage, she softened her expression.

"I can think of nothing I'd enjoy more than having dinner with you tomorrow night…" she resisted the urge to avert her gaze, "alone."

A relaxed smile crossed his face, and he tipped his head. "Well, Ashley," Brady said, maintaining eye contact with Monet. "There you have it."

He turned and looked at Ashley then. "Tonight, we'll do it your way, but tomorrow—"

"I know," Ashley cut him off as she unlinked her arm from Monet's, "she's all yours." Ashley winked at Monet. "Why don't you get freshened up so we can head to the site?" Ashley said as she headed back through the sliding glass door that led into Monet's bedroom. "Watching all the sparks between you two has me missing my man!"

Monet was speechless, and although she'd made a personal commitment to be more open to the prospect of romance in her life, her stomach was a nervous flutter.

"Don't be too embarrassed," Brady said as he walked past her and back through her room to the villa. "Ashley likes to tease—always has."

Monet nodded as she followed him. "I've noticed." She smiled. "I'll just be a few minutes, and then we can get going."

"Okay," Brady said, but as he took hold of the bedroom door handle with the intent to close it behind him, he hesitated, pinning her with an affectionate gaze. "I'm really glad you're here, Monet."

And with that, the door closed.

Fortunately, Monet was standing next to the bed because her legs gave out, and she dropped into a sitting position on the edge of the soft comforter.

She exhaled the breath she'd been holding since the moment Brady surprised her while she was contemplating the mysterious bouquet. Monet's thoughts were in a whirl, and she placed a hand over her frantically beating heart.

This place—the villa and the people living there stirred such a range of emotions in Monet. She often felt nervous and embarrassed, but she also experienced excited anticipation, a giddiness over the prospect of what might happen with a man—Brady.

Monet knew better than to get her hopes too high; disappointment had been a staple in her life often enough to know nothing was certain or guaranteed. Yet, she found herself breaking through the protective layer she'd carefully built over the past five years, something she didn't allow herself to do very often. For the first time since she walked onto that airplane as a fearless and trusting 18-year-old girl full of big dreams, Monet allowed herself to hope.

Brady

Brady watched Monet slip her sandals off and dip her feet into the warm Caribbean Sea. She was beautiful—graceful, and she didn't have the slightest clue that she was. That was one of the reasons he was so attracted to her and why he sat watching her from where he stood on a wooden platform that would soon be the first of 16 private beach cabanas at The Grand Jewel.

Brady spent the past few hours assisting Ashley with the task of showing Monet around and giving her a crash course on where things stood in terms of the interior decorating that had begun. It was plainly obvious that he didn't need to be there for ninety percent of it. Yet, even with Ashley's occasional raised eyebrows and subtle smirks thrown his way, Brady remained undeterred from inserting himself into the tour.

Upon their arrival, Monet's mouth had fallen open at the sight of *The Jewel's* entrance—the resort's nickname among the crew. She'd been genuinely enchanted by the beauty of the Mexican colonial architecture.

When Velma first approached Brady and Cole about the resort, Brady immediately knew he wanted to design the luxury hotel with an updated take on the old hacienda-style homes. Cole was on board from the beginning, and together, they'd exceeded their expectations. Although they were still six months out from the grand opening, construction was ahead of schedule, which allowed Monet to easily visualize the result—not just from the plans and concept images but also from the resort itself.

Once completed, guests would pass through a security gate. Following a short drive down a palm tree-lined, cobblestone driveway, they'd be greeted by a towering three-tiered Cantera stone fountain at the hotel's roundabout entrance.

The blue accents on the hotel's creamy yellow exterior, combined with the soon-to-be streams, thick green lawns, and tropical foliage, would create a tranquil atmosphere, allowing the guests to escape the second they step foot onto the property.

Brady was encouraged at the way Monet seemed to do that very thing—and construction and design weren't even complete. During her entire tour of the grounds, she freely dished out compliments to Brady and Cole in genuine awe of what they were creating. She particularly gushed over the bungalow-style layout of the guest rooms and gazed longingly at the partially finished infinity pool that lay elegantly along the beach.

"I've always wanted to swim in an infinity pool," she'd said.

Brady tucked that piece of information away.

Monet was equally complimentary about both the interior and landscape design. Ashley's eyes lit up when Monet commented that the hotel's central courtyard—with its breezy loggias and newly placed metal gardening trellises awaiting their colorful bougainvillea vines—had a *"Zorro vibe."*

During one of the initial meetings, the trio of friends agreed that they wanted the resort to be rich with both authentic Mexican culture and history, as well as elements of fable.

Monet's praise over what they had accomplished so far wasn't phony either; she listened actively and asked a lot of questions. She was genuinely impressed and interested in every aspect of the resort Brady and Cole designed and that Ashley and an army of workers were bringing to life.

Recalling Monet's approval, Brady took a deep breath, filling his lungs with the fresh, salty air that one can only find near the ocean.

"Considering I missed some time this morning, I'd say it's been a productive few hours," Ashley said as she approached Brady.

"Maybe for you," Brady chuckled. He pulled his attention away from Monet and looked at his friend. "Every time I try to get something done, I get... distracted."

Ashley's light-colored eyebrows slid up, and a delighted sparkle entered her eyes as she scanned the beach and found the source of his distraction. "You're hooked, aren't you?"

He couldn't help himself, and his eyes found Monet again. "I'm something, that's for sure."

"It scares you, though, doesn't it?"

In the same way Brady observed people and could read facial expressions as if he were reading your mind,

Ashley had her own gift of being perceptive. But it could also be because they'd been friends for so long.

"It does, but not in the way you'd think."

"Oh?" Ashley asked as she sat on the edge of the wooded platform. She removed her sandals and let her feet sink into the white sand.

Brady followed her lead and sat.

"I'm not afraid of relationships, or even love," he said, "there's something deeper going on with this." He reached up and unbuttoned a third button on his linen shirt; the breeze coming off the ocean felt refreshing on his skin. Not only was the Cancun sun brutally hot at that time of year, but the feelings Monet was stirring caused him to feel heated and unsettled.

"Something is going on with her," he said, nodding toward Monet. Ashley's gaze followed, resting again on Monet, who was gazing at the horizon while the water rolled over her feet. "An underlying fear. I see it behind her eyes—a lack of security and confidence… it concerns me."

"I've noticed it too," Ashley said. "It's subtle, but it's there."

"I guess I'm just afraid that whatever it is will keep her from…" He sucked in a breath and shrugged.

"Letting you in?" Ashley finished his sentence for him. "Or allowing herself to get close to you?"

"Yeah, something like that." He sighed. "And I realize it makes no sense because we know so little about each other, but I've never wanted the chance to get to know a woman the way I do with her."

Ashley reached over and rubbed Brady's back. "Then try." Her voice was rich with understanding. "I've seen the way Monet looks at you, Brady." She chuckled. "Even if she hasn't realized it yet, she's just as '*something,*'" she used her fingers to make air quotes, "as you are."

Brady smiled. "I've noticed it too."

"You've never been one to hold back," Ashley said. "When you want something, you've always taken it by the reins and plunged headlong into it." She glanced behind her toward the resort. "Look at where you are now."

"Cole has as much to do with where we are as I do."

She nodded. "True, you two make an amazing team, but it was you who inspired him."

"Better not let him hear you say that," Brady teased.

"Oh, Cole knows that the sun rises and sets on him as far as I'm concerned," she said. "But he'll be the first to admit you were the one who set him on his professional path."

Brady smiled softly, acknowledging Ashley's praise with a slight nod. He reached over and squeezed her hand. "Thanks. You've always been one of my biggest supporters. Clear back to our days at the White Rainbow, all through college, up to now."

Ashley returned his smile. "And as one of your best friends, I'm telling you, you should go for it." A playful glint entered her eyes as they shifted toward something behind him.

Brady turned his head, and at the sight of Monet walking toward them, the familiar lightness in his limbs returned, and as had become the case each time she was near, his heart leapt.

"I can't get over how warm the water is—and the color!" Her expression was nothing less than joyful. "Juliet invited me to Aruba for Spring Break last year—and don't get me wrong, the water there is beautiful, but to me, this," she gestured to the ocean, "takes my breath away. The turquoise against the white sand is gorgeous."

Her enthusiasm was contagious, and Brady found himself entirely rejuvenated with a grin he couldn't contain. "It is, isn't it?"

"It looks exactly like one of the tropical posters my brother had in his bedroom growing up," she said as she continued to take in the scenery. "The real exotic beach destination ones."

Brady laughed. "I had one of those too!" Monet had unknowingly given him a fun flashback. "Mine was of a beach in Fiji with one lone palm tree on a white sand beach next to perfectly still aqua-colored water." He could still picture it on the wall of his bathroom from his teenage years. "It had the word *Paradise* printed along the bottom."

Monet's eyes danced with amusement; it was the first time Brady had seen her so relaxed. There was no hint of the fear he'd seen earlier.

"Velma Larsen certainly knew what she was doing when she chose this location for her resort." Monet continued to beam. "The guests will definitely be in *paradise* here."

Brady's eyes locked with the glimmer in Monet's, and something powerful passed between them.

"That's Velma," Ashley said, boosting herself up from where she sat and breaking the moment. "She knows how to pick 'em," Ashley said with a knowing wink, her layered meaning not lost on Brady.

Velma was as clever and sharp as they came, and the fact that she'd hired Monet on the spot was just another example of her gift for *picking 'em.*

"After seeing all of this," Monet said as her hand swept around their surroundings, "and spending time with you all today, it makes me realize how lucky I am to be a part of it."

Ashley smiled. "I think you're right." She held her sandals in one hand and stepped forward, sliding her free arm through one of Monet's as she began to guide them back toward the resort. "All of us are super lucky, but especially Brady and me because we get to spend time with you again."

Ashley shot a sly glance over her shoulder at Brady, and he knew full well she was referring solely to him. And it was true; Monet Everly had left an indelible impression on Brady. *He* was the lucky one to have her in his life again.

As the trio, now not just co-workers but friends, headed back to the construction office to seek out Cole before calling it a day and heading back to the villa, Brady thought about what Ashley had said. She was right; Brady always went after what he wanted, professionally and personally; he'd always been that way.

And as he watched Monet politely listen to Ashley talk about the array of activities she had planned for Monet's first weekend in Cancun, he saw her peek over her shoulder and flash a smile Brady's way, driving home those powerful feelings he'd been having. Monet Everly was someone he wanted, and Brady was ready to do whatever it took to make that happen.

Monet

Monet could smell the spices radiating down the hall from the villa's kitchen, and her stomach grumbled heavy and loud. She hadn't eaten since she landed, sharing an oversized plate of chicken nachos with Ashley at the Margaritaville bar right outside the airport.

The rest of the day, however, had her belly in knots every time she found herself in Brady's company. Monet wasn't complaining; on the contrary, she'd be content to live out the rest of her life staring at the ridiculously attractive man all day. The unfortunate part was that he was to blame for the endless swarm of butterflies in her stomach, and she hadn't been able to eat anything up to that point.

When they'd all returned to the villa after working the afternoon at the resort, Monet immediately escaped to her room to shower and freshen up before dinner. She'd just finished slipping into a short breezy skirt and camisole tank when she heard her phone chime from where it was charging on the nightstand.

Monet had sent text messages to her family and Juliet when she'd first landed, informing them that she'd arrived safely, but it occurred to her that she hadn't checked her phone since. Walking to her bed, she perched herself on the side and picked up her phone. Seeing multiple notifications on the screen, she quickly entered her password and opened her message app.

> Mom: *"Hi sweetheart, so happy you landed safely. Please let me know once you've settled at the villa, ok? Six months will feel like an eternity for me, so don't forget to check in regularly. You may be an adult, but I still worry. I love you. xoxo"*

> Mom: *"Dad says hi, and he loves you too."*

Monet smiled. Even though she'd been gone six months in between visits with her parents while in New York, she still understood her mom's concern. After all, she was living in a foreign country with near strangers.

> Evan: *"Hey Mo! Still jealous you get to spend the next six months in Cancun. I know how much you'll miss me, and since I'm such a good brother, I guess I'll have to visit. Stay safe and call or text me if you need anything. Love you."*

A slight pang pierced Monet's heart. She missed Evan. He'd been there for her when things were at their weirdest and worst with John Wessler. Even though she didn't get to see him as often as she preferred, her brother was one of her best friends, and Monet knew that if she needed him, he'd drop anything to help her. She released a satisfied sigh at the thought of Evan visiting her in Cancun. Maybe he would really come? Monet made a mental note to push the idea with him.

She continued to scroll through her messages, and any melancholy she felt over missing her brother evaporated when her eyes landed on a message (correction, messages—plural) from her other best friend.

1:33pm
Juliet: *"Good thing you texted me. I've been wondering when you'd land. How was your flight?"*

1:34pm
Juliet: *"Ah!!! I just realized you're going to see Brady soon!!! I think I'm more excited than you are. If you can't call, at least text me as soon as you have a free minute and give me a play-by-play of everything that happens so I can interpret it all for you. I am so happy right now. Love you and miss you already."*

4:40pm
Juliet: *"All I can say is you're one lucky chica. I've been swamped at the restaurant and didn't notice until now that you haven't responded. I'm dying to know what happened when you saw Brady. Were there sparks? Flirting? Details Monet, I need them now! Oh, and I hope the work stuff is going well too.* Wink."

6:18pm
Juliet: *"Ok, so you send me an "I landed" text at 2:30 (1:30 to you). It's now 7:15 (6:15 to you... time zones – ugh!) Almost five hours and nothing! Are you purposely trying to break up my relationship with Josh? Because I'm taking out my frustration on him, you know. Text me!"*

6:47pm
Josh: *"Hey Mojo, if you could send Juliet a quick text just to let her know you're alive, it'll calm my fiery fiancé down a bit. Thanks, doll."*

7:30pm
Juliet: *"Six hours, Monet! SIX. I am thoroughly convinced you've either been abducted and are currently being held for ransom, or you've up and eloped with the hot bellhop. Of course, my preference is the latter, but I will one hundred percent never forgive you if you got married without me. Call me or text me now!"*

Monet's empty stomach churned again, but it wasn't only from lack of food this time. She felt bad she'd left Juliet hanging for so long. Even Josh had texted her. Monet sucked in a breath through gritted teeth; Juliet must be pretty wound up.

Just as she was about to press "call" on Juliet's name, there was a knock on her door.

"Monet?" It was Ashley.

"Come on in." She stood and walked toward the bedroom door as Ashley entered.

"Hey, the boys almost have dinner ready."

Monet placed a hand over her belly. "It smells so good; it's making my stomach growl."

Ashley laughed. "Wait until you taste it. I'm not kidding when I say you'll never experience enchiladas the same again."

Monet grinned. "Okay, I'll be right there. I just need to send a quick text."

"Take your time, sweetie," Ashley said. "I just wanted to let you know."

"Thanks."

Ashley smiled and closed the door behind her.

Monet made her way to the bathroom vanity while quickly typing a message to Juliet.

"Not to worry, I haven't been abducted, so your money is safe. And sadly, I did not elope with the hot bellhop. I know that one crushes you, no matter how adamantly you insist you'd never forgive me for it."

1 minute later:
Juliet: *"It's about d*#! time!"*

Monet laughed out loud. One thing about Juliet—no matter how mad, no matter how frustrated, or no matter how upset she became, she would never swear.

"Jewels, I am so sorry! As soon as I landed, Ashley was there, and it has been go go go since. I feel terrible that I left you hangin'. Sad face*"*

Juliet: *"Sigh. You know I would never stay upset with you, especially when you type* Sad face.*"*

Juliet: *"But! I've been going out of my mind. If curiosity killed the cat, I'm dead as a doornail."*

"hahaha. Well, you know how the whole saying goes. Curiosity killed the cat, but satisfaction brought it back. And after you hear what I have to tell you, I'm pretty sure you'll be satisfied and fully alive again."

Juliet: *"Oooh, tell me! Wait, better yet, can you talk?"*

"Please don't freak out, but I can't. Brady and Cole made dinner for Ashley and me. They're waiting on me right now. How late will you be up?"

Juliet: *"Ok, first, you had me at* 'Brady and Cole made dinner.' *When you're making your pros and cons list for this man, this is a definite pro. And even though I'm dying to hear about your day, go enjoy yourself. You can call me anytime, but you're probably exhausted. Just promise to call me the second you wake up. For real!"*

"I pinkie promise, cross my heart promise, and every other kind of promise. I'm just as anxious to talk to you. Brady has me wanting things I haven't wanted for a long time. I've got all these mixed feelings—it's confusing."

Juliet: *"Of course it would be. This is the first time you've been interested in a guy since I've known you. But don't worry; your fears and insecurities are smack dab where they should be: behind you.*
You've got this."

Monet's heart warmed. She adored Juliet. She was the sister Monet never had. Juliet understood Monet better than almost anyone, and simply reading her words of encouragement gave Monet a boost she hadn't realized she needed.

"Thanks, Jewels. How is it you always say what I need to hear?"

Juliet: *"Ha! Not sure that's always true,* wink, *but I have faith in you. Now go! Enjoy your evening and call me in the morning with all the delicious details about what they made for dinner and what Brady gave you for* dessert- *ooh la la!"*

"Juliet!"

Monet giggled over her friend's implication as the swirls in her belly increased. The thought of any physical contact with Brady sent Monet's insides into a flurry of nerves and butterflies.

Juliet: *"Just a little something to think about. Loves."*

"Loves."

Monet set her phone on the counter and quickly did one last refresh, trying in vain to stamp out the visions her best friend had put in her mind. With a deep breath of courage, she exhaled with a smile and made her way out to the delicious-smelling kitchen.

Brady

"Well, I think we need to keep trying," Ashley was saying. "I feel bad for the guy."

"I think we all do," Cole said. "But Jesse isn't budging, babe."

Ashley blew out a defeated breath. "It sure seems that way."

The foursome was just finishing dinner, and the current topic of conversation was the grumpy contractor Velma hired to assist in overseeing the construction site for the Grand Jewel. Ever since Jesse started working with them the previous year, Ashley, Cole, and Brady tried tirelessly to befriend him, but the guy had no interest in it. He'd even turned down the offer to stay in the villa and opted to rent his own place for the duration of the project.

It was clear that Jesse's divorce had left him scarred and bitter, traits he didn't attempt to hide in his daily interactions with people.

"Maybe he just needs a little more time," Monet said from where she sat across the wooden kitchen table. "I've never been married, so obviously I can't sympathize in that way," she said as she fidgeted with one of her hoop earrings. "But I went through something… that shook me for a while, so I get it—in a way." She glanced at Brady and shifted her attention to Ashley and Cole before her eyes landed back on him briefly.

Brady's pulse kicked up; his curiosity was piqued. Monet kept her eyes down as she toyed with the stem of her water glass. Brady glanced at Ashley, whose wide eyes were staring at him. She gave a discreet yet firm nod toward Monet.

Brady shifted his attention to Monet again and spoke in what he hoped was a casual tone.

"Shook you for a while?"

Her eyes glanced at him, and he saw a hint of uncertainty in them.

"Do you feel comfortable talking about it?" he asked.

After a long inhale followed by a deep exhale, Monet shrugged one shoulder. "Sure."

Brady smiled softly as his focus remained solely on Monet.

"Usually, the only person outside of my family that I talk to about this is Juliet." Her eyes traveled back and forth between the friends before settling on Brady again. "But I feel comfortable sharing what I went through with you guys." Monet's thoughtful gaze shifted between Brady and Ashley. "Maybe it's because you two were there when it all started."

"What do you mean?" Ashley asked, with a crease on her forehead.

Monet looked at Ashley and hesitated. She fidgeted in her chair and nervously smoothed her palms over her skirt. Brady's heart went out to her; he could see she was uncomfortable, even though she claimed not to be.

"Monet," he said, drawing her eyes back to him. "You're safe here, you don't have to talk about it, but if you want to, we're pretty good listeners." Brady's heart lifted when Monet returned his smile.

With another deep breath, she exhaled. "John Wessler."

"The Sleaze?" The name was out of his mouth before he could stop it.

Monet puffed a small laugh. "Sleaze-essler. That was the perfect name for him."

Sleaze-essler. Hearing it again still brought the same skin-crawling sensation it had when Brady witnessed the man's disgusting behavior where young, hopeful fashion models were concerned.

"Wow," Ashley breathed with a shake of her head. "Now there's a name I never thought I'd hear again."

Brady watched Monet, pieces of the puzzle beginning to connect.

"He contacted you again, didn't he?" Brady asked. "After that day."

After biting at her lips for a split second, Monet nodded, and her eyebrows rose. "He did."

"What?" Ashley blurted with wide eyes. "No way."

"I remember the guy," Cole spoke up. "Slimy snake."

"My sentiments exactly," Brady said as heat flushed under his skin at the reminder of what John Wessler put Monet through.

Monet chuckled softly. "Yeah, pretty much," she said. "I did reach out to his agency a couple of times right after I got back home to have my photos from the finalist shoot sent to me. But I was told they were property of the agency, and since I'd dropped out, I didn't have any rights to them." Monet huffed. "Isn't that crazy?"

"Sounds like a load of bull," Cole said.

Brady agreed. It sounded more like a pouting child not getting his way.

"Maybe." Monet shrugged. "But unfortunately, aside from my failed attempts at getting my photos, the day I met both of you was not the last I heard from him."

A worried crease puckered Ashley's brow. "I'm almost afraid to ask—but what happened?"

Monet tossed her head, and a low sigh escaped her throat. "It's such a long story. I don't even know where to begin."

"Did he hurt you?" Brady asked. It was a blunt question, but his protective instincts flared.

Monet drew in a shaky breath, and a flash of fear lit her eyes, causing Brady to regret his bold question.

"I'm sorry," he quickly said. "The man just riles me up. Especially where you're concerned."

He didn't miss the satisfied smirks coming from Ashley and Cole. Brady didn't care; he wasn't bashful about his growing interest in Monet.

"It's alright," Monet said. "I'm honestly touched that you would care so much." She gifted Brady an understanding smile. "It reminds me of Evan, my brother. Next to Juliet, Evan is my best friend." Her face clouded over. "But almost more than that, he was the rescuer I needed when things with Wessler became so scary and deranged."

Brady snuck a glance to Ashley and then Cole, who each sat uncharacteristically silent and met his eyes with concern engraved in their own.

"It turns out," Monet began, "Both my family and I underestimated the size of Wessler's ego, and we certainly hadn't anticipated the lengths he would go to when he didn't get his way with me. It was only a week after I'd arrived home when Mr. Wessler showed up at my house."

"What?" Ashley shrieked again. "Are you kidding me? The man came to your house?"

"He did," Monet said. "Initially, I suspected maybe he'd planned it perfectly—to show up right after my parents left for work—but it didn't take any of us very long to realize he had definitely hoped I'd be alone that day."

Brady's heart was in his throat, and heat flushed through his entire body. He didn't like the way this story was headed.

"Thankfully, Evan was home from college, so nothing terrible happened... other than what I'd thought were empty threats."

"What on earth did he threaten you with?" Ashley asked.

"Believe me, I've spent countless hours trying to understand that man's motivation behind what he put me through, and the only thing my family and I come up with is that I bruised his ego." Monet shrugged. "That first day he showed up, he and Evan got into a pretty bad yelling match, and Wessler accused me of ruining his reputation professionally."

"Pfft! What a bunch of bull." Brady was irritated. "You didn't ruin his reputation, Monet."

"I know that now, but at the time, I felt a lot of guilt over not showing up for the music video. Mr. Wessler said the band ended up going with a different agency, and I'd made him look bad."

Ashley's head jerked back, and she caught Brady's eye. He could read her thoughts. She tilted her head as she shook it. "That's not true," Ashley said to Monet. "I remember exactly what happened."

"What do you mean?" Monet asked.

"Wessler checked a new girl into the hotel the same day you left," Ashley explained. "I remember because she was over the top excited about being in the music video that day."

"I remember too," Brady said. "She was very forward and flirty." And arrogant and rude, the exact opposite of Monet.

"For real?" Monet's jaw dropped.

"I'm afraid so," Brady said as Ashley gave a sad nod. "Wessler was right back at it with his slimy ways—didn't miss a beat. I worked there another five months after we met, and he seemed to carry on business as usual, parading in one girl after another as a potential model for his agency."

Monet was silent before she folded her arms across her stomach, giving her head a slow shake. "I shouldn't be surprised."

"Sounds like the guy guilt-tripped you pretty bad," Cole said, breaking his silence.

"Yeah, but he did a lot more than that." She straightened in her chair. "After the confrontation that day at my parent's house, Wessler started sending me flowers. At first, he wouldn't include his name, but we knew who they were from because of the inappropriate and vulgar comments written on the cards." Monet's eyebrows rose. "I don't want to put *those* images in your minds, but just know the comments were terrible—total smut." She focused on her empty plate, exhaling a disgusted puff. "The first time they were delivered, my dad was furious and called the florist, demanding to know why they would agree to write something like that."

"Well, yeah!" Ashley blurted. "Good for your dad. What did the florist say?"

"That they hadn't written it, that the customer came into the shop and wrote it himself before sealing the envelope."

"Ew!" Ashley rubbed vigorously at her arms.

"Which means Wessler flew to Utah to send you flowers?" Brady asked as the fire in his belly flamed.

"Yes."

"Whoa." Cole flinched. "Just so he could put a disgusting note inside. Scary."

"It really was," Monet agreed. "We tried to get the police involved, but they wouldn't do anything at that point. After a while, he switched things up and started sending me other kinds of *gifts*." Monet broke eye contact and dropped her eyes as she squirmed in her chair, tucking both hands under her legs and locking her arms. "Lingerie and other items along the same lines. But things took an even creepier turn when he started following me."

"Oh my gosh," Ashley breathed in disbelief.

Brady caught Cole's eye; a silent understanding passed between them. This was bad.

Monet looked at Ashley. "The first time it happened, I was at the mall shopping with my friend, Lily. We were in line to pay for some perfume I'd picked out, and Wessler walked up to the cashier and told her he'd be paying for my purchase."

Brady's mouth dropped.

"It completely freaked me out. My heart jumped into my throat, and I froze. I literally couldn't move. Thankfully, Lily kept her senses and took my hand, pulling me out of the store until we found a security officer. Lily explained that I'd been harassed for weeks, and the man was in the mall." Monet let out a defeated huff. "By that point, Wessler was gone. Lily and I didn't stick around either; we went straight home."

"I'm in shock," Ashley said. "I can't wrap my head around it. I mean," she scowled, "We all knew the man was a creepy jerk, but I had no idea he was an off-his-rocker predator."

"Same," Cole said. "I didn't see the guy as much as you both." He gestured to Ashley and Brady. "But I wouldn't have guessed he was a full-blown psycho."

Brady sucked in deeply and exhaled. "I guess we were pretty blind," he said. "It was obvious the guy was a predator; just look at how he treated the girls he recruited for the agency." He puffed an irritated breath. "But a stalker? Wow."

"From that point on, I never went anywhere without Evan or my parents." Monet's voice dimmed. "My life changed. I started looking over my shoulder, and every time the doorbell rang, my heart sank... It was miserable."

"Oh, Monet." Brady was angry—furious, but so unbelievably heartbroken that someone so innocent went through such a nightmare.

"Evan was great, though." Monet's countenance lighted, and she smiled. "He and his friends were my protectors. They would go with me to the grocery store, doctors' appointments, to and from my summer job—everywhere."

"Did the weasel ever show up again?" Cole asked.

Monet nodded. "Two more times. Once at a movie theater, and the last time I saw him was the night he tried to..." She trailed off.

Brady's hands curled into fists under the table. He knew he shouldn't pry, but he had to know. "What happened?"

Monet cleared her throat as she flashed a nervous glance around the table. "Well, nothing happened at the movie theater. He was just there in the parking lot when we left, staring at me. Evan called the police, and we filed a report, but nothing much was done again.

"While I was in high school, I always worked at one of those snow cone places that pop up in parking lots during the summers. I'd just graduated, and it was my final summer working there. I'd explained to my boss about the harassment and stalking, and he'd been very understanding and only scheduled me during the day shifts—I just felt safer during daylight hours."

"I don't blame you," Ashley said. "Honestly, I think you were brave to keep working at all after what you've told us."

Monet smiled. "That's kind of you to say," she said. "At that point, even after everything Wessler put me through, I was still determined to try and live as normal a life as I could. Which, let's be honest, wasn't exactly normal.

"Anyway, I ended up having to work the closing shift for a couple of nights, which wasn't as bad as I'd imagined, so I told my boss I'd be open to more night shifts if he ever got desperate. He took me up on the offer, and one night, just after I'd served a group of teenagers and was getting ready to close, Wessler appeared at the ordering window. There were still people in the parking lot, so foolishly I figured I was safe." Monet hesitated and breathed in deeply. Her eyes focused on the table before her eyelids closed, and she exhaled, blowing out a long breath.

"Monet." Brady wouldn't make her relive it. "It's okay; you've told us enough. You don't have to keep going."

Ashley reached over from her seat next to Monet and squeezed one of her hands. "Brady's right, sweetie. We know whatever happened was terrible. You don't need to tell us."

Monet opened her eyes just as a tear escaped and slid down her cheek. A painful tightness struck at the back of Brady's throat. John Wessler should be in prison, locked up where he could never inflict such torment on anyone ever again.

"It's alright." Monet nodded as she wiped the tear away. "I want to tell you. I think it's important that I do. We will be spending a lot of time together the next several months." She locked her gaze with Brady's. "And I just want you to know."

Brady kept a steady focus on Monet. "Okay," he said softly. "Only if you're sure."

"I am." She returned his faint smile before taking another deep breath. "As soon as I saw Wessler at the window, I tried to slide it closed, but he reached in and grabbed my wrist. He kept saying he just wanted to talk to me, but there was hatred in his eyes, and his grip was painful; I genuinely believe he meant harm.

"After a minute or so of struggling, I freed my arm and slammed the window shut and locked it, but that's when I realized the back door to the snow cone stand was propped open. I ran back and closed it before he made his way back there. Wessler started yelling obscenities and banging on the door." Monet's eyes widened with a shake of her head. "I have never been so scared in all my life."

"No kidding," Ashley said, still holding one of Monet's hands. "I would be terrified."

"I scrambled for my cell phone and dialed 911. The operator had just come on the line when suddenly I heard other voices yelling, and the banging stopped."

"What happened?" Cole asked, wide-eyed.

"Evan." Monet's posture slackened, and the deep crease between her eyebrows softened. "He'd been out with a couple of friends that night, and they'd come to get me."

"Oh, thank goodness," Ashley said, slouching back in her chair.

"I wasn't kidding when I said he was my protector; he came to my rescue more than once."

"Did he beat the tar out of the sleaze bag?" Cole asked.

"Almost," Monet said. "Evan landed a couple of punches before one of his friends pulled him off Wessler. It was a good thing too because the police showed up right then."

A wave of relief washed over Brady. "I am so grateful to your brother and that Wessler didn't hurt you—physically anyway."

Monet offered him a sad smile. "Yeah, not physically, but the mental damage from it messed with me for a long time."

Brady understood now. The reason for the fear and lack of self-confidence he and Ashley could see. The reality of it weighed heavy on his heart.

"Please tell me Wessler went to jail or something," Ashley said. "Although, I doubt it, seeing as he regularly came into the hotel."

"Unfortunately, only for one night." Monet sighed. "My boss filed a complaint against him, and I filed criminal charges, but he had this high-profile attorney that got him out and off the hook."

"What?" Ashley spat. "Unbelievable."

"The one thing I did get," Monet said, "was a restraining order against him. It was the only thing his attorney didn't fight."

"You should have taken this to the media," Cole said. "The guy should have been accountable for being a psycho."

"Maybe." Monet lifted one shoulder in a shrug. "But the restraining order seemed to snap him out of it because I never heard from him again, and that's all I ever wanted."

Brady's mind was spinning, and his nerves were rattled. For the life of him, he couldn't fathom what could drive a person to behave the way John Wessler had with Monet. A shot of adrenaline tore through him as a horrible thought crossed his mind. What if Monet wasn't the only woman Wessler had treated like this?

Brady shook his head firmly as his attention turned back to Monet.

"I am so sorry, Monet." Brady exhaled a deep sigh. "I can't begin to imagine how hard it was for you."

Monet gifted him a genuine smile; Brady hadn't seen many of them, and the sight did funny things to his heart.

"Thank you, Brady," she said. "And yes, it was hard. The experience altered my entire view on life, and for a long time, all I wanted to do was disappear—become invisible—which is why I moved to New York in the first place."

Ashley breathed a soft chuckle. "Sweetheart, I mean this in the most respectful way imaginable, but I don't believe you could ever be invisible."

"It may surprise you, but I did a pretty good job of it for a while," Monet said. "It took a very special person to find me—to really see me again." She smiled and looked back and forth between the group of friends. "Someday, I'll tell you that story."

Brady knew Monet was probably spent. Retelling the traumatizing events at the hand of John Wessler undoubtedly took an emotional toll, and he knew it would be best to cut the night short and let Monet turn in.

"I'd like that," Brady said, and Ashley and Cole agreed.

"Well," Cole stood and started gathering plates from the table, "I've got this." He flashed a sly grin Brady's way. "Why don't you and Monet head down to the beach for a little moonlight stroll to help clear her head."

"Oh! You totally should," Ashley said as she stood to help clear the table. "Monet, it's just what you need.

Nighttime walks on the beach are so relaxing—it's a perfect escape."

Though every part of him wanted to whisk Monet away to that walk on the beach he'd been anticipating all day, he didn't want to pressure her.

"Monet's had a pretty long day, guys. I'm sure she'd rather—"

"I'd love to go," Monet cut in. "That is if you're up for it?"

Brady's eyes floated to where Cole and Ashley stood in the kitchen behind where Monet sat. Cole's smile was full of mischief as he quirked an eyebrow. Ashley looked entirely too pleased, and Brady could see she was about to make an undoubtedly embarrassing remark.

"You bet he's—"

"I'm up for it," Brady interrupted, rolling his eyes Ashley's way. "But are you sure you are?" He drew his attention back to Monet.

"You'd think I'd be exhausted from the time change and after such a full day," she said. "But I'm really not tired at all."

It was probably the adrenaline from retelling her horror story. Brady knew the events and emotions of the day would eventually catch up to her, but until then, he'd take advantage of the opportunity for a little one-on-one time with Monet.

"Alright then, if you two really are good to take care of this," Brady gestured to the remaining dishes and leftover food on the table, "then we'll take that stroll."

"Of course," Cole and Ashley said in unison before Ashley giggled. "You two enjoy."

"Yeah." Cole waggled his eyebrows. "*Enjoy.*"

Brady tossed his head with a humorous puff. Cole would tease him mercilessly; Brady had learned as much from his friend over the years. To Monet's credit, she laughed off Cole's gentle teasing. She was a good sport, and Brady liked that about her—just one more endearing quality to add to his ever-growing list.

"Thank you for dinner and such a warm welcome," Monet said as she stood. "I'm not the greatest cook, but it's my turn next time—I'll do the dishes too."

"You don't have to ask me twice," Cole chuckled. "Sounds good to me."

"The nights are beautiful here, Monet," Ashley said. "It never gets too overly cool, but you might want to take a light jacket or something, just in case."

"That's a good idea. I'll just grab a sweatshirt really quick," Monet said to Brady as she walked back toward her bedroom.

Once Monet was out of sight, Ashley moved closer to Brady. "I can't believe that all happened to her," she whispered. "It breaks my heart."

Brady nodded and kept his eyes in the direction of the hallway where Monet's bedroom was. "I'll tell you this," Brady spoke softly as Cole joined them. "It's a good thing I didn't know about this while I was still working at the hotel. I'd be the one in jail."

"It all makes sense now," Ashley said. "The insecurities we both noticed."

"She's such a sweet little thing, too." Cole kept his voice low. "At least she seems like she's recovered ok."

Brady nodded, but he wasn't so sure she had. "I hope so, but I'm glad I know now. I'll need to tread lightly for a while; take it slow."

"Maybe," Ashley said, still whispering. "You should just go off Monet's lead, Brady. I see how she looks at you; there's something there."

Cole chuckled. "I see it too, but I get it," he said. "After what we just heard, you'll want to be careful with her." Cole gripped one of Brady's shoulders. "Just not *too* careful."

Before they could say anymore, Monet returned with a comfy-looking jacket thrown over her arm.

"Ready?" she asked.

Brady was momentarily struck mute as he looked at Monet. There was something different about her, a lightness to her countenance that he'd never seen before. Even more so than earlier when she'd been so carefree while he'd watched her on the beach at the construction site. Her features were softened, her posture strong, and a glimmer of confidence in her voice that hadn't been there before.

"Yeah." He shook himself out of his daze. "Um, thanks again, guys, for cleaning up," he told his friends. "We'll see you a little later."

Monet offered her repeated thanks, and Brady grabbed a beach towel from a stack of dry towels they kept near the shutter doors. He escorted her out the back of the villa and across the swimming pool bridge that would take them to the beach.

After descending a short set of steps, they reached the sand, and Monet bent to remove her sandals just as a light breeze stirred the air around her. Her feminine fragrance flirted with his senses, and he fought the urge to close his eyes and inhale.

As Brady leaned down to remove his shoes, he inwardly groaned. Treading lightly where the irresistible Miss Everly was concerned would test every ounce of self-control he had.

Monet

The beach felt soothing beneath her feet as Monet stepped slowly through the sand. It was soft and cool. The sound of crashing waves, combined with the breathtaking hues of orange and red from the setting sun, steadied Monet's pulse, providing a sense of calm.

She couldn't explain her spur-of-the-moment decision to open up to her new friends about her John Wessler nightmare. As she'd said, Brady and Ashley were there when she'd first met the man and helped her escape. She felt a connection with them in that way.

Even more potent than that, though, was Brady. There was something about him that drew her in. It went beyond his physical appearance—she trusted him. Some might argue it didn't make sense based on the lack of time they'd spent in each other's company, but Monet's heart and mind felt differently.

"You seem different," Brady's deep voice broke into her thoughts.

"Different?" Monet looked at him as they strolled along the beach. "As in good different or bad different?" She smiled.

Brady didn't answer right away but studied her before gently shaking his head. "Not good or bad, just different. As if a burden has been lifted from you."

His words triggered a flutter in her belly, and she giggled softly. "Juliet said the same thing after I'd mustered the courage to open up to her too." Monet smiled and turned her head toward the ocean, where the coral sky was making its final appearance of the night. "Wow, it's beautiful."

They stopped walking, and Brady gazed out across the horizon. "I can't wait for you to see the sunrise," he said. "It makes getting up at 5:00 a.m. worth it." Brady gestured to the dry sand behind them. "Would you like to sit for a while?"

"Sure." Monet started to lay out her sweatshirt as a makeshift blanket, but Brady stopped her.

"No need to get that dirty," he said as he held up the beach towel.

"Ahh." A smile danced on her lips. "I thought maybe you were planning a little moonlight swim."

Brady spread the oversized towel over a dry area of sand and let out a deep chuckle as his mouth slid into a playful grin. "Not tonight."

Monet arched an eyebrow as she took a seat on the beach towel. "Oh?" She set her sandals down next to her in the sand and spread her sweatshirt across her lap. Her lips curled into a smile. "Do you often take moonlight swims?"

"Occasionally." His voice carried a tone of teasing as he sat next to her. "When I want to give Cole and Ash some privacy, I'll come down here for a little moon dipping."

"Moon dipping?" Monet asked.

"Well, that's what I like to call it." Brady gestured toward the sky. "Without all the light pollution you typically get in the city, the night sky here is pretty spectacular." His gaze focused on the moon. "See how bright the moon is already?"

"Oh, wow," Monet said, awed by the big, gorgeous orb beginning to cast a streak of light across the ocean.

Wait.

She turned her attention back to Brady. "So is moon dipping the same as the other type of dipping?" Skinny dipping, to be precise.

Another low chuckle arose from within his broad chest. "Pretty much."

"Hmm." Monet nodded, pulling her widened eyes away from his hypnotic ones, forcing herself to stare up at the first stars beginning to dot the sky—unsure of what to make of the frenzied fluttering now swirling around in her stomach over the image of Brady *moon dipping*.

She heard him clear his throat and, from the corner of her eye, caught a glimpse of him resting back on his elbows before he let out a long, low breath.

"I'm sorry," he said. "It's just, after what you went through, I should be a little more... careful."

Monet's head tilted. "Careful?"

A split second later, understanding dawned on her. Brady was worried that his comment alluding to skinny dipping had offended her. Maybe it should have? And the idea that Brady was concerned caused a sense of relief to expand through her chest. But Monet knew his comment was only a bit of light teasing, and the longer she sat there staring at him, the more desperate she became for him to know it. A sudden burst of adrenaline triggered her next words. "You don't have to be careful around me."

Brady's eyebrows shot up. Despite the increased rate of her heart and the sheer determination egging her on, Monet nearly laughed at the expression of surprise on his face.

"Given everything I went through, it does mean a lot to me that you'd be worried about offending me—or scaring me." She looked away, feeling the temperature of her body rise as the words inside her head struck at the truth. "But the thing is," she turned back to Brady, "all that happened five years ago. I've already processed it." She let out a defeated huff. "I've already lived in fear and tried to hide from the world." Her voice softened. "And I've already lived with a wall around my heart for far too long." Monet dropped her eyes to her hands and toyed with the strings of her hoodie. "It's time I *really* start living."

For the first time in five years, Monet meant the words she'd just spoken. She'd repeated them inside her mind countless times since she met Juliet and had overcome many hurdles with her friend's help. But now, sitting on a tropical beach alongside the irresistible man who had been there when her nightmare began, Monet truly meant it. She was ready to move on, ready to live—really live. A warmth, unlike anything she could remember feeling cascaded from head to toe, and she closed her eyes and exhaled a deep breath.

After a brief moment, she opened her eyes and turned toward Brady, who had boosted himself into a sitting position with his knees bent and feet resting in the sand.

Monet couldn't read his expression, and although she wondered what Brady would make of the glimpse inside her mind she'd just subjected him to, she still felt the slow and steady beat of her heart. She'd meant every word she'd spoken, and it calmed her. Still, the silence was stretching, and the way Brady continued to study her began to chip away at her confidence.

Wondering if she'd made him uncomfortable, Monet opened her mouth to apologize. "Brady, I'm—"

"Okay," Brady interrupted as his hand reached over and gently squeezed hers.

It was a small gesture, but his touch sent a wave of warmth through her hand, up her arm, and straight into her heart.

"Okay?" she asked.

"If you're ready for it," he replied as his fingers laced with hers. "I'll help you start *really* living." The deep intonation of his voice and the way his gaze intensified caused Monet's pulse to pick up.

"I'm ready." Her eyes dropped to their intertwined hands, and she instinctively tightened her fingers around his.

It had been years since Monet held a man's hand in a romantic way. High school, actually. She hadn't been on a date since senior prom, over five years earlier. The realization could have easily sent her into a panic accompanied by heart palpitations and sweaty palms, but the warmth of Brady's grasp and the strength behind it banished all concerns and worries that tried to fight their way into her mind.

"Good," Brady said. "And not a moment too soon." He turned his focus toward the ocean. "Look."

The sun had set, and only the light from the moon lit the water and the beach. Monet's eyes had adjusted to the darkness, and she could see movement near the retreating waves of high tide. She strained to focus even more. "Is that a—turtle?"

Brady chuckled. "It is. I was hoping we'd get lucky and see one tonight."

"Oh my gosh!" Monet let go of Brady's hand and jumped up, intent on getting a closer look.

"Wait," Brady said, reaching up and taking hold of her hand, tugging Monet back down next to him. "We don't want to disturb her; she's here to lay her eggs."

Monet drew in an excited breath. "Really?"

Brady nodded with a broad smile. "This beach is a favorite spot for nesting." He glanced behind them. "We've witnessed quite a few turtle mothers lay their eggs here."

Monet inhaled an astonished huff as she watched the female turtle paddle through the sand. "How often do you see them?"

"It's mainly in the summer months," Brady said. "Not many sea turtles nest in the fall and winter."

After several moments, the mother turtle reached a spot in the sand and, using her hind flippers, started digging a hole that would soon be a nest for her eggs. Monet remained still as she watched, not wanting to interrupt the surreal moment. Without thinking, she linked her arms around one of Brady's. "I can't believe how cool this is."

"In another couple of months, all these eggs will start hatching," Brady explained. "And if you think this is cool, wait until you see that."

Monet's eyes sparkled as they widened. "I would love to witness that."

The two of them continued watching as another two sea turtles fought the crashing waves and made their way up the beach to begin nature's seasonal routine.

As the initial excitement over the appearance of the sea turtles wore off, Monet realized she'd been boldly clinging to Brady's arm. "So," she said as she nonchalantly untangled herself from him. "Earlier, you mentioned a side project you and Cole are working on. Tell me about it."

"Ah, yeah." Brady nodded. "It's actually pretty awesome."

Monet casually slid to the left, putting some distance between them while her mind spun over how comfortable she'd felt cozying up to Brady.

Up to that point in time, Monet would expect her throat to tighten. The terrifying sensation of not being able to breathe would rear its head anytime a man attempted to show her any affection, regardless of how harmless or platonic it was. But an assurance deep within her heart knew that wouldn't happen, not where Brady Nash was concerned. He was safe, and Monet's growing interest in the man caused a different sort of breathlessness to swell within her.

"The whole thing," Brady said, "was all spurred by a day trip Cole and I took right after we'd first broke ground for the resort."

Monet focused her thoughts back on Brady. "Oh?"

"We wanted to do some sightseeing, really dig into the authentic culture and architecture of Mexico, so we took off one Saturday to explore some ruins and get a glimpse into life away from the tourist zone."

Monet sighed. "Now that," she said, "sounds right up my alley."

Brady smiled as he studied her. "Yeah, I thought it might be. I remember you telling me how you loved different types of architecture when we first met."

Monet's heart fluttered over Brady remembering what she'd told him all those years ago—she barely remembered saying it herself!

"Well," Brady said, his eyebrows rising with a slow shake of his head. "That's when we discovered that many of the people of Cancun live in poverty."

Monet's eyes narrowed. "Really?"

Brady nodded somberly. "Yeah, it was pretty shocking. I mean, you expect poor areas in every city or town—it's a sad reality to the world, but neither Cole nor I expected to find so much of it here."

Monet exhaled a thoughtful breath. "I suppose it's ignorance or naivety. Take me, for example. When I think of Cancun, I think of white sandy beaches and pristine ocean water lined by glamorous, exotic hotels. You just don't think of that part of it. You know?"

"I do know," he said. "But once I saw it, it stuck with me, and it stuck with Cole too, because we both had the same idea; great minds and all that." He chuckled, and Monet smiled.

"About a month after our discovery of the *real* Cancun, Cole and I launched a little side project to help restore some of the most run-down homes and other structures."

Monet's lips parted as she sucked in a quick breath, and goosebumps raced up her arms. She was speechless.

"At first, it wasn't a huge deal. Cole and I convinced a few of the crew to help out, and every other weekend we'd head into town and fix a leaking roof or a broken window, that type of thing." He chuckled again. "Eventually, Velma caught wind of what we were doing and wanted to get involved. *Whatever you boys need,*" Brady quoted. "She helped kick it up a notch, and before long, we were restoring and even rebuilding entire homes."

"That's incredible," Monet breathed in awe. "What an extraordinary act of service—and kindness."

"Like I said earlier, it keeps me grounded. Cole too." He shrugged. "And I love doing it. Especially when you see how genuinely gracious and grateful the people are."

Monet was so captivated and impressed by what Brady had revealed to her that she'd almost entirely forgotten she sat on a moonlit beach with sea turtle mothers preparing their nests.

"I would love to see what you do," Monet said. "And I may not be the best with tools, but I'd be willing to help while I'm here."

Brady's head tilted, and an enchanting grin spread across his lips. "I just might take you up on that."

"You better!" She laughed. "I'm not kidding, Brady. I would love to help."

"It's a date then," he said. "We have a crew working pretty much full time now—thanks to Velma. Cole and I usually try to get out there every weekend we have free, but sometimes we have clients back home that need our attention."

Brady pushed himself off the beach towel and offered Monet his hand. "Would you like to get your feet wet?"

"Of course!" Monet willingly took his hand and stood.

Brady didn't let go; instead, he interlaced his fingers with hers and led her down the slight slope to where the tide was high, and the water flowed peacefully back and forth.

The feeling of the ocean was soothing as it rolled over her feet and ankles. "It's like bathwater."

Brady chuckled deeply. "Now you know why I enjoy a little *moon dipping* every now and then."

Monet giggled softly as her playful side bubbled its way to the surface. Reaching down, she scooped up a handful of warm Caribbean water and tossed it playfully at Brady. "You and your moon dipping." She laughed. "You're a big tease!"

Brady didn't flinch as the water fell in droplets on his shirt. "Oh, you think so?"

It was dark, but the moon lit his face enough for Monet to see an impish smile of his own, and in the next instant, Monet's adrenaline spiked, and a long-buried excitement took flight in her belly as Brady took a step toward her. "You think I'm a tease?" he taunted, scooping up his own handful of water and splashing her.

Monet squealed and took off running, only stopping to splash him again.

"I do!" She laughed as the two continued to playfully soak each other.

Monet couldn't remember the last time she'd felt so light. Every part of her felt weightless: her chest, her limbs, and even her mind. She was happy; for the first time in a long time, Monet felt happiness radiate to her very core.

Losing herself in the joy of the moment, Monet scooped up an especially large handful of water and tossed it, hitting Brady directly in the face.

"Oh!" Monet stifled a giggle with her hand.

Brady wiped the salt water from his face and arched one drastic brow. "I see how it is."

He advanced on her then and, in two short strides, was in front of her.

Monet suppressed another giggle. "Sorry about that."

Before she could say another word, Brady took hold of one of her arms and squatted down, wrapping his free arm around the back of her legs and flinging her up and over his shoulder.

"What are you doing?" Monet managed through her laughter as she ceremoniously pounded on his back.

"The way I see it," Brady said as he stepped into deeper water. "What's fair is fair, and seeing as you've all but drenched me, I'm just repaying the favor."

"You wouldn't!" Monet was still laughing even though she knew what he intended to do.

"You don't have your phone tucked in your skirt or anything, do you?" Brady asked.

"I don't know. Maybe I do!" Monet teasingly fibbed.

She heard Brady chuckle. "In that case," he said, finally stopping in knee-high water, "I guess we'd better not take any chances."

Brady lifted Monet off his shoulder, keeping his hands at her waist as her body slowly slid down his. Monet hadn't stopped smiling since she'd first splashed him. However, as her eyes met Brady's while he was lowering her feet into the water, her smile faded, replaced by an unfamiliar warmth spreading slowly from her belly and throughout her limbs.

Instead of releasing her, Brady held her close. Monet sensed a shift in the air between them as they stared at one another.

"I can't tell you what it was like," Brady said in a low, provocative voice that caused her heart to thud hard in her chest. "You have no idea of the feelings I experienced when I saw you standing there."

Monet swallowed. "Standing where?"

"In the lobby of our firm," he said. "When you first turned around, my breath abandoned me, and it was as if my heart froze and then leapt all in the same moment."

"Much like what I'm experiencing right now, then," she boldly admitted.

Through the darkness, she saw a slow smile forming across his mouth. "You have no idea how happy I am to hear you say that because I don't think I can wait for another second to do this."

In the next instant, his hands moved from her waist to cradle her head, sending Monet's pulse into a frenzy, and as Brady guided her lips to his, she found it nearly impossible to breathe. He kissed her once, somewhat tentatively. His lips felt soft, warm, and tempting, but she sensed he was holding back.

It had been years since Monet had allowed a man to kiss her, and a fleeting worry caused a tightening sensation in her ribs. She trusted Brady implicitly, but she feared he sensed her inexperience.

Rallying every shred of self-confidence she possessed, Monet leaned into him, and he kissed her again. This time, his kiss lingered, teasing and coaxing her lips into accepting his.

Slowly and gently, Brady's mouth worked a spell of passion over her, filling Monet with sensations she had never experienced before. She was warm, nearly feverish, and every nerve in her body was awakened with new life.

Monet gripped his forearms, abandoned all timidity, and met his kiss with her own hungered eagerness. Brady responded, weaving his fingers through her hair; he guided her head to a different angle and deepened the kiss. The flavor of his mouth was intoxicating, and the longer he kissed her, the more insatiable her thirst for him grew.

Is this what she'd been missing all these years? The exquisite pleasure of it—the mad pounding of her heart, the goosebumps rippling over her skin, the warmth bathing her limbs—was this what came from letting go of the past? In the next beat, Monet knew she would not have experienced these bliss-filled sensations with just any man. It was the man bestowing dream-worthy, passionate kisses upon her who ignited such passion within her.

All too soon, Brady abruptly broke the seal of the kiss but kept her face in his hands as he studied her.

"Monet." His voice was deep and husky, and his chest rose and fell harshly. "Your kiss tastes even sweeter than I imagined all these years, and you are utterly addictive."

Monet's breath hitched, matching his rhythm as she struggled to regain her breath.

"That's why I need to get you back to the villa, before my good sense abandons me."

Monet wanted to protest and boldly seek out his mouth again, but she knew he was right. Better to keep the encounter to a first kiss and not allow it to lead to something she was unprepared for.

"Okay," she whispered, her breathing finally evening out.

Brady released her, but he took hold of her hand, leading her out of the warm water and back to their spot on the beach. There, he gathered their towel and quickly shook it to rid it of sand.

Monet suddenly found it difficult to look at him, somewhat embarrassed over how willingly she'd accepted his affections. She also worried she'd appeared a novice in the art of kissing. In an attempt to avoid eye contact, she focused on the mother turtles, still busy with their task.

"Hey," Brady said, stepping closer to her as he draped the towel over his arm. He placed his free hand on the back of her head and gently pulled her face closer to his. "Just in case you were wondering," he whispered with his mouth a breath away from hers. "Kissing you is by far the most enjoyable thing I've done over the past five years."

He kissed her tenderly, and she willingly accepted.

"We'd better go," he said, pulling his lips away.

Monet nodded. With one sentence and one small kiss, Brady chased her momentary insecurities away.

Monet bent and picked up her sweatshirt and sandals before Brady again took her hand in his, and they made their way down the beach.

Their conversation was easy, and Monet felt at ease in Brady's company. Soon, the soft and inviting lights of the villa appeared.

Monet secretly hoped Ashley and Cole had turned in for the night. She could feel the delicious effects of Brady's kiss and suspected her inexperienced lips were flushed and plump to prove it.

Once they'd rinsed the sand from their feet using the beach shower installed at the base of the steps leading to the villa's swimming pool, exhaustion from the long and eventful day seemed to wash over Monet almost instantly.

After floating on a cloud of pure exhilaration for the past hour, Monet's mind and body were ready for a reprieve. It felt as if weights had been strapped to her feet, legs, and arms, and her strides turned to shuffles. She sensed Brady practically pulling her over the swimming pool bridge as she fought against the extreme fatigue that was overtaking her.

She watched Brady toss the beach towel on a nearby lounge chair before turning his charming smile on Monet.

"Come here."

Before Monet could protest, Brady swept her up again, but this time, instead of throwing her over his shoulder, he cradled her tenderly in his masculine arms.

Monet let out a giggle. "Is my exhaustion that obvious?"

She felt his chuckle rumble deep within his chest. "To be honest, I'm impressed you made it this long," he said, keeping his voice low. "You've had a big day."

Instead of going in through the large shutter doors leading into the villa's main living area, Brady carried Monet down the path that led to her private terrace.

She should have made more of a fuss over Brady carrying her, but she was too tired to complain. And besides, anyone would have to be out of their mind to complain over being held so protectively by Brady. Without the sea air filling her senses, she could smell the subtle scent of spice-scented soap and feel the warmth from his body next to hers. In truth, Monet could easily fall asleep in Brady's arms, content and safe.

"Here we are," Brady said, setting Monet on her feet. His hands encircled her waist, pulling her close again. "This is where I say goodnight."

It must have been her extreme fatigue, for the confidence she'd unleashed on the beach while in Brady's arms seemed to vanish. Monet's breathing picked up, causing her mouth to go dry, and she dropped her eyes to where her hands gripped his arms.

Brady's low chuckle immediately made her look at him again. "Don't get shy on me now."

In the next instant, he took hold of Monet's chin and kissed her. The feel of his perfect lips on hers ignited her courage, and she willingly accepted and returned his moist, alluring kiss. It only lasted a moment, but it left Monet breathless.

Brady reached for the handle of the sliding glass door and slid it open.

"In you go, while you still can," he said.

"You can cut through my room," she said, feeling her fatigue again.

Brady's eyes crinkled softly at the corners. "I've gotta close the pool and take care of a few other things out here first." He gestured back toward the pool deck.

Monet's lips curled into a soft smile as her eyelids began to droop. "Okay."

"Goodnight, Monet."

"Goodnight."

Monet watched Brady walk down the short path before she closed her sliding door and locked it.

The room felt cool and inviting; soft, intimate light emanated from the bamboo lantern chandelier hanging in the center of the room. Monet dropped her sandals near the armoire and pulled out a soft pair of cotton pajama shorts and a matching tank. The thought crossed her mind to ditch her whole bedtime routine and climb directly into the big, inviting bed calling to her. Monet didn't think she'd ever felt so tired—so relaxed.

She glanced at the clock sitting on the small nightstand beside her bed.

11:10, which meant it was just after midnight in New York. Even though Monet knew Juliet would be more than okay with her calling that late, Monet was so unbelievably tired, and once she spilled the delicious beans that Brady had kissed her, Monet knew the conversation with her best friend would be a long one.

She sluggishly changed her clothes and did a minimal face wash and a quick tooth brushing before she turned the lights out and fell into bed. The fluffy down comforter felt heavenly, like being swaddled in a cloud of comfort.

Monet reached for her phone that had been charging on the nightstand and swiped the screen, bringing it to life.

She opened the text thread with Juliet and, with the last bit of energy she had left after such an exhilarating day, typed:

"I think it happened, Jewels. The past is finally behind me."

With the memory of Brady still fresh on her mind and in her heart, Monet exhaled a contented sigh.

"I'm finally free."

Brady

The mornings in Cancun were some of Brady's favorite times. He'd always been a morning person, so getting up at the crack of dawn to go for a run wasn't a chore; it was something he looked forward to each day. But he hadn't slept well, so it had taken extra effort to drag himself out of bed and pull on his running shoes that morning.

After he'd said goodnight to Monet, he'd put the mesh cover over the swimming pool, made sure the security system was on, and locked up the villa, but Brady was still on a high from the time he'd spent with Monet on the beach. His thoughts had been scattered, and he'd felt rejuvenated—alive. No woman had tempted Brady the way Monet did, and now that he'd kissed her, he knew his hunger for her would be nearly insatiable.

His night of tossing and turning was in large part due to his inability to get the memory of Monet's silky skin and lush, full lips out of his thoughts long enough to settle down, but the other thing that kept Brady from a blissful night's sleep was the guilt he battled.

What if he'd moved too fast? He and Monet had only been alone in each other's company a handful of times over the past five years; the last thing Brady wanted was for Monet to think he was a player. On top of that, she'd just revealed her traumatizing experience with John Wessler;

Brady's timing probably wasn't the best, but he couldn't help himself.

Thoughts such as these taunted him most of the night and still plagued him as he dropped into a lunge on the back patio just as the sun peeked above the horizon.

"Well, well, well." Cole's amused chuckle echoed from his throat.

Brady inwardly groaned. He knew Ashley and Cole had seen him scoop Monet up and carry her to her room. He'd noticed them star-gazing on their bedroom terrace but had chosen to ignore them.

"Morning, Cole," Brady grumbled.

"I am *so* happy I got to witness that," Cole taunted with an all too pleased grin fastened across his face.

"I'm going to pretend I don't know what you're talking about." Brady shot his friend a deadpan look. "And I suggest you stretch out; I'm not waiting for you."

Cole slapped Brady on the back as he laughed. "I'm just messin' with you, man." He stretched his arms out and started a set of arm swings. "It's none of my business, but I am excited for you," Cole said. "I know you've been pining for her since you first met."

Pining?

"I wouldn't go so far as to say I was pining for Monet all these years."

Seeing Cole's raised eyebrows and hearing his scoff, Brady quickly continued. "Okay, I will admit, for a few months after we met, I couldn't get her out of my head—I even contemplated looking her up." He stopped stretching. "The first time I saw her at the firm, it felt like my eyes were playing tricks on me." He glanced at Cole, noting his all-too-satisfied smirk.

Brady dropped his head with a slow shake and a huff. "I guess you're right." He looked back at his friend. "But, dude, she's amazing. I just hope I didn't scare her off last night."

"Oh ho ho," Cole chuckled, "from the way she cozied right up to you when you scooped her up like Prince Charming himself, you have nothing to worry about."

"I hope so," Brady said as he finished his pre-run routine.

"Why didn't you look her up?" Cole asked.

Brady's mouth slid into a lopsided smile, and he gave a one-shoulder shrug. "Honestly, I didn't think she'd be interested."

Cole's face distorted into a mix of horror and shock. "Dude! Are you being serious right now?"

Brady gave a sheepish nod. "It doesn't matter, though," he said. "She was going through so much with Wessler; the last thing she would have wanted was me knocking on her door."

"Yeah, well, I beg to differ, my friend," Cole said as the two started walking toward the beach.

Brady did feel a tinge of regret in not reaching out to Monet all those years, especially after how willingly she'd accepted his affections the night before. But his Grandma Nash had taught him something long ago: *"My boy, there's no use cryin' over spilled milk."* Brady smiled at the memory of his spunky, five-foot-two grandma. It seemed she always had a wise saying primed and ready for any occasion. And she was right. You can't change the past, but you can influence the future.

"I guess the only thing that matters," Cole broke into Brady's thoughts, "is that she's here now, and you're getting a second chance."

Brady chuckled. "I was thinking the very same thing."

The two reached the water's edge. Brady turned toward the spectacular sunrise, inhaling the invigorating salt air. "I can't wait to experience this with Monet," he said. "I was so tempted to wake her up this morning and invite her to join us but decided better of it."

"Yeah. Ash agreed that we should let Monet sleep. She's probably fighting some jet lag," Cole said as the two broke into a light jog along the beach.

"I was thinking," Brady said, "that we run to the Jewel, check on things with the weekend crew, and then maybe join the girls in town?"

Cole laughed. "You're falling fast, dude. I'll call Ash and let her know."

"Do you think she'll mind us crashing her plans?"

"Nah!" Cole, now breathing heavier, said. "She's rooting for you and Monet as much as I am."

The two friends picked up their pace, and Brady could feel his pulse quicken as his own breathing became deeper. He loved running. He loved the feel of the packed sand under his feet and the refreshing morning air in his lungs.

With each stride, any stress knotted inside him would loosen and evaporate. And then, about twenty minutes into his run, the endorphins would release, and Brady would feel like he was flying. Every part of his body working in perfect rhythm. There was little else that could compare.

As they continued their four-mile run toward the construction site, they passed a few early morning beach vendors who were already about their business of trying to sell their goods to tourists who were out early to see the sunrise.

Velma's villa was on a private beach, where vendors weren't allowed. Brady wouldn't have minded, though. He couldn't help but feel a certain admiration for them. There was something profoundly authentic and humbling about the local vendors in Cancun. During the months Brady and Cole had spent there, they had become adept at spotting the occasional scam artist among the throng of honest craftspeople. It was the locals, those who infused their livelihood with their talents—be it through exotic hair braiding, weaving blankets and baskets, crafting jewelry, or offering fresh fruits and portraits—that truly captured the essence of Cancun for Brady.

Brady's musings were interrupted when his attention was suddenly drawn to an older gentleman wearing a faded linen shirt, worn sandals, and a wide-brimmed straw hat. He was standing next to a cluster of lounge chairs further up the beach. The people occupying the chairs seemed enthralled by whatever the vendor was selling.

As Brady and Cole got closer, Brady could see dozens of necklaces wrapped around one of the man's arms. "Hold up," Brady puffed out, his voice reflecting the exertion of running.

Cole stopped and placed his hands on his knees to steady his breathing while Brady quickly jogged over to where the man was causing such a stir.

"May I?" Brady asked, drawing the vendor's attention to him and pointing to one of the necklaces. "*¿Puedo?*"

"*Sí.* Yes, yes. You like? Handmade." The man slid the necklace off his arm and handed it to Brady. "For you, eight dollars," the man said in broken English.

Brady studied the necklace, turning it over in his hand and examining the impressive craftsmanship. It was long and made of highly polished sand-colored tube-shaped beads, but the thing that made it so unusual were the eight evenly spaced black pendants hanging from it. They were a type of black rock, all chiseled into the shape of soft-ended spears. The necklace had a tribal look and feel, like something you might also see in Africa. It was striking, and Brady loved it.

"Woah," Cole said, coming to stand next to Brady. "That is wicked looking."

Brady rubbed his fingers along the black spikes. "Super cool, right?"

"Are you thinking of getting one?" Cole asked as the vendor attempted to hand one to him.

"You like?" the man asked Cole.

"Oh no, no, *gracias*." Cole threw his palms up.

"I like," Brady said as he unzipped the back pocket of his running shorts and pulled out his cell phone with his card holder attached to the back. He removed 200 pesos from behind his credit cards and paid the man. "*¡Excelente!*"

"*Gracias.*" The man nodded humbly before counting out the two dollars in change.

Brady quickly waved his hand toward the man. "No, no. You keep it."

Once again, the man gave his thanks, tucked the money into the worn pocket of his pants, and turned back to the other waiting customers.

Brady lifted the necklace over his head and placed it around his neck. The beads hung low on his chest, and the spikes fanned over his t-shirt.

"It's a gift," he announced.

Cole's eyebrows shot up. "A gift?"

"For Monet."

Cole started laughing. "I can't see her wearing something like that; it's pretty savage and exotic."

Brady glanced down at the necklace. "Of course not. I'm not giving it to her to wear unless it's part of a costume or something, but I think Monet will love it—just to have."

Cole nodded. "Cool."

He slapped Brady on the back. "Let's get back at it."

Cole took off in a jog down the beach, and Brady followed. He hoped he was right and that Monet would like her gift. His pulse quickened as his feet pounded the sand, and Brady smiled. He knew she would appreciate its unique beauty. In that way, the necklace was much like Monet—unique and beautiful.

"Um hum," he mumbled to himself. "She's going to love it."

Monet

The brightness seeped through Monet's eyelids, gently rousing her from her dreams. Slowly, she opened her eyes, allowing memories from her dreams to linger. She'd been dreaming of Josh and Juliet's wedding, an event that had been nothing short of magical. A soft smile tugged at her lips as she lay there, gratitude filling her for the inspiration the dream had provided. She finally had a clear direction for her best friend's wedding.

As her mind cleared, she rolled to her side and gazed out the sliding glass door that led to the swimming pool and beach. The view was as spectacular as she'd imagined it would be. The sun sat just above the horizon, lighting the soft, fluffy clouds with soft hues of pink and purple mixed with vibrant yellows and oranges.

Seeing the sunrise reminded her of Brady—as if she'd need any other reminder. The feeling of being held in his arms was still fresh, and the taste of Brady's kiss lingered on her lips. As she recalled the time spent with him the night before, she marveled at how easily she'd melted into him when he'd first kissed her.

"Ahh!" Monet flipped to her back and yanked the comforter over her head as the euphoria over that first brush of Brady's lips on hers gave way to embarrassment.

What had she been thinking? Monet had been in Cancun less than twenty-four hours and was already making out with Brady—the man she would be working with for the next six months! True, she'd harbored a crush on him for years, but to behave so boldly? The longer she thought about it, the more the heat swept up her neck and face, even reaching her ears. Tossing the covers off, she quickly sat up and grabbed her phone. "Juliet," Monet said aloud. She needed her best friend.

Ignoring the multiple text notifications on her home screen, she dialed. The phone rang once.

"Ahhhh!"

Monet jerked her head back as she held the phone away from her ear.

"Tell me, tell me, tell me!" Juliet was almost screaming.

Monet flinched but slowly brought the phone back to her ear and couldn't help but giggle. "Okay, okay. But you have to stop yelling."

Juliet laughed. *"I'm sorry. But you can't send a text like the one you did last night and not expect me to freak out. I am not a patient person; you know this."*

Monet smiled. She did know it. When Juliet cared about something or someone, she cared about that thing or person with everything she had—heart, mind, and soul. Given that Juliet had been there for Monet through some pretty challenging times, it wasn't a surprise that her best friend would feel almost as emotionally invested in Monet's *"the past is behind me,"* revelation as Monet herself.

"Hmm…" Monet inhaled and exhaled. "Where to begin?"

"How much time do you have?"

Monet glanced at the clock. *10:16.* "Well, we aren't doing any work today since it's my first weekend here. Ashley mentioned going into one of the flea markets in Playacar, but I think we'll hang out by the pool first."

"Aaannd," Juliet drew out the word, *"I'm not jealous of that."*

Monet laughed. "I wish you were here to come with."

"Aw, me too, and I'm just teasing. I am so happy for you right now."

"My point is, I think I've got plenty of time to talk. It sounds like it will be a pretty relaxed day."

"Okay, then I want to hear everything. Start when you first landed, and don't leave anything out."

Monet rested against the padded headboard and snuggled under the cozy comforter; she knew this wouldn't be quick.

And she was right. She spent the next forty-five minutes giving Juliet her play-by-play of everything that had happened up until Monet had watched Brady walk down the path to the swimming pool after saying goodnight. Juliet was always good at dissecting hidden meanings, pointing out subtle hints, and, best of all, soothing fears and insecurities.

"This man." The emotion welled in Juliet's voice. *"I don't even know him—never met the guy, but I adore him."*

Monet smiled as her throat grew thick. "Even if he breaks my heart?"

"Even if he breaks your heart, which he won't," Juliet said. *"But even if he did, I will always admire him for giving you the courage to finally let go."*

Monet breathed a sigh. "When you put it that way... You're right."

"I do have to admit," Juliet said, *"I wish I were there. I've been waiting four years to see a man pierce that wall, and the fact that I can't witness it with my own eyes... Ahh! Let's just say it's making me extra fiery. Poor Josh."* Juliet laughed. *"But I love you, and I will simply have to be content with your daily calls."*

"Daily?" Monet smiled.

"Non-negotiable."

"Deal," Monet said.

"Oh!" Juliet blurted in the way Monet had come to recognize. An idea had just popped into her best friend's mind. *"I will get to witness it! Don't forget, Josh and I are making a trip to Cancun before the wedding."*

"At least one, right?"

"Of course!"

"But maybe last night was just a one-time thing, you know? When we first met, Brady and I both obviously felt a spark... maybe we were just getting it out of our system."

"Uh-uh, nope, you're not going there," Juliet scolded. *"Even if Brady was that type of a guy, which I doubt, you're not. Right?"*

"I don't—I don't think so." Monet had little to no experience with men, but she was pretty sure she wasn't a man-eating seductress—as she'd heard it called once.

"You don't think so?" Juliet puffed an astonished laugh. *"Okay, let me ask you this, do you feel like you were just getting it out of your system, as you put it?"*

Monet scrunched one side of her face and stared at the ceiling, thinking.

"Hmm..."

"You silly girl," Juliet said through the phone. *"I can picture you with your contemplative face right now. Speaking of which..."*

Monet heard some muffled sounds, and soon her cell phone switched to FaceTime. Monet accepted, and Juliet's familiar face appeared on the screen.

"We should have done this earlier," Juliet said. *"It's easier for me to read your thoughts."*

"Are my facial expressions that telling?"

"Only to those who know you best." Juliet's smile was warm. *"Now, let me ask you again, do you feel like you were just getting Brady out of your system last night?"*

The tension Monet hadn't realized she had in her shoulders loosened, and she shook her head. "No." The tone of her voice was soft. "And it didn't feel like Brady was just getting me out of his system either." Her forehead drew into a pucker. "Quite the opposite," she said. "It felt like the beginning of something."

Juliet's beautiful face lit with delight. *"Yes!"* She placed one hand over her heart and looked heavenward. *"I knew there was a reason everything fell into place so flawlessly; you and this job—it was meant to be. You and Brady are destined for each other."*

Monet giggled. "I love it so much that you believe in destiny, Juliet. I think you and Ashley will become fast friends. She thinks it's fate that brought us together again."

Juliet's eyebrows rose. *"Clever girl. And she's right."*

"I wish I were as confident as both of you, but I'm not sure I'm even ready for... for whatever this is between Brady and me."

"Of course you're not sure." Juliet's features softened. *"I don't think anyone ever really is,"* she said. *"Look at Josh and me. After the heartbreak I'd gone through before meeting him, I was done with romance, but all it took was one glimpse of that flirtatious smile and some playful banter, and I was hooked. Love has a way of finding us, often when it's the furthest thing from our minds."*

Monet smiled softly with a slight nod. "I know you're right; you always are." She puffed a small chuckle. "I just don't have the experience, you know? My last real date was when I was eighteen years old." She blew out a defeated breath. "Brady has probably dated hundreds of women by now." Juliet's bark of laughter caused Monet to jerk back. "What?"

"Hundreds of women?" Juliet tilted her head dramatically. *"Ya think?"* The question dripped with sarcasm.

"You know what I mean." Monet rolled her eyes. "It just intimidates the daylights out of me when I think of how experienced Brady obviously is when it comes to—women."

"Oh, Monet." Juliet's tone softened to understanding. *"You are one hundred percent justified in how you're feeling. The intimidation and fear are okay—natural, don't let me or anyone else push you into something you're uncomfortable with."*

"Then what do I do?" Monet asked. "Because I really like him, and last night was the happiest—the most alive I've felt in years."

An empathetic smile slid across Juliet's lips. *"You follow your heart,"* she said. *"That's what you do. Everything else will fall into place."* She lowered her voice as her eyes twinkled with a hint of mischief. *"After all, from what you told me, your kissin' skills came rather naturally."*

Monet dropped her face into her free hand as the embarrassment over the memory of kissing Brady burned her skin. "I can't even think about it."

"Why ever not?" Juliet giggled. *"That's one of the best parts!"* She continued to laugh. *"Obviously,"* she waved her hand dismissively, *"enjoying each other's company, the mutual respect, the common interests, all of that is wildly important to any healthy relationship."* She hesitated and exhaled a dreamy sigh. *"But the physical attraction, the way you make each other's heart race, the craving to touch one another—that heat, the passion—it's to be savored and enjoyed just as much as the other stuff,"* Juliet said. *"So let yourself think about it, relive it, and dream of it happening again."*

Monet sat listening to her adorable friend, and as was usually the case when Juliet offered her advice, Monet found her anxieties diminishing. A familiar warmth bathed her limbs, and she inhaled a deep, satisfied breath. Monet wasn't in this alone; she had Juliet to help her navigate the new and unfamiliar territory of romance and men. She also knew that if the occasion ever called for it, Ashley would be another ally for Monet.

Ashley knew about the trauma Monet experienced at the hands of John Wessler and was kindly sympathetic. Since becoming reacquainted with the feisty blonde, Monet had, on several occasions, noticed how Ashley and Juliet shared many of the same personality traits. She wondered how she'd been lucky enough to find two friends so similar.

"Thanks, Jewels," Monet said. "Thank you for always being there for me. Sometimes I wonder what path my life would have taken if I hadn't met you; I owe you a lot."

"Oh, now, you can't start that or I'll get all emotional, and I'll cry!" She swallowed and fanned her face with her hand. *"But you don't owe me anything. I just love you to pieces. You have become so dear to me, and I want to see you as happy as I am."*

"You can't do it either!" Monet said as tears welled.

"Okay, okay," Juliet laughed through her emotions. *"Enough serious talk. Show me that gorgeous room you're staying in. So far, I've only seen the headboard of your bed!"*

Monet tossed her comforter aside and pulled herself together.

"Oh, Juliet, my room—the whole villa," Monet said as she flipped the phone around, "it's a little slice of paradise."

*

As Monet lay on the cushioned-top lounge chair, watching the gentle rolling waves of the mesmerizing turquoise water, she smiled, remembering Juliet's animated reaction to the villa's kitchen as she'd given her a virtual tour. Juliet had cooked in some mighty luxurious kitchens over the years, but Monet knew the vibrant traditional Mexican-style kitchen would have her friend itching to cook up something as spicy as the kitchen's décor itself.

Ashley and Monet started their day sunbathing by the pool. They'd eaten a light breakfast, discussed the Grand Jewel, and shared ideas. Eventually, they moved to the beach. The gentle caress of the tropical ocean breeze, carried by the whispering waves, beckoned to both of them. So, they arranged themselves beneath the shelter of a thatch-covered umbrella, savoring the unhurried pleasures of the day.

Monet's mind wandered to the night before, and her attention turned down the beach to where she and Brady had sat talking before witnessing the mother turtles lay their eggs. She hoped the eggs were safe.

Monet fought the memory of their time spent in the ocean; her shyness in recalling the intimacy between them was still too overwhelming. But as she stared toward the water, Juliet's words came to her mind. "*... relive it, and dream of it happening again.*"

Monet gave in and allowed her mind to conjure up their playful water fight and the teasing that led to Brady tossing her over his broad shoulder... the feel of his solid muscular back as she playfully pounded on it... the way his hands held her waist as her body slid down his... the provocative tone to his voice as he spoke... the way his strong hands cradled her face as his head descended and his mouth—

"Oh!" Monet drew in a breath.

"You okay?" Ashley asked from where she lay on her lounge chair next to Monet.

Monet inhaled deeply, attempting to calm the frenzied fluttering in her stomach and steady her galloping heart.

"Uh," she stuttered before huffing a nervous chuckle and looking at her friend. "Yeah."

Ashley slid her oversized sunglasses up and rested them on her head before her eyebrows arched. "So." A sly grin formed on her face. "How'd it go last night?"

Monet awkwardly turned her attention to the bottle of SPF 50 tanning oil lying on her towel. "Um," she swallowed as she popped the lid off and pumped a couple of squirts onto her leg, "it was... nice. We saw turtles."

Ashley puffed a giggle, drawing Monet's attention back to her. "You saw turtles?" Ashley bit her lip.

"We did." Monet continued to reapply her sunscreen as the nervous lump in her throat grew. She swallowed again. "The mother turtles were nesting."

"Oh, how fun!" Ashley gushed. "I'll never forget the first time Cole and I saw our first turtle nesting," she said. "It was seriously the coolest thing I'd ever seen."

Monet nodded as she replaced the cap on the bottle. "Me too. I was pretty in awe of it all."

"And... besides the turtles, anything else particularly juicy happen?" Ashley's voice held a hint of teasing.

Monet's head whipped toward Ashley, who was looking at her with a knowing, playful glint in her eye.

Does she know?

Maybe Brady talked to Ashley and Cole after he said goodnight. He didn't seem like the type to kiss and tell, but perhaps he had?

Again, her recent conversation with Juliet popped into her mind; Monet could trust Ashley, and although they hadn't been reacquainted long, Monet felt they were becoming friends.

Monet tilted her head as her own eyebrows raised. "I feel like you already know the answer to that."

Ashley laughed. "I have a hunch," she said. "Don't get mad, but Cole and I were stargazing on the terrace when you two came back."

Monet's eyes bulged, and her mouth dropped open, coaxing another laugh out of Ashley.

"The terrace with the telescope?" Monet asked as a tingle of heat swept under her skin.

"Yep," Ashley said. "That's our bedroom."

"Oh." Monet swallowed. "Then I guess you probably saw Brady carry me to my room?"

"Um, hum."

Monet rested her head against the lounge chair and draped her arm over her face. "Oh my gosh!" She couldn't help but laugh. "How embarrassing."

"Embarrassing?" Ashley nearly shrieked. "That was the most romantic thing I've witnessed in a long time—aside from Cole," she quickly clarified. "I almost swooned right there and then."

Monet's arm still covered her eyes as she shook her head. "I can't believe you guys saw that."

"Oh, don't you be worried about that," Ashley said. "Brady oughta be the one worried." She laughed. "Cole will probably never let him live it down!"

"Ugh," Monet moaned.

Ashley continued to laugh as she reached over and pulled Monet's arm off her face. "I promise, it's really not a big deal," she said. "But what I wanna know is, what happened after Brady swept you off your feet?" She bit her lip. "Did he kiss you?"

"Ashley!" Monet halfheartedly scolded as she sat up and threw her legs over the side of her lounge chair.

Ashley's eyes popped wide. "He did!" She fell against the lounge chair and placed a hand over her heart. "I knew he had it in him."

"Fine!" Monet tossed her hands up. "He kissed me."

Ashley drew her shoulders to her ears and squealed. "Wee! I am so happy!"

Monet felt her unease melt away over Ashley's exuberant reaction. How could she not? Ashley's joy was contagious.

Monet inhaled as she tipped her head back and closed her eyes. "The truth is," she said with a sigh, "it was divine."

"Divine?" Ashley sighed. "Must have been some goodnight kiss, huh?"

Monet slowly opened her eyes and looked at Ashley. "Oh, it was," she nodded, "but our first kiss... Mmm, that was utter bliss."

"First kiss?" Ashley abruptly sat up. "Brady kissed you twice?"

Monet's eyebrows drew up as she bit her bottom lip. "Yeah... three times if we're counting."

Ashley's arms shot out with her hands spread wide. "Three?" she blurted.

Monet chewed on her thumbnail and gave a knowing smile. "Um, hum."

"This is the best day of my life," Ashley mumbled to herself before focusing on Monet. "Please. You have to tell me *everything!*"

Monet laughed. She was growing quite fond of Ashley and her animated personality. For so long, Monet had only shared her innermost secrets with Juliet. Finding another friend that she felt comfortable enough to talk to was refreshing.

"Alright," Monet said as she rested her back against the lounge chair. "But I hope you won't think less of me."

Ashley jerked her head back. "What? Why?"

Monet shrugged one shoulder. "I've only been here a day, and I haven't known Brady that long."

"That doesn't matter." Ashley gave her head a shake. "You and Brady have been crushing on each other for five years."

Monet mimicked Ashley's shock as her head drew back and her forehead puckered.

"The way I see it, anyway," Ashley said in response to Monet's doubtful expression. "I *know* Brady has thought about you over the years and was thrown for one big, flustered loop when you showed up at the firm and has been pleasantly distracted ever since." She eyed Monet. "You can't tell me, even with all you went through, that you haven't felt the same."

Monet smiled. "Maybe." She had thought of Brady over the years and was thrown for the same crazy loop when she first saw him. "Yeah, I guess you're right. I never got over my crush on the hot bellhop."

Ashley laughed.

"I just never *ever* thought I'd see him again." Monet sighed. "It's all pretty surreal."

"Like I keep saying," Ashley pretended to flip an imaginary long strand of hair over her shoulder, "it's fate."

Monet chuckled as she reached into her beach bag, pulled out two water bottles, and handed one to Ashley. "I can't wait for you to meet Juliet," she said. "You two are a lot alike."

"Ooh, I like her already," Ashley teased. "When will we get to meet her? Sooner than later, I hope."

"I hope so, too," Monet said before she took a drink from her water bottle. "She and her fiancé, Josh, want to visit before the wedding."

"Oh, for sure," Ashley said. "And how fun! I think it's the coolest thing that they are having their wedding during the grand opening—and that you're in charge of it!"

Monet puffed out a breath. "I still don't know what they're thinking." She shrugged. "But I'll do my best."

"And don't forget," Ashley said. "I'd love to help."

Monet smiled. "I will most definitely take you up on that."

"Now." Ashley's eyebrows waggled. "Tell me about last night, and don't leave anything out."

*

Over the next couple of hours, the two friends chatted openly about the romantic night Monet and Brady shared. Ashley was giddy with delight and would often interject stories of her and Cole's own romantic history. Even after four years of marriage, Ashley and Cole remained deeply smitten, and their enduring love gave hope to Monet's heart.

Ashley also shared how she and Cole had waited for the right woman to come into Brady's life. Contrary to

Monet's assumptions, Brady hadn't dated a multitude of women. In fact, there were only a handful—and of those, just a couple that Ashley deemed somewhat serious. Throughout the conversation, Monet had to fight to keep her expression neutral and ignore the way her muscles tightened and the feeling of her stomach turning to stone whenever Ashley mentioned Brady with another woman.

Since her arrival at Nash and Perkins Architect Firm two weeks earlier, Monet realized she'd unearthed emotions she'd long kept buried. This newfound awareness heightened Monet's insecurities about her own lack of experience in the realms of dating and romance.

"I suppose," Monet began, "one of the reasons I feel anxious about how easily I gave in to Brady's affections is how little I know about him."

Monet's gut told her he was a good man, and she couldn't ignore the calm and contentment she felt in his company, but what did she really know about him? Very little.

Ashley gave a reassuring smile. "I can understand that," she said, "but that piece will come in time. It would be one thing if last night was a one-time thing, but it wasn't." Ashley's face softened. "This—you and Brady—is the beginning of something really great."

Monet smiled with a faint nod. She felt it was, too. She only hoped she could trust her feelings.

Ashley's cell phone chimed, and she reached into her beach bag and pulled it out.

As she read the screen, she started laughing. "You see?" She handed the phone to Monet. "He can't stay away."

Cole: *"Hey Sunshine, you called it! Our boy can't wait until tonight—wants to meet up and go into town with you and Monet. We're leaving now. xx"*

Monet's face flushed, but her embarrassment immediately gave way to a drumming in her chest. Her face lit up, and she couldn't contain her smile.

"You called it?" Monet handed the phone back to Ashley.

"Pfft. Totally." Ashley chuckled. "After we saw him sweep you up in his arms last night, I knew he'd be hard-pressed to stay away from you for too long."

"So," Monet loosened her hair from its messy bun, "they're running back from the resort?"

"Yeah," Ashley said. "It usually takes them about fifteen or twenty minutes." She giggled. "Unless they're racing, then they make it back faster."

Monet ran her fingers through her hair before pulling it back up and securing the hair tie around her messy bun again. She smiled over Ashley's remark and quickly reached into her bag, took out a tube of clear lip gloss, and swiped her lips.

"Don't worry," Ashley said. "You look hot, as in smokin'."

Monet let out a disbelieving huff. "Not quite."

To steer the subject off herself, Monet cleared her throat.

"Can you tell me about Brady's family?" Monet asked. "Does he have any siblings?"

Ashley snorted. "Oh yeah." Her eyes widened. "He sure does."

Monet's forehead raised over Ashley's reaction.

Ashley sucked in a deep breath and released it. "Beau Nash." She dramatically shuddered. "Brady's only brother—sibling, actually."

Monet frowned, and her brows knit together. "That name sounds familiar."

"Probably because he was named most eligible bachelor last year by *Vurve* magazine," Ashley said. "Didn't you mention Juliet's family is connected to *Vurve* somehow?"

Monet blinked a few times. "Um, yeah," she stuttered. "Juliet's uncle and brother own *Vurve*." She slid her sunglasses onto her head. "But wait—" Her forehead furrowed even more. "Brady's brother is Beau Nash?"

"The very one." Disgust laced Ashley's words.

"The founder of BeauFuel Protein?"

"Um hum." Ashley's lips were pursed.

Monet's gaze shifted, and she stared flatly at the open air. "Wow."

She'd never met Beau, but thanks to her friendship with Juliet, Monet was well aware of who he was; he ran in some of the same circles as the Quinn family. The entrepreneur had developed a new protein powder that was taking the health industry by storm. He was ridiculously successful and wildly attractive. Judging from the images Monet had come across of the gentleman, it was evident that he could only be Brady's older brother. If Monet were guessing, she'd place him in his mid to late thirties.

"And let me tell you," Ashley said. "I break into a cold sweat whenever that man is near me."

Monet pulled herself out of the daze. "Because he's so handsome?" she teased.

"I will give him that," Ashley said. "He looks like an older version of Brady, but they're as different as night and day." Ashley huffed. "Beau Nash is as sullen and brooding of a man as you'll ever meet."

"He can't be that bad," Monet said.

"Sweetheart, you have no idea." Ashley tossed her head. "The only thing Beau cares about is his family and his company."

Monet was thoughtful for a moment. "Now that you mention it, Juliet might have said something about him not being the friendliest man."

"Brady says he wasn't always this way," Ashley sighed. "I've only met him a handful of times," she said. "He's very supportive of Brady—always checking in, flying out to construction sites, and such."

"He can't be all bad then." Monet smiled softly.

Ashley's eyebrows arched high. "Just you wait." She shook a finger at Monet. "You'll meet him soon enough, and you can judge for yourself."

"Is he expected to visit?"

Ashley shrugged. "He usually gives Brady a day or two notice before he shows up. But I know he'll be here for the grand opening regardless."

Monet was suddenly distracted by the sight of Brady and Cole down the beach in the distance. The two appeared to be slowing the pace of their run as they made their way closer.

"Looks like they're back," Monet said as a fluttering began deep in her belly. As nonchalantly as possible, Monet slid her sunglasses back over her eyes and glanced down at her body to ensure her swimming suit hadn't shifted in any of the wrong places and that she remained suitably covered.

"Now there's a sight for sore eyes," Ashley said as she slid her sunglasses down her nose and peered over the top. "A sight for *any* eyes, really."

Monet didn't have to ask; she knew what Ashley meant and was indeed grateful her eyes were currently shielded.

Walking toward them were Cole and Brady, both of whom had discarded their shirts and shoes and wore only shorts. Cole boasted a healthy, burly physique, but it was Brady who Monet couldn't help but shamelessly ogle from behind her sunglasses.

He was so incredibly handsome, his square jaw, his strong cheekbones, and his masculine lips. At the sight of them, Monet bit her own, remembering how Brady's felt and tasted. She continued to study him; his skin was bronzed and glowed with the exertion from running; his arms and chest were so well-defined and muscular that his body appeared almost flawless. But it was the necklace he wore that gave him an untamed, savage appearance, and Monet loved it.

The exuberant greeting happening between Ashley and Cole seemed to fade away as Brady's eyes locked onto her.

"Hi." The sound of his voice caused tiny goosebumps to travel the length of Monet's arms.

"Hi." Monet's heart thumped harder.

Brady silently used his pointer finger and motioned for her to "*come here*" as a flirty grin played on his lips.

Monet glanced at Ashley and Cole, who were preparing to take a dip in the ocean. Cole shot her a wink before he led his wife toward the water.

Monet reached for her lace cover-up and slipped it on as she stood.

Brady's eyes quickly traveled the length of Monet as she stepped closer to him, but it didn't make her uncomfortable—which was new.

He lifted the unusual-looking necklace over his head. "I got you something."

Monet's eyebrows arched beneath her sunglasses, and her pulse kicked up even more. "You did?"

"One of the local vendors was selling these down the beach." He held the necklace out for Monet to see. "Something about it caught my eye and," he shrugged, "I thought you might like it."

Monet bit down on a smile as she accepted the necklace from Brady.

He'd bought her a gift! And not just any gift; something beautiful and unique. "It's gorgeous."

"The man told me that it's handmade," Brady said. "I know it's not something you will wear, but—"

"I love it, Brady," Monet cut him off. "I'm between apartments right now," she said. "But when I have my own place again, I'll display it or incorporate it into my decor somehow."

She ran her fingers over the soft ends of the black spikes before looking at Brady again. "Thank you."

Brady's smile was wide. "Here." He took the necklace from her and draped it over her head. "Just for fun."

Monet laughed as she admired the spikes fanning across her chest. "It definitely looked better on you."

"Come on in, you two!" Ashley hollered from where she and Cole were wading in the shallow ocean.

"How about it?" Brady used his thumb to motion toward the water. "I could stand to cool off."

Monet nodded. "I'll be right there."

Brady gifted her another smile before making his way to the water.

Monet walked back to her lounge chair and lifted the homemade native necklace from over her head. She tenderly ran her hands over it as warmth spread throughout her chest, and she giggled. Men had gifted Monet all types of jewelry and other expensive items over the years in an attempt to win her affection, but Brady's gift was different. The fact that he recognized Monet would appreciate the local vendor's handmade necklace touched Monet deeply, and she knew she would cherish it forever.

Brady

The day was a scorcher as the foursome browsed the shops of the local flea market in Playa Del Carmen, a small town near the villa. Not only was Brady battling the afternoon Cancun sun, but the sight of Monet walking alongside Ashley in front of him also had him wishing he could strip off his shirt right in the middle of the dirt-lined street and pour his water bottle directly over his head.

He'd about lost his mind earlier when he and Cole had come upon Monet and Ashley sunbathing on the beach. He'd tried to play it cool but couldn't stop himself from admiring every inch of Monet: the feminine lines of her neck and shoulders—visible with her hair pulled up— the curve of her waist, and her long, sleek legs freshly kissed by the sun. It was almost too much. Brady knew some beautiful women, women whose sole ambitions seemed centered around looking flawless; take Bethany Hawk, for example. But none held a candle to Monet Everly—not to Brady.

"Hold it together, dude," Cole chuckled. "You look like you're about the pounce on the poor girl."

Brady blew out a frustrated breath and tossed his head. "She's getting to me, man," he said. "The physical attraction... it's off the charts."

Cole laughed. "It was like that with me when I first met Ash." He gripped the back of Brady's neck with one strong hand. "I feel for ya."

"And what are you laughing about?" Ashley asked her husband as she slowed her pace, allowing Brady and Cole to catch up. Monet followed suit and turned toward them.

"Just how Brady's about to—"

"Melt from the heat," Brady cut Cole off as he glared at his friend. "It's a cooker out here." He unbuttoned his linen shirt a few more buttons.

Brady noticed how Monet's eyes traveled over the opening of his shirt and lingered on his chest. He cracked a smile as she rolled her bottom lip beneath her teeth. The innocent gesture gave Brady a boost.

"Are you girls about ready to head back?" he asked.

Monet drew a quick breath, and her eyes jumped to his face. "Um," she adorably stammered. "I just want to stop in this one last shop." She motioned toward one of the open-aired shops with Mexican embroidered dresses hanging from the entrance overhang. "I'll be quick."

"I think there's shaved ice up ahead; anyone want?" Ashley asked.

"I'd love one," Monet said. "If you wait, I'll come with you."

"No need," Brady said. "I could go for one myself. I'll grab yours too. Take your time."

"If you don't mind," Monet said. "Thank you." She gifted him the smile he loved so much.

"I'm in, too," Cole said. Cole took his wife's hand, and with Brady following, they left Monet to her shopping.

The three friends made their way up the street full of tourists searching for the perfect souvenir or a taste of authentic Mexican cuisine and sweets. It didn't matter how often Brady visited the local flea market; he never could get enough of it. He loved the atmosphere, rich with the presence of locals and brimming with handicrafts and vintage goods.

Although he enjoyed browsing other street markets that were a bit more off the beaten path, Brady savored the unique energy of mingling with travelers from all over the world as they haggled with vendors for a good price.

They passed a woman selling fresh coconut milk, and Brady was tempted to stop, but Ashley seemed set on shaved ice, which soon came into view. The line wasn't too bad and was partially shaded by a tall palm.

"What flavor should we get Monet?" Ashley asked as they studied the handwritten sign displaying the half-a-dozen flavors.

Cole snorted. "That's easy." The deep chuckle that followed tipped Brady off.

"Dude," Brady grumbled.

"*Nashion* Fruit."

Ashley laughed, but Brady heaved a deep sigh and tried not to crack a smile.

"You gotta admit that was pretty good," Cole said with a wide grin.

"That was so bad, man." Brady shook his head, but his amusement showed as he rolled his eyes.

The line moved quickly, and Brady stepped up to order.

"One banana colada and one," he shot a side-eye glance at Cole, "*passion* fruit."

A low chuckle emanated from Cole's chest, but Ashley's startled gasp cut into their banter.

"Oh my gosh!" Her hand clutched Cole's forearm.

"Ash, what is it?" Cole asked.

Ashley's rounded eyes were locked on something, and Brady immediately followed her gaze.

"John Wessler," Ashley breathed the words at the exact moment Brady saw him.

Not thirty feet away from where they stood, sifting through a stack of colorful woven rugs, was the slimy modeling agent that had inflicted unimaginable torment on Monet.

"No. Freaking. Way," Cole huffed.

"How... how is this possible?" Ashley's voice cracked with disbelief.

The words Cole and Ashley were saying were drowned out by the ringing in Brady's ears as the heat of rushing blood pulsed through his head. He continued to stare at the man, and his body grew hotter as his heart pounded furiously against his chest.

Brady's hands balled into fists, and he stepped toward the vicious snake when Cole's strong hand grabbed his arm.

"What are you doing?" Cole's voice was firm.

Brady whipped his head toward Cole, but he didn't answer. He didn't know what he was doing. He'd never felt this rush of anger before.

"Let it go, Brady." Gone was his best friend's typical easy-going manner. Cole was serious. "Monet is literally only a few shops away. You cannot make a scene."

"Cole's right, Brady." Ashley's forehead was wrinkled. "We can't let her see him."

They were right. Brady couldn't let Monet see the sleaze. "He can't see her either," Brady mumbled.

"*Doscientos pesos, por favor.*" The young woman behind the stand offered Brady the two shaved ice cups.

Brady blinked rapidly. "Right." He reached into his back pocket and pulled out his phone, where he retrieved two hundred pesos from the cardholder attached to it.

"Thanks—*gracias*." He took the shaved ice and turned to his friends.

"Keep an eye on him," Brady said. "I'll try to guide Monet back toward the villa."

Ashley and Cole agreed as they paid for their own ice treats.

"Watch your phone," Cole said. "We'll catch up."

Brady glanced one last time at John Wessler before making his way back down the street in search of Monet.

He couldn't believe it. Of all places in the world, John Wessler was visiting the same flea market in Cancun, Mexico, as Monet. Brady doubted even Ashley could claim it was fate. It felt more like good old-fashioned bad luck, or an even darker thought crossed his mind. Wessler followed her.

He shook the thought from his head. Wessler appeared to be accompanied by several older men, and his demeanor was too relaxed. If he'd been there for Monet, Brady doubted he'd have brought a group of peers to witness his crazy behavior.

At least Cole and Ashley were on the same page as him: Monet couldn't know. Brady's heart sank at the thought of what it might do to her if she ran into the man. From what she'd confided in them, it had been a long, hard road to recovery from the despicable man's harassment.

Brady quickened his step. Protecting Monet from her painful past was now the most important thing to him, and he would do whatever it took to keep her safe.

Monet

Monet studied herself in the mirror, admiring the beautiful embroidered Mexican dress she'd purchased from the flea market that afternoon. She chose an off-the-shoulder peacock blue with white, green, and yellow floral stitching.

Brady was taking her to dinner, and she hoped he wouldn't think she'd gone too touristy on him with her choice of clothing. But Monet loved learning about the world's different cultures, and now that she was living in Mexico for a few months, she was ready to immerse herself.

She pulled her hair into a loose, low-side bun and began fastening flowers into it. Monet had bought several rose flower hair clips from the flea market and adored how they looked. If she stretched her imagination wide enough, she might convince herself that she resembled a woman native to Mexico. To Monet, they were some of the most beautiful women in the world.

The hair clips got Monet thinking about their shopping trip and how odd Brady had acted when he'd returned with their shaved ice. It was clear that something had unsettled him. She hadn't thought much of it when he mentioned Cole and Ashley were checking out some other shops and would meet them later. But the way Brady kept looking over his shoulder and the hurried pace at which he guided Monet back through the streets toward the villa worried her.

She'd asked him if everything was alright, and he'd assured her it was. Brady just wanted to get back and check on a few things at the Jewel and confirm their dinner reservations. Monet wasn't entirely convinced, but she didn't press the issue. She was still getting to know Brady, and if something was bothering him, she decided it was best to leave him be until he was ready to talk about it.

The soft knock on her bedroom door, followed by a muffled "Can I come in?" drew Monet away from her thoughts, and she hollered from inside the bathroom.

"Of course, come on in, Ashley."

Monet quickly fastened the last flower near the top of her bun just as Ashley appeared at the door and gasped.

"Monet!" Ashley threw her hand over her chest. "You look stunning! Like those folk dancers we saw performing today in the market."

Monet laughed as a light blush colored her cheeks. "You don't think it's too much, do you?"

"Not at all!" Ashley said as she stepped into the oversized bathroom. "It makes me wish I'd have picked up one of these dresses too."

A relaxed smile crossed Monet's face as warmth over Ashley's genuine reaction calmed her. "Let's go back to the flea market and get you one," Monet said. "I saw a lavender one that would look lovely on you."

Ashley's lighthearted expression morphed into a brief scowl, but she quickly shook it off. "Um," she began, rolling her bottom lip with her teeth. "I'd love that." She shrugged. "They have those dresses for sale all over; maybe we can find a place closer to the villa."

"Sure." Monet sensed something was off. "But... is everything alright?"

Ashley's face instantly brightened. "Of course." She stepped behind the stool where Monet sat and began fiddling with the flowers in Monet's hair. "These are beautiful. I find myself wanting long hair just so I could wear them."

"Your hair is long enough." Monet knew something was on Ashley's mind but could tell she didn't want to talk about it. "Here, you sit down." Monet stood, and Ashley took a seat on the stool as Monet picked up one of the smaller dark red roses. "This one matches your sundress." She clipped the rose just above Ashley's ear. It was true that Ashley's hair was short, but Monet could easily fasten the rose to it.

"See," Monet said with a smile, "it looks beautiful on you."

"Wow, it actually does." Ashley adjusted the rose a bit. "I've never even thought to try them." She looked at Monet through the mirror. "Thanks."

"You're welcome." Monet tossed her a wink.

"Oh!" Ashley suddenly jumped up. "The reason I came in was to see if you were ready. Brady asked me to check on you."

"Well, as long as you think this is okay," Monet gestured to her dress and hair, "then I'm ready."

"You look perfect," she said. "A little hot and a little spicy! Brady is gonna lose his mind."

Monet tilted her head skeptically and let out a short breath. "I doubt that."

Ashley chuckled as she shook her head. "Still the humble hottie, I see," she said. "Trust me; he won't know what to do with himself."

Monet picked up her small purse and followed Ashley out of the bedroom.

"Have you been to the restaurant he's taking me to?" Monet asked.

"Many times," Ashley said. "*Forbidden* is a favorite of ours—a lot of people, actually. You're going to love it!"

"Forbidden?" Monet cocked her head with a sly smile. "Sounds intriguing."

"Oh, it is." Ashley's eyes twinkled. "Just wait."

The astonished "Whoa!" coming from Cole drew their attention toward Ashley's animated husband as he walked into the open-air living area from the swimming pool.

"Dang! *Señoras muy bonitas*," Cole said in an exaggerated Spanish accent.

Ashley laughed. "Cole likes to pretend he knows Spanish."

"Humph!" Cole's head jerked back as he strode toward his wife. "That was perfect." He looked at Monet. "Wasn't it, Monet?"

Monet drew her shoulders up. "I'm no expert, but it sounded good to me."

"See!" He wrapped his arms around his wife and picked her up, nuzzling her neck.

Ashley giggled and tried to push him away. "You need a shave! Your whiskers are too prickly!"

Monet smiled as she watched the happy couple. Although Josh wasn't as boisterous as Cole, Ashley and Cole reminded Monet of Josh and Juliet—two couples deeply in love. A lighthearted feeling fell over Monet, giving her hope for her own romantic future.

"Go grab your suit," Cole said as he set Ashley down. "Let's take a dip."

"You read my mind. I was thinking the same thing." She kissed her husband lightly on the lips before she turned to Monet.

"Have fun tonight, sweetie." She waved a finger at Monet. "And I want all the juicy details tomorrow."

Monet's eyes bulged a split second before her heartbeat spiked.

Ashley and Cole both laughed as they made their way to their bedroom.

"You'll get used to it." Brady's low masculine voice caused a delicious chill to run over her arms, and Monet gasped softly as she turned to face him.

He wore a pale yellow button-up linen shirt with the sleeves rolled up to his elbows and cream pants. Brady's shirt fit him perfectly and showed off his muscular physique, visible even beneath his clothes. He appeared freshly showered since his hair was still damp, and Monet found herself stunned by his pure magnificence.

"To the teasing, I mean," Brady clarified.

Monet nodded as she swallowed the excess moisture gathering in her mouth over how attractive Brady was.

"I know, I know." Brady shook his head and glanced down at his clothes. "My standard outfit—linen." He chuckled. "It works best for the humidity."

"Oh... no!" Monet realized he'd mistaken her awestruck silence for critique, or maybe it was the way she was shamelessly staring at him. "I was only thinking how—" *tempting, irresistible,* Monet cleared her throat, "—handsome you look."

One corner of Brady's mouth twitched before a knowing smile spread across his lips. "Thank you." He stepped toward her. "And let me repay the compliment and tell you how lovely you look this evening."

Brady had her locked in, and she couldn't pull her eyes away from his, regardless of how strong the urge to do so was. He reached down, took her hand, and raised it to his lips. "*Impecable*," he whispered in an alluring Spanish accent before his lips pressed to her skin. The gesture caused her stomach to flutter and goosebumps to race over her arms.

Brady straightened but kept hold of her hand.

"Thank you," Monet managed to say. "You don't... think it's too much?"

Brady raised a teasing eyebrow. "Let's take a look." He still held her hand and tugged so that her arm would raise to the side. He took a small step back and scanned her from head to toe before spinning her around, which made

Monet laugh. Once she faced him again, his smile transformed from teasing to sincere.

"You are the most beautiful woman I have ever known, Monet." His tone was low and warm. "You take my breath away."

Monet stared at him—her own breath stolen as her heart pounded wildly against her chest. She was completely entranced by him and wondered how any woman could ever resist him.

"Wow," she breathed. "You best be careful, Mr. Nash. You could make a girl swoon using words like that."

"Not just any girl." His charming smile appeared. "Only you."

Butterflies took flight in her belly, and warmth coated every inch of her. Monet had received her fair share of compliments in her life, but none had touched her heart the way Brady's did at that moment. His words were genuine and full of sincerity.

She bit her bottom lip as her eyes drifted to Brady's masterful ones. Memories of their intimate moments the night before sent her pulse racing. Monet wondered what would happen if she leaned up and kissed him.

Before she could contemplate the gutsy move further, Brady unknowingly intervened, sparing her the humiliation.

"So," he asked as he squeezed her hand before letting it go. "Are you ready for the dinner of your life?"

"Dinner of my life?" Monet drew her eyebrows up. "That's a pretty bold claim there. And you forget, my best friend is a culinary master."

Brady chuckled. "I see the bar is set pretty high, then?"

"I'm afraid so," Monet teased with a shrug.

"Well then," Brady said as they walked to the villa's front door. "Challenge accepted." He opened the door and gestured for Monet to precede him.

She adored his playful nature and how at ease Brady made her feel. Delighting in the lighthearted banter between them, Monet smiled at him as she passed through the doorway. "I look forward to it."

*

Monet sat, taking in the atmosphere of *Forbidden*, the open-aired waterfront restaurant Brady had taken her to, and she couldn't suppress the frenzied swirls of excitement spinning in her stomach. As the music from the live band wove a spell of enchantment with the sultry sounds from the Spanish guitar, Monet mused how the muted bamboo and rattan lantern chandeliers, along with the intimately spaced tables lined with cream-colored lounge couches rather than chairs, conjured the very essence of romance.

Their table was positioned along the edge of the open-aired room and overlooked the ocean. Although it was dark, the lights from the restaurant reflected like sparkly ripples on the water.

"I've never eaten at a restaurant where we sit on couches before," Monet said to Brady, who sat beside her on the low, cozy modern-style couch.

Brady raised an eyebrow. "Not even with Juliet, the culinary master?"

Monet laughed. "No, not even with Juliet," she said. "Although I'm certain she has."

"Good evening, you two," a woman wearing a black top and black slacks greeted. "My name is Sophia. Welcome to *Forbidden,* a dining experience you'll never forget."

Monet turned to Brady, who tilted his head with a shrug. "I told you."

Monet smiled. "We'll see."

"Is this your first time dining with us?" Sophia asked.

"I've had the pleasure many times," Brady said. "But it's a first for Monet, here." He looked at Monet but kept talking to Sophia. "She's given me the challenge to make this the dinner of her life."

Sophia drew her head back, and both eyebrows rose as she turned her attention to Monet. "Is that so?"

A slight tingling crept up Monet's chest and across her face, and she let out a nervous chuckle. "Sort of... I guess."

"Well then..." Sophia gave Brady a conspiratorial smile. "Let's see what we can do. How about our world-famous mango daiquiri to start?" Sophia asked. "It is literally paradise in a glass."

"I'd love one if you can make it virgin." Monet bit her lip and awkwardly glanced at Brady.

After her experience with John Wessler, Monet made the firm decision she'd never do anything to intentionally put herself in harm's way, and that included drinking alcohol. Monet knew what too much of it could do to a person, and she never wanted to lower her inhibitions; she always wanted to have her wits about her—in every situation.

"Make that two," Brady said as he shot a quick wink at Monet.

"You got it," Sophia said. "Two mango mocktails coming right out."

Brady and Monet both gave their thanks, and Sophia moved on to her next table as Monet picked up the menu.

"Now, let's see what all the fuss is about." Monet let out an exaggerated sigh but wore a broad smile.

As her eyes landed on the beautifully printed menu, realization hit. It was in Spanish. She could make out a few words: *Hummus... Alaskan King Crab... Soup... Salad, Salmon—*

"Do you need some help?"

Monet glanced to her side to see Brady staring at her. His lips were curved and matched the humor in his eyes.

"It was the—" he pointed to his forehead but focused on Monet's, "wrinkled brow that gave it away."

Monet couldn't help but laugh. "I guess I need a crash course in Spanish," she said. "Especially since I'll be here for a while."

"You'd be surprised how much you'll learn just by exposure," Brady said. "And not to worry, Cancun is a top tourist location, so most people here know enough English to get by."

Monet opened her small purse and pulled out her cell phone. "I did download Google Translate." She turned the screen toward Brady and laughed. "It helped me in the flea market today."

Brady chuckled. "I used a translator app when we started the job, too, but I soon found out it's not always accurate." He puffed a laugh. "Let's just say I embarrassed myself a time or two. But you won't need it tonight anyway." Brady held Monet's gaze. "You've got me."

The bright green of his eyes was mesmerizing and so full of warmth. Monet smiled softly and nodded.

Brady pulled his attention from Monet and focused on the menu. "How hungry are you?" he asked. "Could you share an appetizer with me?"

"The last thing I ate was the shaved ice this afternoon," Monet said. "So I could definitely go for an appetizer."

"Do you want me to read you what they have, or do you trust me?"

She tilted her head and tapped a finger against her lips. "Hmm..." She smiled. "I'm feeling a little daring this evening, so I'll let you order... Just nothing too spicy," she quickly added. "I've got to ease into that."

"I know just the thing, something a little sweet with a little spice," he said. "And what about your main dish? Seafood? Pasta? Steak?"

"I'd love to try a seafood dish with a little Mexican flare," Monet said. "Do they have anything like that?"

Brady's eyes lit up. "They do," he said. "One of my favorite dishes here."

"Ooh, I'll have that," Monet said as Sophia arrived with their drinks.

"Here we are." She placed the mango daiquiris in front of them. "Have you had a chance to look at the menu?"

"We have," Brady said.

"I'm leaving the decision to him," Monet added. "Since I'm not too fluent in Spanish."

Sophia teasingly cocked one eyebrow. "Brave girl." She directed her attention back to Brady. "So, what are we having?"

"The stuffed piquillo peppers to start," he said. "And two orders of your lobster tacos."

Sophia beamed with approval. "Two of our bests," she said, looking at Monet. "You won't be disappointed."

After Sophia gathered their menus and left, Monet pulled her drink closer and took a sip. "Mmm, wow." She took a longer sip. "That is so good." The flavor was a sweet and tangy mix of mango and pineapple. "I don't know what the traditional *Forbidden* mango daiquiri tastes like, but the virgin version is amazing."

Brady chuckled. "I see we're off to a good start this evening," he teased. "One point for Brady, then?"

Monet laughed. "You've already scored way more points than that, Brady."

Brady's expression brightened, and he smiled. "Is that right?"

Monet felt warmth spread through her chest and quickly reach her cheeks. She rolled her bottom lip between her teeth and nodded. "The truth is, there's no need to keep track because I already know this will be the dinner of my life."

"And why's that?" he asked in his deep, alluring tone.

Monet was lost in his eyes again. They held such power, and her wits abandoned her under his gaze. "Because I'm with you." Her eyes widened as soon as the words slipped out.

She pulled her straw to her mouth and took several long sips to try and cool the heat traveling over her face but quickly pushed it away, wondering if they'd mistakenly added alcohol.

At the feel of Brady's hand caressing her cheek, Monet turned to look at him. "Monet," Brady said. "I feel the same."

Monet could barely hear him due to the music suddenly increasing in volume, and before she could respond, she realized why. The band had dispersed amongst the diners and were serenading individual tables. The musician playing the electric violin was in front of them, weaving an electrifying trance over the crowd as he played an energetic version of "Bailando" by Enrique Iglesias in time with the other band members.

The restaurant was alive, and Monet could feel the electricity in the air. That, coupled with the affectionate way Brady had caressed her cheek and the words he had just spoke, caused a new wave of adrenaline to invigorate her.

Before she knew it, people were on their feet, dancing—a few more enthusiastic patrons even climbing on top of tables. Monet laughed as Brady took her hand and pulled her from the couch and out onto the open-aired deck, where he spun her around.

"When in Rome," he said as he pulled her close.

"Do as the Romans do," Monet finished.

"That's what they say, right?" he asked as they continued to dance.

"Definitely!" She laughed again.

Brady continued to lead her through some lively dance steps, spinning her around and holding her close, swaying in time with the music. Monet couldn't have kept the wide grin from her face even if she'd wanted to. She hadn't danced much over the years, but occasionally, when Juliet would drag her out to a nightclub or during some social event Juliet's family was hosting, she would enjoy dancing in a group with Josh or Juliet's brother Sawyer. Luckily, she didn't have two left feet and was able to keep up.

A short time later, the song ended, and the band announced they'd be taking a short break before the "show" started.

"Show?" Monet asked as she and Brady took their seats at the table.

"You'll see." He winked.

A young man wearing a similar black outfit as Sophia stopped by the table with their appetizer.

"Stuffed piquillo peppers, huh?" Monet asked after the man left. The plate held six large red peppers stuffed with what looked like white cheese. "Is that cheese?" Monet asked as she dished a pepper onto her plate.

"It is," Brady said. "Goat cheese."

Monet sliced a piece of the pepper and took a bite. The sweet, tangy pepper mixed with the rich, creamy cheese flavor was delicious. She'd never been a huge fan of goat cheese, but if she were ever going to eat it, it would be like that.

"So?" Brady asked as he took a bite of his own pepper.

"Mm! So good," Monet said. "When Juliet visits, I'll need to bring her to this place."

"Oh?" Brady asked. "Is your friend planning to visit you?"

"That's right!" Monet's eyes rounded, and she pointed at Brady. "I didn't tell you," she said. "Juliet and her fiancé, Josh, are getting married at the Grand Jewel in December."

"Wait," Brady said. "Velma told us about the wedding for the Quinn family. Your Juliet is Juliet Quinn?"

Monet giggled over how Brady's head dipped as his mouth fell open.

"The one and only," she said. "And erase any notion of Juliet being a wealthy snob; she is as kind and down to earth as they come."

"Not like her mother, then?" Brady cocked an eyebrow.

Monet's head jerked back as her forehead furrowed. "No!" she blurted. "Polar opposites. Juliet and her brother take after their dad."

Brady nodded. "I've heard Sawyer Quinn is a good guy. Sounds like his sister is, too."

"It's true," Monet said as she sliced up another piece of pepper. "I'm curious; how have you heard about Sawyer?" she asked. "Just through the media?"

Thanks to what Ashley revealed earlier on the beach, Monet knew Brady's brother was acquainted with the Quinns, and she hoped her question would give her a segue into asking about the mysterious Beau Nash.

Brady had just taken a bite of food but shook his head as he used his napkin to wipe his mouth. "No." He took a sip of water. "My brother worked with him a year or so ago."

Monet feigned surprise with slightly widened eyes. "Oh?"

"Yeah," Brady chuckled, rubbing his forehead. "My brother, Beau," he clarified before clearing his throat. "He was named *Vurve's* bachelor of the year last year."

Monet raised her eyebrows dramatically. "Wow."

Brady puffed a laugh. "It's true. Embarrassed him to no end." Brady shrugged. "I get it, too. It's even a little embarrassing for me to admit that about him, and if you knew Beau," Brady laughed. "Let's just say he almost didn't do it."

Monet smiled. Brady's laughter was contagious, and she couldn't help but giggle over the image of the insanely handsome—and, according to Ashley—grumpy Beau Nash being embarrassed by anything.

Monet shook her head while smiling. "I can't believe Beau Nash is your brother."

Brady flashed Monet a playful smile. "So, you know who my brother is?"

"Juliet mentioned him a time or two," she said. "He's attended a few events hosted by the Quinns." Monet picked up her drink and rested against the couch before focusing on Brady. "You look so alike." She gave a slow, disbelieving shake of her head as she continued to study him. "If I had known your last name, I might have wondered if you two were related."

Brady cocked his head. "You didn't know my last name?"

"No," she said. "I realized it right after we said goodbye that night at the White Rainbow."

Brady slowly nodded. "Yeah, I guess you wouldn't have known; we didn't talk about it."

"I thought about asking the front desk when I left the next morning, but to be honest, I was so afraid that Wessler was on to me and might show up in the lobby that I left as quickly as I could."

Brady's smile softened. "I don't blame you for that." That teasing glint entered his eyes. "I guess I'll let you off the hook for not contacting me all those years, seeing as you didn't even know my last name." He winked.

Monet huffed a laugh. "That's very kind of you. Thank you," she teased as a spike of playful adrenaline gave her more of that long-forgotten courage. "But what's your excuse?" Monet's heart rate spiked, and a nervous swirl brushed her stomach. That was a bold question, and was she ready for the answer?

Brady chuckled and dropped his head. "Cole asked me the same thing... but he didn't like my answer."

The swirl in Monet's belly opened into a pit, and her heart dropped through it, but she tried her best to keep her features even. "And why's that?"

Brady looked at her. "I didn't think you'd be interested in hearing from me again."

Wait, what? Monet's head jerked back, and she blinked a few times. "Are you being serious right now?"

Brady laughed. "That is exactly what Cole said."

"But," Monet stumbled. "Really? You didn't sense my interest that night?" She felt a slight flush under her skin.

Brady grinned. "I felt a connection with you—but, Monet, I don't think you understand how entirely out of my league I felt you were—still are, actually," he said. "I was a nobody college student, and you were this gorgeous woman who just put John Wessler in his place." He paused, studying her. "I honestly didn't think I'd have a shot."

Monet stared back at him, momentarily at a loss for words. Who wouldn't be interested in Brady Nash—the younger version or the older mature version? In Monet's mind, there was no version of Brady that a woman wouldn't want—or at least want to get to know better.

Monet finally broke through her daze. "But," she tried to shake the insanity out of her mind, "I was just an 18-year-old high school graduate with no set plan for the future," she scoffed. "And as far as *gorgeous*, beauty looks different to everyone." Monet's chin dipped. "And besides, the real truth is, I'm the one batting way out of my league." She peeked at him as she fiddled with the daiquiri straw and stirred her drink a few times.

Brady's eyebrows raised as his lips pulled into a flirty smile. "I guess we both misjudged the other then."

"I guess we did," she said as she tried to calm her galloping heart. What was happening to her, and who was this person who felt free enough to admit such personal—and embarrassing secrets?

Monet took the cocktail menu from its place perched on the center of the table and fanned herself. "Still getting used to the humidity." She released a nervous laugh.

It was only a half fib; she was still getting used to the Cancun climate, but her skin burned from her admission.

"Well." Brady lifted his glass in a toast. "Here's to what Master Oogway says."

Monet's forehead puckered, and she let out a giggle. "Master Oogway?"

"From Kung Fu Panda," he said, like it was the most obvious thing in the world.

"Ohh," Monet laughed again. "The turtle."

"Elderly tortoise, yes," Brady said as Monet played along and lifted her glass.

"Yesterday is history, tomorrow is a mystery, but today is a gift. That is why it's called the present. And getting a second chance with you is the greatest gift I could ever ask for."

The sincerity behind Brady's words and the passion in his eyes caused Monet's heart to flutter and her stomach to flip. This man was dangerous, but not in the way Monet had feared for so many years. Instead of physical or mental danger, the only thing in danger now—was her heart.

Brady

Brady watched Monet, hoping his confession wouldn't scare her. As hard as he tried to keep his attraction and growing feelings reined in, he couldn't seem to help himself.

The woman had only been back in his life for mere days! He let out a baffled huff, mystified by his intense feelings. How could he be falling this quickly for someone?

"What?" Monet's voice broke into his thoughts.

"Oh," he said, shaking his head. "It's nothing." Brady wanted to confess his growing feelings for Monet, but his better judgment won out. Admitting he saw their meeting again as a second chance for them was enough—for now.

"Alright, you two." Sophia arrived at the table with the same server who had brought their appetizer. "Two lobster tacos."

The young man placed Monet's dish in front of her before doing the same for Brady.

"And in case you're in the mood for a little extra spice..." Sophia set two small bowls filled with coleslaw next to their plates, "spicy slaw."

Monet used her fork to spear a tiny sliver of cabbage and sampled it. After a couple of slow chews, her eyes widened, and she covered her mouth to muffle a squeal, which caused Sophia to chuckle.

"It's another specialty here at *Forbidden*," she said. "Made with napa cabbage, lime, cilantro, and a generous amount of serrano peppers."

"That's hot!" Monet fanned her mouth before she grabbed her water glass and took a sip.

"I should have warned you," Brady said. "I've gotten so used to the spiciness found in the dishes here that I didn't even think about it."

"Oh, no." Monet shook her head as she set her water back on the table. "It's okay. It wasn't that bad," she said. "I just wasn't expecting it."

"Is there anything else I can get you?" Sophia asked.

"I'm good," Brady said, turning to Monet. "What about you?"

Monet glanced around the table before smiling at Sophia. "I don't think so, thank you."

"Okay, you two enjoy," Sophia said as she left them to their meal.

"These smell incredible," Monet said as she lowered her face to her dish and inhaled before scooping one of her tacos up and taking her first bite. "Mmm!" She covered her mouth with her fingers. "Oh my gosh," she mumbled through her food.

"Good, isn't it?" Brady asked as he dished some spicy slaw onto one of his tacos and rolled it up.

"This would give Juliet a run for her money," Monet said. "But if you tell her I said that, I'll deny it," she laughed.

The two ate in comfortable silence for a few minutes, enjoying the music and romantic ambiance of the restaurant. Although the lighting was muted, Brady could see the relaxed smile fixed across Monet's face and how her eyes lit up as she scanned the restaurant and focused on the band.

When Brady first saw Monet back at the villa, wearing the dress she'd purchased from the flea market that day, he nearly lost his composure. The color brought out the mesmerizing blue of her eyes. Coupled with the way it sat just off her freshly sun-kissed shoulders, her already stunning features, and her playful nature, it had almost been too much. Brady had never given himself so many silent pep talks in his life as he had in the past 48 hours.

"So," Monet said, breaking into his thoughts, "tell me more about your brother. Is he still a bachelor?"

"Yeah." He nodded, taking a sip of water. Was Monet interested in Beau? He inwardly groaned. She must be. Every woman was.

"Juliet didn't really talk about him a lot, but," Monet scrunched one side of her face, "she did mention he's kind of a grump."

A bubble of laughter spewed from his mouth, and he nearly choked on his water.

"Sorry!" Monet blurted as she tried to suppress a giggle. "Was that too blunt?"

Brady lifted his napkin to his mouth and dabbed. "No," he chuckled as the tightness in his chest loosened.

"It's refreshingly honest. *Kind of a grump* is the perfect description."

Monet laughed again, and as Brady watched her take another bite of her food, his chest tugged, and he gave a slight shake of his head. Of course Monet wasn't interested in Beau.

"He wasn't always the way he is now—brooding and unapproachable," Brady said. "Beau used to be the life of every party: outgoing and fun. He cared about his family, friends, everyone—even strangers." Brady smiled over the memories of his chivalrous big brother. "Beau was like that in high school and college, too, always looking for ways to serve the community." He inhaled before exhaling and furrowing his brow. "But something happened before he started the company that changed him—before all the wealth and success."

Monet mirrored Brady's wrinkled forehead and tilted her head. "Do you know what happened?"

Brady shrugged. "No, not for certain," he said. "I have my suspicions, but Beau shot me down whenever I asked about it."

"I'm sorry," Monet said softly. "I can't imagine if Evan suddenly changed and started shutting me out."

"That's the thing," Brady said. "Although his temperament isn't the same, Beau still puts family first. He's the first to congratulate me on a new project, checks in with me at least once a week, and has never missed a grand opening of one of our hotels." Brady sighed. "He's just never wanted to talk about what caused him to change."

"Sounds like a good brother." Monet smiled. "It could be he's just not ready to share yet," she said. "Obviously, I don't know what he went through, but I know what it's like to withdraw into myself because of fear—or pain." Monet's voice was soft and rich with understanding. "He'll get there." She reached over and let her fingers brush the side of Brady's face.

The affectionate gesture and tender assurances caused a delicious warmth to travel under his skin and flow to his heart. *Keep it together, Brady,* he silently repeated.

Monet dropped her hand and turned her attention back to her food. Saving him—again.

"What about your parents?" she asked. "Do they live in Arizona?"

At the mention of his parents, Brady's heart lifted even more. He adored his mom and dad.

"They do," he said. "And I promise I'm not just saying this because they're my parents, but they are honestly the best, most down-to-earth people." Brady smiled. "They live in a quiet little neighborhood in Tempe. My mom is an elementary school teacher and has been most of her life. And my dad is an airline pilot."

"Airplane pilot?" Monet's eyes lit up, and Brady nodded.

"Wow," she said. "That's pretty cool. How long has your dad been a pilot?"

Brady's forehead lifted. "Uh," he puffed a drawn-out breath, "as long as I can remember," he said as he searched his memories. "My dad got his license before I was born, and from what they tell me, was hired on at Western Airlines shortly before it was merged with Delta."

Monet smiled. "You've probably flown all over the world then."

"Yeah, that is one of those awesome perks when your dad is a pilot, and he did fly us all over, but mostly the U.S. I didn't get to Europe until I'd graduated college."

"Lucky. I'm still hoping to make my way there eventually," she sighed. "It's on my bucket list."

Brady laughed. "You're pretty young to have a bucket list already."

"Not really," she said. "I think most people probably have one; maybe they don't term it a *bucket list*, but maybe a *wish list* or, like Juliet, *hopes and dreams list*." She tossed her head and grinned. "She's the one who encouraged me to start making mine."

"I think that's great," Brady said, "and you're right. Come to think of it, I do have some things I'm itching to do. Maybe my list could be called my itch list."

Monet's smile was enchanting, and her laugh was contagious. "Your *itch list*," she repeated. "That's a clever one."

"I will say you have piqued my interest, though," Brady said with a raised eyebrow. "What grand adventures are on Monet's itch list?"

Monet was sipping her tropical drink and set her glass down before resting back against the couch. "Well." She chewed her bottom lip. "I've only added a few things; I'm still working on it."

"*Well*," Brady mimicked, leaning back against the soft cushions, "I already know Europe is on there."

"It is." Monet smiled. "Now that you mention it, all the things I've listed so far have to do with traveling... There are the obvious ones: go on a gondola ride in the canals of Venice. See the Pyramids of Egypt and ride a camel along the way." She giggled. "Greece, *of course*."

"Of course," Brady chuckled.

"Ooh, I'd love to visit Fiji and stay in one of those over-the-water bungalows!"

Brady couldn't stop grinning as he listened to Monet go on about the traveling she dreamed of doing in her lifetime. She was animated and beautiful, and every word she spoke held genuine excitement. Brady found himself wishing he could be the one to experience those places with Monet.

If Brady had his way, he'd book them a trip to Fiji and be on the first plane out after the grand opening—even sooner if he could.

"I think I might have to steal a few of those for my own itch list," he teased, only half-joking. "Or maybe," his pulse kicked up, "I could tag along with you."

She drew her eyebrows up, gave a flirty tilt to her head, and said, "Where should we go first?"

"Fiji," he said casually.

"Good choice," she teased.

Brady knew the conversation was all in light fun and joking, but what was that old saying? *Many a true word is spoken in jest.* In this case, he knew that applied to him, but he hoped it was more than just teasing from Monet, too.

"So," Brady said, attempting to steer the conversation in a different direction. At the rate his thoughts were headed, he'd have the two of them booked on a trip together before they ordered dessert. "Tell me about your parents."

Monet's features softened. "The best," she said, smiling. "Something we have in common, it sounds like."

Brady's eyes widened. "Well, if I remember clearly, I think your dad gave Wessler quite an earful the night we met, so he must be awesome."

"I can't believe you remember that!" She tossed her head. "Wow, that whole thing was crazy, wasn't it?"

Brady's eyes widened as he nodded. "It was, but I was just thinking," he said. "Aside from the crazy, it was the day we met, so it was also a pretty great day for me."

A relaxed smile crossed her face as her cheeks flushed lightly pink. "Aside from the *crazy*, it was a pretty good day for me too."

Brady's chest warmed at Monet's confession.

"But, yes, my dad is pretty awesome," she said. "He doesn't have quite as exciting a job as an airline pilot, but he works in IT as a project manager for a company developing new AI software; he's super techie."

Brady drew his head back. "AI? That's very cool."

"It really is, but some of the stuff they're developing honestly freaks me out," Monet said with a laugh. "When a computer program can mimic human behavior—" she shuddered. "I just don't know if I'm ready for that yet."

"And your mom?" Brady asked.

"Aww, my mom," Monet sighed. "She's an angel on earth. She works as a librarian at my old high school, and the kids adore her."

Brady gave a slight tilt of his head, his eyes twinkling with mischief. "Both of our mothers work in schools. I'd say the fates are trying to tell us something."

Monet laughed. "I see Ashley is rubbing off on you."

"No," Brady said, his expression softening, but there was no teasing to his tone. "*You* are rubbing off on me."

Monet blinked several times before dropping her eyes to her plate and twisting the long, dainty chain around her neck. Brady had flustered her, and the fact made him smile.

"Um," she puffed a nervous giggle. "I wonder if that's a good thing."

"Oh," he said as he picked up his glass and prepared to take a sip. "It's a very good thing."

Those alluring blue eyes turned back to him, and he could see a hint of something— doubt or maybe surprise, but soon they softened, and she smiled.

"And what is your brother doing these days?" Brady asked, hoping to ease her embarrassment from yet another flirtatious comment on his behalf.

"Evan is living in Seattle," she said. "He graduated from college there and was offered a job as a video game designer working for a Seattle-based company, so he stayed." She sighed. "I miss him."

"Yeah, I know what you mean," Brady said. "I wish I could see Beau more than I do, but our work schedules make it hard."

"Well, maybe they'll visit us while we're here," Monet said. "A little tropical getaway never hurt anyone."

Brady chuckled. "I'm sure Beau will visit—at least once."

"Evan said something about coming to see me too." Her forehead wrinkled. "I hope he really does."

"I hope so, too." Brady smiled as an idea took root in his mind.

A familiar cheer erupted from the bar and Monet's eyes shifted to the sounds of the hoots and hollers, and a broad smile crossed her face at the sight of white sparks emitting from tall party sparklers.

"What are they doing?" Monet asked above the noise.

"Anytime someone orders a bottle of tequila, it gets delivered in an ice bucket lit with sparklers." Brady gestured toward the bar. "They make it a big deal, and it even gets its own parade."

They watched as the waiter placed the bucket holding the bottle of liquor and two tall party sparklers on a tray and started weaving through the tables, followed by a line of staff members waving crackling sparklers above them. The energy in the restaurant was electric, and Monet easily fell into the spirit, clapping and cheering along.

"This is insane!" She laughed. "I love it!"

Sophia appeared amongst the celebration and leaned in close to the table. "Can I get you two a refill on your daiquiris?"

"I think I'm good with water, thank you!" Monet said above the noise.

"I'll stick with water too. Thanks," Brady agreed.

"Alright, things are about to get wild in here, but wave me over if you need anything."

Brady nodded his thanks, and Sophia moved on to her next table.

As if on cue, the rich, smooth sounds of the electric violin danced over the air. The diners burst into another round of applause and cheers as the violinist animatedly began to play.

Monet leaned in closer to keep from yelling. "This sounds so familiar!"

For a moment, Brady was distracted as a warm vanilla scent swirled around him, inviting him to take a deeper breath.

"Uh! It's on the tip of my tongue." She giggled and turned her attention back to the musician.

Brady knew the song but wanted to let Monet discover it on her own. Suddenly, right in time with the chorus, the other band member joined in, and Brady watched as recognition washed over Monet's delighted face.

"Lady Gaga!" She turned to him and began singing the words to *Alejandro* with the crowd.

Brady was enchanted. Seeing Monet so lighthearted and uninhibited caused his heart to lighten even more. He marveled at her free and easy behavior since she'd shared her experience the night before. Brady's mom always said *opening up does more good than bottling up,* which proved true with Monet.

He shifted closer to her. "Dance with me."

Several other diners were already on their feet dancing, singing, and having a great time.

Monet smiled at him and nodded. Brady slid out from around his side of the table, and Monet did the same. Most people were dancing in the aisles around their tables, but Brady led Monet out to the open-air deck again and pulled her close as they swayed in time to the music.

The same alluring fragrance of vanilla filled Brady's lungs, and its sweet, rich scent transported him to another time and place. Memories flooded his mind, taking him back to his childhood when his mother would bake cupcakes and fill the house with the same comforting aroma. He'd only been around Monet for a short time, but he had quickly come to associate the fragrance with her.

The rhythm of the music picked up, and at the same time, staff members began handing out party sparklers to a few people on the deck.

Brady reluctantly stepped back from Monet as Sophia handed each of them one.

"Pretty awesome, isn't it!" Sophia shouted above the noise.

"It's amazing!" Monet's smile was radiant as she took her sparkler and waved it in front of her.

Sophia chuckled and shot a wink at Brady before she left. She obviously remembered the challenge to make this the dinner of Monet's life, which Brady felt pretty confident about by that point.

The music volume continued to increase, and one of the band members spoke in a thick Spanish accent over the microphone. "Are you ready?"

The crowd cheered in unison, and Monet laughed as she continued waving her sparkler. Brady knew what was coming, and he gently took hold of Monet's elbow and pulled her away from the outer railing. She didn't question him but stepped back, smiling up at him the whole time.

"Tres—" the band member hollered, and the crowd joined in. "Dos—uno!"

In the next instant, giant white sparklers lining the restaurant's roof hanging over the ocean erupted, burning brightly and casting a beautiful glow over the restaurant and the water.

Monet squealed. "This is unreal!" She giggled as she took in the sight of the sizzling fireworks. "Here." She handed her sparkler to Brady. "I need to get my phone!"

Brady chuckled as he watched Monet hurry off to the table and retrieve her cell to capture the moment while he maneuvered their now dwindling party sparklers.

"I think she's impressed." Sophia appeared with a small bucket and gestured for Brady to dispose of the sparklers. "From what I've seen, she hasn't stopped smiling all night."

"Yeah," Brady said as his eyes searched out Monet. "Well, you can't go wrong with *Forbidden*. You guys never disappoint."

"Sophia!" Monet was beaming. "This place is so much fun! It's like a dance club and exotic restaurant all rolled into one." She glanced at Brady. "I'm having such a great time!"

Sophia laughed and shot Brady a sly look. "So, he did good then?"

Monet looked at Brady with a tender smile. "Yeah, he did really good."

The way she gazed at him made Brady's heart spike, and he struggled to resist the urge to pull her into his arms. "Challenge won then?"

Monet giggled. "I already told you; just being with you beats any other night out I've had."

"Ooo!" Sophia chimed in with wide eyes. "That's my cue." She smiled at them. "Let me know if you need anything."

Brady and Monet spent the rest of the night dancing, talking, and relishing each other's company. He had never felt so at ease with a woman nor experienced such intense emotions of protectiveness and longing to make someone happy. Witnessing Monet's carefree and joyful demeanor that evening, Brady was determined to ensure the new chapter of Monet's life would be filled with more of the same.

Monet

As Brady and Monet sat in the driveway of the villa in the open-air Jeep, the warm breeze caressed her skin, and the waves crashing on the shore echoed in the distance. The sky was a canvas of stars, each twinkling brightly like a diamond.

Monet rested back on the headrest as she stared at the sky, but she rolled her head to the left and couldn't help but stare at the man sitting beside her. The only light came from the stars and the dim glow from inside the villa, but she could easily see that his profile was perfect, and from what she'd witnessed so far, everything else about him was, too.

"I wanted to ask you something," Brady said softly, meeting her gaze.

"Hm?" Monet was relaxed, and the activities from the day were catching up to her.

"Please don't take this in any other way than how I'm intending it," he said.

Monet huffed a small chuckle. "Okay... I think."

"From everything you've told me, it doesn't sound like you've dated much." He paused. "Am I right about that?"

Monet was grateful the night sky hid the blush she could feel on her cheeks. Brady's question caught her off guard.

She looked away and nodded. "You'd be right about that."

"I don't mean to pry or make you uncomfortable," he said. "I sort of put the pieces together on my own; after everything you went through, I figured dating was probably the last thing on your mind."

"Um, hum," she said as she glanced at him. "I had no desire to."

Brady's smile was soft and kind. "I think that's a pretty normal reaction, and nobody would blame you either."

Monet returned his smile and let her head lean against the headrest again as her drowsiness crept back in. "Why do you ask?"

Brady shrugged one shoulder. "I was just thinking—" he stammered, "you probably want to then... you know... date around."

Monet bit back a giggle. She sensed he was the uncomfortable one. The way he stuttered the question caused a flutter in her belly.

"Not really, no," she said. "Even before John Wessler, the thought of dating a bunch of different guys never appealed to me." She sighed. "I know a lot of people think it's healthy to date around and have different experiences to help you learn and grow." She shrugged. "I just always thought if I met someone I like and he likes me back, why not go for it?"

Brady nodded, and an easy smile broke across his lips. "Funny you say that; I've always felt the same." His shoulders relaxed, and he settled back against his seat.

Monet's eyelids were heavy, and the lull of the distant ocean was making it increasingly hard to stay awake. Despite her exhaustion, she didn't want to go inside.

"I don't want this night to end," she whispered.

Their eyes were locked on to each other, and Brady inched closer.

"Then it won't." His voice was low, and Monet's heart, beating slow and steady, began to hammer as Brady reached across the console and undid her seatbelt.

"You won't be needing this anymore." He leaned in and let his lips brush her cheek, causing her breath to quicken.

"Can I kiss you?" he whispered against her ear, sending a wave of goosebumps rippling down her arm and over her body.

Monet couldn't resist him and turned her face so their lips hovered excruciatingly close to each other.

"Yes."

The word was embarrassingly breathy, but she didn't care. Monet wanted nothing more than the feel of Brady's lips against her own.

She felt his lips curve upward an instant before his mouth was on hers. Brady kissed her softly at first, almost cautiously. His kiss was tender and unhurried; the feel of his mouth was warm—tempting, and the gentle way his lips caressed hers left her desperately wanting more and awaking a deeper need.

Breaking through any timidity she might have felt, Monet reached up and caressed the side of Brady's face with her hand before tangling her fingers in his hair, eliciting a deep groan from the back of his throat. He deepened the kiss, coaxing her lips apart. Monet gasped, melting into breathless quivers as his mouth ground against hers. A burning desire rose within her, and she met him, hesitantly at first, but as his affections continued to stir her blood, she let her body respond.

Suddenly, Brady broke the seal of their lips but kept his hand at the back of Monet's head as their foreheads rested against each other. Monet's hand slid down his face and rested on his chest. Her breathing matched the pounding of his heart.

"You need to go inside now." Brady's voice was raspy and rough, and the way he said it caused a delicious shiver to trace over her body.

"Okay."

Monet didn't want to go, but she knew she needed to. The crazy desire Brady stirred within her was new; she'd never experienced such an intense need to touch and be touched. Monet was further convinced of Brady's high character—and willpower. She trusted it was time to end the night if he felt it was.

Monet started to pull back from him, but he stopped her.

"I don't have many temptations," he said. "But you, Monet Everly, are one."

Brady's confession caused another shiver of delight to rush through her, and she timidly bit her lip as a small smile spread across her lips.

The two climbed out of the Jeep and made their way into the villa, where Brady walked Monet to her room. The romantic atmosphere they had experienced under the stars had left Monet feeling like she was floating on a cloud.

The kiss they'd shared moments before still lingered on her lips, but instead of feeling self-conscious, Monet relished in the memory of their intimate moment.

"Thank you," Monet said while her fingers softly grazed the flowers in her hair, "for tonight."

She heard Brady chuckle before he closed the short distance between them. The air between them was instantly charged, and he gently took her chin and tipped her face so that their eyes met.

For a moment, Monet was struck by how utterly handsome he was. She marveled at how lucky she'd been to be the recipient of his affections.

"It was my pleasure," he mumbled as he stole one last kiss. It was sweet and gentle, conveying a tenderness that made Monet's heart leap again.

Brady watched as Monet turned, opened her door, and disappeared into her room.

*

As Monet lay in bed, the sensation was much the same as it had been the previous night. The smell of the sea and the lush vegetation flowed in through her open window; she felt the plush, elegant comforter around her and the soft pillow beneath her head. Persistent thoughts of Brady's kiss also invaded her mind—the warmth of his lips, his taste, and how he made her feel. It was like nothing she'd ever experienced before, and she knew she was falling for him.

She silently scolded herself for it; it was too fast, especially for her, but she couldn't help it. There was something about Brady that drew her in and made her feel safe and cared for. Maybe she was crazy, but she felt there was something special between them, and for the first time in forever, she wanted to explore it further and see where it would lead.

Monet

Over the following weeks, Monet's days were filled with a flurry of resort meetings, design approvals, vendor appointments, and daily errand runs. Despite her hectic schedule, Monet cherished stolen glances and kisses shared in private with Brady.

Cole and Ashley had joined forces to play matchmaker for Monet and Brady, conveniently missing meetings that left the pair alone or opting for romantic dinners for two more often. It was amusing how often they found reasons to give Monet and Brady space.

It was sweet, really, and Monet was more than happy to share any alone time with Brady that she could. From what she could tell, Brady felt the same. And no matter how hard they tried to keep their blossoming interest in each other a secret, all the workers seemed to know and were unusually giddy about the whole thing—everyone except the grumpy Grand Jewel contractor, Jesse.

Despite Monet's relentless efforts to include the man in their small friend circle, she couldn't break through his icy walls. She was determined, though, and she hadn't given up yet.

*

As the week wore on, the Grand Jewel remained ahead of schedule, with Friday just around the corner. The whole crew had been working long, hard hours, including Monet.

After her first weekend in Cancun, Brady, Cole, and Ashley swiftly put their business hats back on. They'd all been working seven days a week, but due to Monet's upcoming birthday, everyone had decided to take the upcoming weekend off. Despite her passion for her job, Monet eagerly anticipated some well-deserved R&R.

It was thrilling to be a part of something as grand (no pun intended) as the resort they were building. The fact that Ashley trusted Monet's taste and ideas made the experience that much more exciting, not to mention the fun she was having.

Ashley and Monet would often scour shops a little off the beaten path in search of authentic trinkets and decor to add to the resort. The two women were alike in that way; they'd envision something and hunt until they found it. That was what had taken Monet away that Thursday morning.

Velma was adamant that The Jewel be a family resort, but they'd decided to include an adult-only swimming pool. They'd gained popularity over the years, and Brady and Cole knew it would be short-sighted not to add one into the design. When Monet first saw the plans, she'd had some ideas about the color scheme for the private pool area. She wanted to create a cozy and inviting ambiance for those wishing for a more soothing atmosphere.

Monet had already brought in some beautiful wicker chaise lounge chairs with jungle green cushions, and she'd found a woman in a nearby village who handmade the most exquisite throw pillows. The pillows were brightly colored with Mexico's vibrant hues, perfectly matching Monet's vision for the chairs.

Monet was on her way back from meeting with the woman when she received a text message from Ashley asking if she'd stop into one of their favorite lunch spots, Señor Frog's, and pick up lunch; Cole had his weekly craving for their spicy chicken and blue cheese sandwich. Brady had taken Jesse out to lunch, so Monet was borrowing Cole's Jeep.

She pulled into a parking spot and made her way down the street to the beachfront restaurant. The sun was scorching, and Monet was grateful she'd worn a light and breezy sundress.

She reached into the small purse she had crisscrossed over her body and removed the hair tie she'd purchased during one of her first daily work outings with Ashley. Monet had underestimated the Cancun heat and quickly learned the importance of always wearing your hair up or always carrying a hair tie with you. The one she'd bought that day had a white lily attached to it, and Monet loved how feminine she felt wearing it.

She quickly pulled her hair into a semi-tidy bun and secured it with the small accessory before walking into the open-aired restaurant. It was early afternoon, so the lunch crowd had already started to thin out.

Monet walked up to the podium, where the young hostess greeted her.

"Hey there," the woman said.

"Hello." Monet returned the woman's warm smile. "I'm here for a pickup order." Her gaze flickered to Ashley's text message. "Looks like it's under my name, Monet Everly."

"Got it," the hostess said. "I'll go and grab that for you."

Monet smiled. "Thank you."

A light breeze blew through the restaurant, bringing an unsettling chill as a voice cut through the air.

"Well, hello there, young lady."

Another shiver skirted her body as Monet spun around to see a face she recognized but couldn't quite place. It didn't take long before she realized he was the man she'd sat beside on her flight to Cancun a month earlier. His features were soft, and his smile was sincere; Monet couldn't make sense of her body's reaction to him. She did her best to tamp down the rising unease she felt and pasted on a friendly smile.

"Mr..." she searched her mind for the man's name.

"Hamlin," he said with a chuckle.

"Mr. Hamlin." Monet puffed a nervous laugh as her heartbeat quickened.

"And it's Monet, right?" he asked.

"Wow." Her eyebrows rose. "I can't believe you remember."

"Of course I'd remember, darlin'." He grinned. "Monet isn't too common a name."

Monet cleared her throat and fiddled with the strap of her purse. She didn't know why this man made her uncomfortable, but he did. She glanced toward the kitchen, and a nervous quiver touched her stomach when she didn't see the hostess.

"How's everything with the resort coming along?"

Monet whipped her head in his direction but instantly remembered she'd told him about it on the flight.

"Oh..." she stammered. "It's going well. The resort is beautiful, and we're ahead of schedule."

"That's fantastic," he said. "I'll have to check it out after it opens. Maybe even have one of our old geezer getaways there one of these times." He winked.

Monet's eyebrows arched. "That's right, you were meeting some old friends," she said. "Must be some trip! Have you been here the whole month?"

He nodded. "Retirement has its perks."

An involuntary shudder shook Monet, and cold prickles ran over her arms as she sensed someone approach behind her.

"My my my, look who we have here."

Monet's world swirled, and her heart lurched hard inside her chest as a shot of painful adrenaline seared her veins at the hauntingly familiar voice.

No...

Monet's entire body stiffened, and her eyes remained locked on Mr. Hamlin, whose expression quickly morphed from carefree and friendly to deep concern as his forehead creased and the smile fell from his lips.

Even if she wanted to turn and look at the man behind that unforgettable voice, her body had taken control and froze. Monet's breaths became more rapid, and the humidity wasn't the only cause behind the sweat gathering on the nape of her neck and forehead.

"Aren't you even going to say hello?" There was a hint of disgust behind his words.

"Monet?" Mr. Hamlin asked. "Are you alright?"

Her voice had abandoned her, and her mouth felt like it hadn't tasted water in a week. She slowly let her eyes float to the man who had stepped beside Mr. Hamlin.

John Wessler.

"What do you know, Bobby? She's speechless." Wessler's voice dripped with mockery.

Monet's head spun again, and the floor seemed to move beneath her feet. She grabbed onto the hostess stand for support. Her mind couldn't make sense of what was happening. Was she dreaming? Why was he here?

"Miss Everly," the chipper hostess broke into the deepening fog that was beginning to consume her. "Sorry about that wait."

"Miss Everly?" Monet heard Mr. Hamlin say.

Wessler chuckled, and the sound caused a wave of nausea to slosh around in her stomach.

"The one and only, Bobby," he said.

"*This* is Monet Everly?"

It was the last thing Monet heard before her vision blurred, and suddenly there was darkness.

Brady

Brady's blood had never boiled as quickly as when he'd entered Señor Frog's and seen John Wessler talking to Monet. The heat pulsing through his veins was almost painful as his eyes bore into the back of the man's head, but as his attention shifted to Monet, Brady's heart was in his throat before it plummeted into his stomach.

"Monet!" He rushed forward, shoving the two men in front of him so hard that one of them lost his balance.

He dove forward and landed on his knees just as he caught Monet's body from landing on the wooden floor of the restaurant.

"Jesse!" he yelled as he cradled Monet's unconscious head in his lap. "Call 911!"

"There's a clinic up the street on the left," the hostess said to Jesse. "I'll get the doctor on call."

"Monet, can you hear me?" Brady patted her cheeks and held his cheek to her lips. "She's breathing!"

"Here." One of the servers handed Brady a cool towel, and he gently used it on her forehead and neck.

"Monet, open your eyes, sweetheart." The tightness in Brady's chest was almost suffocating.

"Mmm..." Monet released a small moan of discomfort as her eyes fluttered open. "Wh... what happened?" She focused on him. "Brady?"

"Monet!" An instant release of tension in Brady's limbs caused his body to slump. He held her face in his hands and kissed her forehead. "You scared the life out of me."

Brady felt Monet's hand cover one of his. "I'm alright."

Brady tenderly helped her into a sitting position.

Monet placed a hand on her forehead and shook her head. "I feel a little dizzy."

"*Perdón*. Excuse me. Everyone, please step aside," a man said, his voice thick with a Spanish accent.

Brady turned to see a gentleman with the hostess and assumed he was the doctor she had gone to fetch.

"I'm Doctor Vela." He crouched beside Monet. "Can you tell me your name, señorita?"

Monet nodded. "Monet Everly."

The doctor spent the next few minutes examining Monet while Jesse firmly instructed the small group of onlookers to return to their meals. He still wore a wrinkle of worry on his brow, and Brady's interest was piqued. For the first time in all those months of working with the man, Jesse dropped his surly demeanor and, in his place, was a concerned and assertive friend.

"Let's get you into a chair," Doctor Vela told Monet. "Do you feel like you can do that?"

"Yes, I think I'm fine now," she said as Brady assisted her.

They walked to a nearby table, and Monet sat down.

"Do you remember anything before passing out?" Doctor Vela asked.

Monet's forehead puckered a split second before her eyes widened, and Brady heard a short intake of breath. The pained expression she held shifted to Brady, and he watched her swallow.

"John Wessler is here."

At the reminder, Brady whipped his head toward the hostess stand, but Wessler wasn't there. Brady frantically scanned the restaurant as his body tensed.

"If you're looking for the men who were talking to Monet when we walked in," Jesse said, "I heard one of them say something about not being allowed near Monet, and he ushered the other man out."

"Wait," Monet mumbled, and Brady refocused on her. "Hamlin... Robert Hamlin."

Brady's brow furrowed as Monet huffed. "Wessler's attorney."

"Why would..." Brady trailed off when he noticed Jesse and Doctor Vela's questioning glances. Monet must have seen them, too.

"Someone I hadn't expected to see surprised me," she said to both of them. "The shock must have been too much." She flashed a tight smile. "I really am okay now, thank you."

"You may feel a little confused and dizzy for a few hours," Doctor Vela said before turning to Brady. "Keep an eye on her for the rest of the day, and make sure she rests."

"I will. *Gracias*, Doctor."

"*Gracias*," Monet said softly as the Doctor gathered his things and left.

"Are you sure you're alright?" Jesse asked as he sat in the chair the doctor had vacated.

Monet smiled. "Yes, thank you, Jesse."

"I thought you were meeting with someone about pillows today," Brady asked Monet.

"I did," she said. "I was on my way back when Ashley asked me to pick up lunch."

Brady acknowledged with a slight nod.

"I'd be happy to take their lunch back," Jesse offered. "That way, you can go back to the villa and rest."

"I think I'm fine to go back to work," Monet said.

"Not a chance," Brady spoke up. "You heard the doctor. You need to rest."

"I'm with Brady on this one," Jesse said. "Are you in Cole's Jeep?"

Monet nodded. "Uh-huh."

"Why don't I drive Cole's Jeep back? I'll grab something and take Ashley and Cole their lunch, too."

Brady's eyebrows shot up. Something had definitely gotten into Jesse. He was never this helpful and agreeable outside of work. Brady was pretty sure he knew what that something was—Monet. He couldn't pinpoint it exactly. Brady didn't think Jesse had a romantic interest, but she affected him; it was obvious in his concern and willingness to help.

"I guess that would be best," Monet said. "I do feel a little... off."

"It's settled then," Brady said. "Thanks, Jesse."

After Monet had unnecessarily apologized to the hostess for the tenth time over causing a scene, Brady and Monet made their way to his Jeep that he'd parked about halfway up the tourist-packed street.

As soon as they'd started walking, Monet found she was still a little light-headed, so Brady kept his arm around her waist. They hadn't spoken about John Wessler, but Brady knew being surprised by the man was already taking a toll.

Once they reached the Jeep, Brady opened the door and helped Monet into the passenger seat before walking around to the driver's side.

A small knot formed in his belly as he slid into the seat and fastened his seatbelt.

"I'm sorry, Monet," he said as he turned the key, bringing the engine and the blessed air conditioning to life.

Monet turned to him. "Why?" She huffed a small, defeated breath. "You didn't bring him here."

"It's not that." He scratched the back of his neck and released a disgusted sigh. "I knew Wessler was in Cancun."

Monet's head jerked back, and her forehead furrowed. "What?"

Brady shook his head. He should have told Monet that they'd seen Wessler in the flea market that day. They'd thought they were protecting her, but the shock of seeing him wouldn't have been so traumatic if she'd known.

"That day in the flea market," he said. "We spotted him."

"Cole and Ashley saw him too?"

Brady nodded. "Yeah. When we were getting shaved ice."

"Hmm." Monet was thoughtful for a moment. "I see."

Brady's heart ached. "We should have told you," he said. "We thought..." He trailed off with another disgusted puff. "We thought we were protecting you."

Monet dropped her eyes to her lap and fiddled with the silver bracelet she wore. "I know," she said softly. "I really do understand that."

"Still," Brady said. "If you'd known there was a chance you'd run into the man, you'd have at least been mildly prepared."

Monet laughed, but it was laced with sarcasm. "I don't think anything would have prepared me for seeing him again."

"I'm sorry you had to face him alone." Brady reached across the console to hold her hand, but at his touch, Monet flinched and pulled away.

"I'm sorry," Monet said quickly. "I didn't mean to..." She trailed off.

Brady pasted on a soft smile. "It's okay."

The last thing he wanted to do was make Monet feel bad, and he understood her reaction. Facing John Wessler again would undoubtedly bring out her insecurities.

As Brady shifted the Jeep into drive, heading for the villa, he couldn't help but worry about the impact of what had just happened. He hoped it wouldn't set Monet back too much. More than anything, he wished that John Wessler would disappear back into whatever hole he crawled out of so Monet would never have to see him again.

Monet

"Hey, it's me again. I hope you're okay," Monet said to Juliet's voicemail. "I've tried calling all afternoon. I really need to talk to you, so call me back, okay?"

Monet ended the call on her cell phone and tossed it onto her bed. She'd been trying to keep it together ever since she and Brady got back to the villa.

At the thought of Brady, a dull pain touched the back of Monet's throat, and she had to fight the same tears she'd been keeping at bay for hours. She'd hurt him when his touch had startled her earlier. Monet saw the flash of surprise and hurt in his expression. Just thinking about it caused her stomach to twist.

"Ugh." She plopped down on the bed and let herself fall backwards, flailing on top of the comforter. It wasn't Brady that caused her to pull back; it was seeing that vile man! His appearance stirred all sorts of uncomfortable memories and unearthed insecurities and fears that Monet had hoped were behind her.

She needed to talk to Juliet. Maybe it was unhealthy to rely on a person so much, but Juliet was the one who helped Monet through some of her darkest times. She'd become like a security blanket for Monet; Juliet always knew the right things to say to help her feel better.

The problem was, she couldn't reach her best friend, and she'd been trying for hours.

A firm knock on her bedroom door caused Monet to sit up and turn toward the door.

"Hey," Brady's voice floated from the other side of the door. "Can I come in?"

Monet smiled. Over the past month, even though the two of them had gotten closer, Brady was always the gentleman; he never barged in on her and continually respected her privacy.

"Of course," she said.

The door slowly opened, and he stepped in.

Jesse had relayed the incident at the restaurant to Ashley and Cole when he'd returned with their lunch. Ashley had left immediately and returned to the villa, where she hovered over Monet like a mother hen for the next couple of hours until she'd gone to fetch Cole from the resort.

During her time with Monet, Ashley described what had happened when Monet first blacked out at the restaurant. Brady and Jesse walked into Señor Frog's to see the two men talking to Monet; it was at that instant she lost consciousness. From how Jesse described it, Brady rushed forward, knocking Wessler and Hamlin out of the way in time to catch her before Monet hit the floor. Apparently, Wessler took the brunt of Brady's strength, knocking him to the ground.

The thought of Brady heroically coming to her rescue that way evoked a warm, tingling sensation that engulfed her entirely, and as Brady made his way toward her, that warmth also penetrated her heart, replacing her anxiety with a sense of calm. She felt safe.

"Hi." She looked up at him from where she still sat on the side of her bed.

"May I?" He gestured to the spot next to her.

"Of course," she said softly.

Brady sat beside her, and Monet noticed how he clasped his hands together in his lap. "Are you feeling any better?" he asked. "Did talking to Ashley help?"

Monet smiled at him. "It did." But not in the way Brady thought it helped. Ashley had become a dear friend to Monet, and Monet genuinely benefited from the advice Ashley gave, but when it came to John Wessler, Juliet was Monet's true confidant.

Digging deep within herself, Monet summoned her courage and fought against the insecurities John Wessler's appearance had reawakened. She gently reached over, untangled his hands, and laced their fingers together.

Brady's posture visibly relaxed, and a slow smile spread across his lips.

"I wanted to thank you," she said. "Jesse told Ashley and Cole what happened." She paused, holding his gaze. "You caught me when I fell."

His green eyes studied her so intensely it felt like he was peering into the depths of her soul.

"I will always catch you when you fall, Monet," he said. "If you will let me."

His words made Monet's breath hitch, and tears gathered behind her eyelids.

"Whatever you do," Brady said, "don't let Wessler win again. He already stole too much time away from you... Don't give him another second of your life."

"How do I do that?" she asked as a tear escaped and traveled over her cheek. "I don't want to give in to it, but..." She trailed off, and Brady gently wiped the tear away with his thumb. "When I think about him—seeing him there today stirred so many memories and feelings." She shook her head quickly. "How do I get rid of that?"

Brady took both of her hands in his. "Somehow, you realize he's just an old, messed-up man." Brady huffed a chuckle. "You are so much stronger than he knows; don't give him any more power over you." Brady raised her hand to his lips and placed a tender kiss on her fingers. "I know it's easier said than done, though."

Monet nodded. "It is. But I know you're right."

"There is something," Brady said, "that might help."

Monet looked at him with wide, hopeful eyes.

"When Beau and I were young, we spent a lot of time with our grandma Nash." He smiled. "She was a pistol."

"Is she still alive?" Monet asked.

"No," he said. "She's been gone for about four years."

"I'm sorry," Monet said.

Brady grinned again. "It was shortly after Beau's company started to take off," he said. "His personality began to change, and whenever we tried to confront him and talk about what was going on, Beau blew us off, even my grandma.

"A few months before she died, I remember her giving Beau this stern pep talk… We'd all gathered to celebrate her birthday; Beau was silently sulking over something, and out of the blue, my grandma said, *Beau, snap out of it! This isn't like you.* She told him she understood if he didn't want to talk about it, but *he needed to get a grip.*" Brady laughed. "And then she said something I've never forgotten. She said *One sure way to forget your troubles is to go out and do something nice for somebody else. Lose yourself in service, Beau, and you'll find yourself again.*"

Monet smiled, and her heart lifted. "Pretty sage advice," she said. "And did Beau do it?"

Brady's head tipped, and he smirked, which made Monet laugh.

"That's right, grumpy Beau Nash is still grumpy."

"Unfortunately, yes," Brady chuckled and lifted his shoulders. "Maybe one day."

Monet smiled again. "Hopefully."

"But," Brady pointed his finger at Monet, "I think the same thing might help you."

Monet's eyebrows rose.

"My grandma was right; serving others really does help you feel better—lighter."

Monet nodded. "What do you have in mind?"

Brady's eyes twinkled, and a silly grin stretched across his face. "Seeing as this is your birthday weekend, I'll keep it a secret for now. One of a few surprises I have in mind."

Monet cocked her head and dramatically arched one eyebrow.

"A *few* surprises?"

"It's your birthday. You shouldn't expect any less."

Monet's belly flipped as it fluttered. Brady Nash was a dream. The way he treated her made her feel special and important. Monet realized at that moment how much lighter she felt since he'd come into her bedroom to talk to her. Maybe Monet didn't need to rely on Juliet as much right then. She had Brady.

The reminder of Juliet caused her brow to furrow.

"What is it?"

"Oh," she mumbled. "It's Juliet. I haven't been able to reach her all day."

"Really?" he asked. "Is that unusual?"

Monet huffed an embarrassed laugh. "I know; it shouldn't be a big deal," she said. "It's fine, I just..." she stuttered. "It's just she..."

"She's your best friend," Brady cut in. "And after today, you want to talk to her."

Monet inhaled, followed by a light exhale. "Yeah." She looked at Brady. "But also, this—" she motioned with a finger between them, "this helped... Thank you."

Brady slowly brought his hand to her face and cupped her chin.

"You are most welcome." His voice was soothing but alluring at the same time. Slowly, he pulled her face toward him and placed a soft kiss on the tip of her nose.

Monet's stomach clenched. She'd thought he was going to kiss her, really kiss her—on the mouth. This was Brady, though, ever thinking of her feelings, and after the events of the day, he'd undoubtedly be careful with her for a while. Monet hoped not too long.

"Now," he said as he stood and pulled her up from the bed. "Even though your birthday isn't for two more days, we're starting the celebrations early."

Monet giggled. "Is that right?"

"Yes, it is," he said. "It's not every day that Monet Everly turns twenty-four. We're starting tonight."

Monet couldn't keep her own silly grin off her face. With each passing second in Brady's company, her anxieties evaporated.

"Oh! Are you making your famous Brady Enchiladas?" Monet loved them.

Brady laughed. "No, but you like them that much, huh?"

"I do," Monet said. "Maybe you can make them for me on my actual birthday?"

A mischievous glint entered his eyes. "We'll see." He winked. "But I have something even better planned for tonight."

"Even better than your enchiladas?" Monet shook her head. "Not possible."

Brady chuckled. "I have a feeling you're going to change your mind about that in about two minutes."

Monet tilted her head. "Why's that?"

"Run on out to the kitchen and see what we've cooked up for you." Brady nodded toward the bedroom door.

Monet's eyebrows squished together, and she glanced at the door and back to Brady.

"Off you go," he said. "I'll be right behind you."

A sudden burst of energy shot through her limbs and propelled her forward.

"Oh, and Monet," Brady said, causing Monet to turn back to him.

"Happy early birthday."

Monet smiled, her curiosity egging her on. She stepped out of her bedroom and into the hall that led to the living area and kitchen when her ears picked up the sound of a blender whipping around. Her mind raced. Cole must be making his famous piña coladas. But as she reached the end of the hall, she spotted Cole and Ashley lounging on the couch, sipping a different kind of fancy tropical drink—these ones were blue.

That's when she heard a blessedly familiar voice.

"I have died and gone to culinary heaven!"

Juliet!

Tingles spread over Monet's skin, and her gaze drifted to the kitchen, where she saw her best friend with an array of fruits, vegetables, and other foods laid out before her on the colorful kitchen island.

"What!" Monet squealed, rushing toward her friend.

"Surprise!" Juliet laughed as she met Monet halfway. The two friends threw their arms around each other, and Monet's heart leapt.

"I can't believe you're here." Monet was almost in tears. "No wonder I couldn't reach you!"

"I can't believe it's only been a month," Juliet said with her dramatic flair. "I feel like I haven't seen you for a year!"

"Not quite a year, sweet thing," a masculine voice chuckled.

"Josh!" Monet almost yelled as he walked in from the pool deck through the open shutter doors. "You're here too."

"Of course I am, Mojo," he said as he scooped Monet up and hugged her. "It's your birthday."

Josh set Monet down, and Juliet grabbed her hands and held them out to Monet's sides.

"Look at you. You're all sun-kissed and beautiful," Juliet said. "I'd say Cancun most definitely agrees with you."

"Well, now, I'll be the judge of that," a voice Monet would know anywhere said from behind her.

"Evan?" Monet spun around and couldn't believe what she was seeing. She jumped into his embrace, throwing her arms around her big brother's neck as her heart swelled with joy. Tears she'd held at bay all day fell freely, her emotions spilling over.

"Happy birthday, Mo," he said next to her ear as he hugged her.

"But," she faltered, struggling to gain control of her overwhelming emotions, "my birthday isn't until Saturday."

"What did I tell you?" Brady called out, standing beside Cole and Ashley with a triumphant smile. "We're starting the celebrations early."

Monet stepped back from her brother and turned to Brady as her mind instantly connected the dots. "Did you?" She trailed off as she gestured to her friends and brother.

"He did," Juliet practically sang.

"Brady reached out a couple of weeks ago," Evan added. "He wanted to surprise you for your birthday."

Monet's emotions were tangled in her throat, and her chest felt tight as if it would burst from the way her heart pounded against it, nearly stealing her breath. She kept a steady gaze on Brady as she stepped toward him. His emerald eyes delved into hers, almost sensing her intent.

Taking a breath to steady herself, Monet whispered, "Come with me."

Brady

Once again, Brady found himself caught in a fierce inner battle. It was a struggle that he had fought multiple times since Monet's arrival in Cancun; he grappled with where to draw the line and how to restrain his physical desires, considering everything that she had been through.

Brady knew that he needed to tread carefully, but the crux of his dilemma lay with Monet herself. Every time he'd kissed her, she had returned the kiss with equal passion; he'd felt no hesitation.

And how often she gazed at him with those piercing blue eyes, eyes filled with a glimmer of barely restrained hunger that left him powerless to resist her. It was the same way Monet looked at him right before she tugged his hand, pulling him out of the living area and down the hall.

Brady worried, though, that she was simply confusing gratitude with adoration.

And yet, Brady couldn't help but feel drawn to her irresistible allure. Monet captivated him like no other woman, and it was this conflict he fought.

Monet led Brady into her bedroom, and the second they were inside, she spun around. With one hand, she closed the door while gently pushing Brady's back against it with the other.

"Monet," he started to say, but her fingers against his lips stopped him as she stared into his eyes.

The world outside seemed to disappear, and all Brady could see was Monet.

Without a word, Monet's fingers covering his lips began to trace them, sending Brady's heart into a wild pounding. His eyes dropped to her mouth, and the desire to taste her sweet lips became overwhelming. Brady's hand moved to the back of Monet's head as he slid his fingers into her hair and pulled her closer. Her intoxicating caramel scent filled his senses, and his breaths became deeper.

"Do you want to kiss me?" His voice was low and husky.

"Yes," she whispered before she captured his mouth with her own.

Monet's kiss was warm and feminine, alluring and utterly intoxicating. Brady's arms were around her at once, pulling her tight against his body, causing a deep sigh to vibrate in her throat. Monet's hands ran up the sides of Brady's face and slipped into his hair, stoking an even deeper hunger within him.

Moving his hands to her waist, Brady spun Monet around so her back was against the door. He crushed her against him, drawing deeper kisses from her mouth as she completely melted against him.

She was driving him crazy! Her taste, her fragrance, the feel of her soft body beneath his palms—Monet Everly was entirely addicting, and Brady was lost in the sweet warmth that permeated her body and vibrated every nerve in his.

Monet's lips left his mouth and drifted to his jaw—to his neck and back to his mouth, sending tingles of passion through every limb. Brady felt her hunger; it matched his own, and they couldn't get enough.

With a ragged groan, he broke the seal of their kiss; Monet's lips were swollen and moist, tempting him further. Their breathing was heavy and rapid as their eyes remained locked on each other.

"You have seduced me," Brady whispered in a raspy voice. "Mind and body."

Monet's teeth skimmed over her bottom lip as a small smile touched the corners of her mouth. "I can say the same," she breathed. "I can't believe you did that for me."

Brady's throat squeezed. He didn't want Monet to feel like she had to repay him with her affection.

"You make everything better, Brady."

The sincerity in her voice and the genuine honesty in Monet's eyes spoke to his heart, and he immediately regretted where his thoughts had gone. In the short month that Brady had gotten to know Monet, he had learned one thing: she was honest. He made a silent promise to himself never to doubt her intentions again.

"We'd better get back out there," Brady said as he reluctantly released Monet, and they both stepped back from the door. "Before your brother comes looking for me," he teased with a wink.

Monet smiled, her adorable blush coloring her cheeks. Brady ran one hand through his hair before he reached for the door handle, but Monet's hand on his arm stopped him.

"Wait," she said. "I... it's just... after today," she stammered. "Aside from you." Her lips relaxed into a tender smile. "Having Juliet and Evan here is exactly what I need."

"I know." His smile mirrored hers. "Perfect timing."

Monet gazed at him as she slowly skimmed one fingertip along his jawline. "Perfect," she whispered.

Her touch was his undoing, requiring superhuman strength not to devour her again.

Brady cleared his throat and took her hand as he opened the door.

"So," Brady said, leading Monet down the hall to the living area where he was sure five curious amigos and amigas waited. "Is it safe to say your first surprise was a hit?"

Monet grinned. "A hit is putting it mildly," she said. "That surprise officially beats all surprises; nothing will ever compare to it."

"Oh ho ho," Brady chuckled, his eyes twinkling. "That's a pretty bold statement. You sure about that?"

"One hundred percent!" She laughed.

"Looks like I've got my work cut out for me, then." He lowered his voice as they entered the living area and leaned in next to her ear. "Because I plan to top it."

Monet

It was all she could do to pull her attention away from Brady as they stepped into the villa's living area. The warmth of his breath against her ear, along with the words he'd spoken, stole Monet's breath, causing her body to warm. She would have fanned herself, but the five sets of eyes focused on them was like a glass of cold water tossed on her.

Monet's focus slowly shifted from one to the other as she assessed what they might be thinking of her brazen act of leading Brady to her bedroom.

Juliet's and Ashley's eyes held the same sparkle of pure giddiness, undoubtedly hoping that what they imagined had happened between Monet and Brady actually had.

Humor danced in Cole's eyes as if he was enjoying a private joke. Evan's eyes were on par with what Monet might expect: confusion. The grimace on his face gave it away.

Monet made the split-second decision to simply carry on; it wasn't anyone's business what she and Brady did, although she knew Evan would begin interrogations the second they were alone. Monet would deal with that when the time came.

Juliet tossed an understanding wink to Monet and came to her rescue. "Who wants a refill?" she asked, lifting her glass of the tropical blue drink.

"I do!" Ashley mimicked Juliet's wink. "I hate to say it, love," she said to Cole, scrunching one side of her face. "But these might be my new favorite."

"Ahh!" Cole dramatically threw a hand over his heart. "You said my piña coladas were your forever favorite."

Everyone laughed as Cole and Ashley continued to playfully banter while they made their way to the kitchen, where Juliet poured refills.

Brady gave Monet's hand a squeeze before letting it go. "I have heard nothing but rave compliments about your cooking, Juliet," Brady said as Juliet handed him his first glass.

"If these drinks are any indication," Ashley took a sip, "I'd say we're in for quite a treat tonight."

"Oh?" Monet's eyebrows rose as she glanced at Juliet.

"What do you think all of this is for?" Juliet asked, motioning to the various foods and spices on the counter. "I'm thinking we'll start with some ceviche, then move on to shrimp tacos with a mango salsa. And for dessert, I'll whip up a batch of homemade churros."

Monet giggled over the way Brady, Ashley, and Cole's mouths dropped in unison. Evan, familiar with Juliet's cooking skills, chuckled. Meanwhile, Josh's chin raised, and a proud glimmer gleamed brightly in his eye.

"But!" Juliet quickly added, "not until I've caught up with my bestie first."

Juliet stepped around the kitchen island and took Monet's hand. "Why don't you all enjoy your drinks by that gorgeous pool for a bit?" she suggested to everyone else.

Juliet's curious gaze flickered to Monet. She knew something was going on between Brady and Monet, and her best friend was aching to hear the details. Monet was grateful, too; it would give her a chance to talk to Juliet about what happened earlier that day at Señor Frog's.

"I'm next," Evan said, pointing a stern finger in her direction. "You and I have some catching up of our own to do." His forehead was raised, and his jaw was tight. Evan was in full-blown protective mode—Monet hadn't dated since high school, and after everything her brother witnessed at the hand of John Wessler, she wasn't sure how Evan would take to the idea of Monet and Brady's blooming romance.

"The villa only has one extra bedroom," Brady said, "but it has two beds, so Evan and Josh are going to stay there and—"

"I'm staying with you!" Juliet squealed as she led Monet away from the group.

Monet glanced over her shoulder at Brady and smiled. It wouldn't take long for them all to fall in love with Juliet's infectious bubbliness, just as Monet had. With that thought, she let Juliet lead her away, eager to catch up on everything since they'd last seen each other.

*

After Juliet had gushed over how lovely Monet's bedroom was and taken in the exquisite view of the beach and ocean, the two women crawled onto the bed. They started chattering the way they always did when one or the other needed to talk.

"Okay." Juliet grabbed one of the fluffy white pillows and cradled it next to her stomach. "What happened?" The excited twinkle in Juliet's eye had diminished and was replaced by worry lines across her brow.

"Did Brady tell you?" Monet wondered if Juliet knew what happened earlier that day.

"No," Juliet said. "Nobody has told me anything, but I can tell that something is off."

Monet let out an astonished puff. "You always could read my thoughts."

"Yeah, well, it was a lot harder this time." A sly smile appeared. "A certain hot bellhop is doing a pretty good job of keeping my girl distracted."

Monet's eyes floated to the bedroom door; the memory of Brady's kiss was still fresh, and she rolled her bottom lip beneath her teeth as a heated flush crept over her skin.

"That good, huh?" Juliet teased.

Monet sighed. "Yeah."

Juliet mirrored Monet's sigh but quickly shook her head. "We'll get to that later," she said. "Tell me what happened."

Monet inhaled a deep breath before exhaling. "I saw John Wessler today."

Juliet's face twisted in a variety of horrific ways. "What!" She blurted the word so loudly Monet was sure everyone heard. "John Wessler is here," Monet watched as Juliet tried to process it, "in Cancun?"

Monet nodded. "Yeah."

"Oh, honey." She tossed the pillow off her lap and moved closer to Monet, taking hold of Monet's hands. "Are you okay?"

Monet lifted one shoulder and toggled her head back and forth. "Maybe."

Juliet exhaled an understanding breath. "Do you feel like telling me what happened?"

"Of course," Monet said. "I've been trying to reach you all day," she huffed a laugh.

Juliet's posture slumped. "I'm so sorry, Monet," she said. "Brady wanted to surprise you, so we've been on the plane—"

Monet cut her off with another laugh. "You don't have to apologize, silly," Monet said. "You're here! That's way better than talking to you on the phone." Monet dropped her eyes to where Juliet still held Monet's hands. "And besides," she glanced at Juliet, "Brady talked to me."

Juliet's eyebrows rose as she slowly tilted her head. "And?" A smile pulled at the corners of her mouth.

Monet's eyes found their hands again, and she fiddled with Juliet's engagement ring as she sighed. "And he's wonderful." She let go of Juliet's hands and scooted so that she rested against the bed's headboard.

Juliet's gaze turned soft, and a gentle expression touched her face. "Tell me."

For the next hour, Monet shared everything she could with Juliet about her time in Cancun, as well as her encounter with John Wessler and his attorney. She detailed the stifling shock she'd felt when she first saw him, all the way up to the moment Brady had surprised her with Juliet, Josh, and Evan. As expected, Juliet was emotional over everything Monet had experienced since she'd arrived in Cancun: the ups and the significant downs that had occurred that day. However, the joy and contentment that Monet felt since reconnecting with Brady and her new friends brought Juliet immense happiness.

"There is nothing in this world," Juliet said, "that I want more for you than to find what I have with Josh. The fact that Brady planned this surprise birthday weekend for you," she chuckled and swung her head, "inviting us here, knowing what that would mean to you," she hesitated with a dreamy sigh. "He's something special." She tucked a loose strand of hair behind Monet's ear. "Just like you."

Tears welled in Monet's eyes. She loved Juliet so dearly. "I hope so."

"Why is it that whenever we talk like this, we end up in tears?" Juliet laughed through her emotions.

Monet joined in, chuckling as she hopped off the bed. Together, they walked into the bathroom, searching for tissues.

"You really are okay, though?" Juliet asked as her laughter subsided. "After seeing *him* today?"

Monet pulled a tissue from the wicker holder sitting on the counter. A tightness in her chest caused her a moment of breathlessness as the memory of John Wessler's face flashed in Monet's mind. She inhaled a deep breath and blew it out slowly.

"Monet?" Juliet asked as concern once again etched over her expression, and she frowned.

"I'm okay," Monet said, reaching out and taking Juliet's hand. "Just a little jittery still."

Juliet's eyes were soft and gentle.

"You're allowed to be *a lot* jittery," she said. "I'm here if you need to talk."

"I know." Monet wrapped her arms around her best friend and hugged her tight. "I love you, Jewels."

"I love you too."

"Now," Juliet said as they ended their embrace. "Seeing as we're sharing a room, you can fill me in on all the fun, *spicy* stuff tonight." She waggled her eyebrows, and Monet laughed. "But I need to get dinner started. After all, this is the beginning of your birthday celebrations, and I plan to kick it off right!"

Warmth oozed through Monet's limbs, and her restless heart leapt over the memory of Brady declaring it her birthday weekend. No matter how tasty Juliet's dinner would undoubtedly be, the thought of receiving another one of Brady's passion-filled kisses already had Monet's mouth-watering.

*

After Monet had given Juliet a quick tour of the kitchen, Monet made her way outside to the pool, where Brady and the others were relaxing on that Thursday afternoon.

Evan was reclined on a double chaise poolside lounger, his sunglasses perched on his nose as he soaked in the warm Cancun sun. The crystal-clear waters of the swimming pool sparkled in the afternoon light, casting dancing reflections onto the surrounding palm trees.

Brady caught Monet's eye and shot her a seductive wink as the corners of his lips curved upward. Monet smiled but quickly glanced in Evan's direction. Her brother was perceptive and had always worried about her, especially the past five years. He'd undoubtedly noticed the sparks between her and Brady, and after Monet dragged Brady to her bedroom, she knew Evan was anxious to know what was going on.

Monet gestured to Evan, and Brady replied with an understanding nod.

"You two wanna help me with something?" Brady asked Cole and Ashley.

"Sure!" Ashley hopped up from sitting with her feet dangling in the swimming pool. "Is it a present for Monet?" she teased.

"Maybe," Brady said. "Cole, come on. You too."

Cole, who had been resting on a lounge chair with his eyes closed, mumbled, "I already know what you're giving her.

"I still need your help," Brady insisted.

"For what?"

Brady sighed. "Dude, just come inside."

"Alright, alright," Cole whined, somewhat irritated.

Monet giggled softly as she watched Cole drag himself into the villa before she turned her attention to her brother.

"Hey," Monet said as she took a seat on the open spot next to him and rested back against the plush cushion.

"Hey, Mo." Evan pushed his sunglasses up to rest on his head and glanced around the pool deck. "Where did everybody go?"

"I think Brady might have another surprise planned." Monet smiled. "He conned Ashley and Cole into helping him with something."

"Ah." Evan nodded with a slight chuckle. "I'll take advantage of having you all to myself then." He smiled. "Something tells me I might not get that many chances while I'm here."

Monet's cheeks warmed, and she pulled her eyes away from her brother and gazed out at the ocean as her body tensed. She knew what Evan was implying, and Monet realized this discussion would be as awkward as she'd feared.

"How's everything going with your job and the resort?" Evan asked. "I know you were nervous about it in the beginning."

"Oh, Evan." Monet sighed. "I absolutely love it," she said. "The resort is stunning, and the work is so fulfilling. I get to be part of creating these beautiful spaces that people will enjoy. It's incredible."

A loving smile crossed Evan's lips. "I knew you'd feel better once you got here." He reached over and gave Monet's hand a gentle squeeze. "You deserve to be doing something you love and are passionate about."

Monet returned his smile, but it wavered as Evan's head tilted, and he looked at her pointedly.

"So," he said. "Tell me about Brady." Evan's left eyebrow was arched, which meant he already knew but wanted to hear it from Monet. She'd experienced the arched brow more than her fair share over the years.

Monet managed to pull her eyes away from Evan's probing ones and smoothed her sundress before tucking her hands under her legs. "Well," she began, keeping her eyes down. "He's a brilliant architect... and he's been super supportive of my ideas—"

"Monet," Evan cut in before his hand reached over and took hold of her chin, guiding her face so she was forced to look at him.

He didn't have to say anything; the tilt of his head and the quirk at the side of his mouth told her he knew she was stalling.

Monet took a deep breath, digging deep for the courage to share her true feelings with her protective older brother.

"I really like him," Monet admitted softly.

Evan let go of Monet's chin and smiled. "That's new."

"I know," Monet said. "I never thought..." She trailed off, shaking her head.

"I never thought either," Evan said. "I hoped and wished for it every day," he admitted. "But everything that happened after the modeling contest took such a deep toll on you I questioned if you'd ever trust a man enough to fall for one."

At the mention of John Wessler, a slight sting pierced Monet's stomach. She needed to tell Evan she'd seen the man that day, but she worried over his reaction. Knowing Evan, he'd scour the entire city of Cancun until he found him. Monet decided that conversation would need to wait.

"You're falling for him, aren't you?" Evan asked.

Monet puffed a small laugh as she avoided his gaze, and her cheeks flushed. "Pretty obvious, isn't it?"

Evan leaned back as he let out a knowing laugh. "For him too, Mo."

Monet's heart leapt. "You think?"

Evan's grin widened. "Monet, I've only been here a few hours, and I can see the guy is whipped—a complete goner."

She looked down, feeling her blush creep to the tips of her ears. "The truth is, I think we both had a little crush on each other all those years ago when we first met."

Evan's chuckle was more of a disbelieving huff. "It's still crazy to me that Brady is the bellhop from that night. But Monet," his voice softened, becoming more serious, "this is the first time you've been interested in a guy since high school." He reached over and gave her hand a reassuring squeeze. "Just be cautious."

Warmth spread through Monet's chest, and she squeezed his hand back. "I will be. But it's been good—different than what I always expected."

Evan's brows furrowed. "How so?"

Monet shrugged. "I think having such an impressionable experience with Wessler at such a young age has given me this unhealthy fear that all men would want the same things from me—that my so-called looks defined me in the eyes of men, and that's all they would see."

"I hope you know that's not true, Monet," Evan said.

"I do now." She smiled softly. "You have always been one of my biggest supporters, Evan. Mom and Dad, too," she said. "But you're my family, and I think it took having a stranger like Juliet to come into my life and tell me the same things you were."

Evan nodded. "I can see that."

"I owe so much to her for taking me under her wing and showing me that I am so much more than what John Wessler made me believe."

"And Brady?" Evan asked.

"Brady has been really good for me too." Monet's shoulders relaxed, and an easy smile played on her lips. "He's patient and understanding, and he does so many nice things for me; he shows me that I matter to him," she said. "He's helping me to heal and to let go of the past."

Evan's eyes softened as he wrapped one arm around Monet and pulled her close to him before he kissed the top of her head. "Then he's got my vote," he said. "Sounds like a good guy."

Monet easily melted into her brother's embrace as they both relaxed on the double-cushioned lounge chair.

"Just remember, I'm here for you if anything ever goes wrong or you need me."

The familiar warmth of her brother's presence spread through Monet's body. Having him there and having his support with her growing interest in Brady meant the world to her.

"Now," Evan said, unwrapping his arm from around Monet, "I have something I need to tell you." A nervous edge tinged his tone, and Monet felt the mood instantly shift.

"Okay," Monet said hesitantly.

Evan cleared his throat, pushing himself upright against the cushion. "Um..." He choked out a strained chuckle. "This is harder than I thought."

"What is it?" Her voice sounded small, almost lost in the wave of her thoughts.

"I've started dating someone," he finally said.

"You've started dating someone?" she repeated, her relief manifesting in a playful smack on her brother's arm.

"Ow!" Evan drew his arm back, and his forehead scrunched. "What was that for?"

"For scaring me!" Monet snapped. "I thought you were going to tell me you'd lost your job or you were sick or something."

"What?" Evan's face twisted as he rubbed at his arm. "No!"

The relief Monet felt, coupled with the irritated expression on her brother's face, triggered a small giggle.

"I'm glad you think it's funny," Evan said, frowning.

"I'm sorry," Monet said, rubbing his arm. "But I didn't hit you that hard."

Evan watched his sister for a moment before rolling his eyes and letting out a chuckle. "Actually... once you hear who I'm dating, you'll probably want to smack me again."

Monet stopped giggling, and her brow furrowed. "Why?"

"It's Lily." Evan flinched and leaned away from her, anticipating her reaction.

Lily?

"Lily Penrose?" Monet's mind was whirling. "My best friend from high school?"

Evan nodded as he watched her closely. "Yeah."

Monet stared unflinching at her brother, her face frozen except for the blink of her eyes. She hadn't spoken to Lily in over four years, ever since she'd moved to Seattle to attend college.

Seattle.

The realization pulled Monet out of her shock. "You both live in Seattle."

"We do," Evan said.

"How...?" She trailed off before her forehead wrinkled, and she shook her head. "How long?"

Evan's eyes widened as he inhaled deeply, puffing his cheeks before he let out a breath. "Three months."

Monet tossed her legs over the side of the chair and jumped up. "Three months, and you're just telling me now?"

"Woah," Evan said as he stood and grabbed Monet's hands. "Take it easy, Monet."

Her body tensed, and she pulled her hands away as she started pacing.

"Lily was my best friend, Evan," she spat. "Who, might I remind you, abandoned me!"

"Mo." Evan sighed with a tilt to his head. "You know that's not true."

The frown on Monet's face didn't lessen, but she stopped pacing and looked at her brother.

"You know why Lily moved away," Evan said. "She ran away from the guilt she felt."

She took a deep breath, steadying herself. "I know." Monet shook her head. "I tried everything I could to convince her what happened with Wessler wasn't her fault."

Evan took a hesitant step towards Monet. "It took her a while, but she understands that now," Evan said. "Instead, she feels guilty that she wasn't there for you. Lily wants more than anything to be close with you again," Evan said.

A dull ache settled in Monet's chest. She'd wanted the same thing for so long. Although Juliet was the best friend Monet needed and loved so much, Monet still missed Lily.

She didn't know the right thing to say, so Monet simply nodded.

"I'm sorry I didn't tell you sooner," Evan said. "But I wanted to tell you in person."

Monet sighed as her tightened muscles loosened. "It's okay."

Evan pulled her in for a hug, and Monet willingly went.

"I love you, Mo," Evan said.

"I love you too."

Evan had always been there for Monet; he'd always supported her. How could she ever be upset with him? Lily was a lucky girl.

"Well," Monet said as they ended their embrace. "You know I want to hear everything." She smiled softly. "How you met up again, how serious it is, and... I'd love to hear what Lily has been up to these past few years."

Evan placed an arm around his sister's neck and began guiding her toward the path that led to the beach. "Let's take a stroll," he said. "I've got a lot to catch you up on."

As they walked down the white sandy beach, Evan filled Monet in on his life with Lily in Seattle over the past few months. As Evan spoke, the hurt Monet felt over Lily faded even more. The two sounded perfect for each other. It had been a secret that Monet had kept until that day: that Lily had always been head over heels for Monet's big brother. The knowledge that they were dating brought a sense of serenity to Monet, and even with the traumatic events from earlier that day, Monet's heart was light.

Brady

It had been an early morning for Brady. Juliet had been wonderful since her arrival at the villa two days earlier. Monet's best friend had spoiled them all rotten with her exquisite gift of cooking. Breakfast, lunch, dinner, and endless fruity drinks had kept them all pleasantly content—and full! But it was Monet's birthday, and not only did Brady want to give Juliet a reprieve, but Brady had this day covered.

He might not be a master chef like Juliet Quinn, but Brady could whip up a pretty decent meal when the occasion called for it, and Monet's birthday was just such an occasion.

Over the few short weeks Brady had become acquainted with Monet, he'd watched her throw herself into learning everything she could about the Mexican culture. She loved dressing in the vibrant colors and patterns of the country; she listened to the music and attempted to speak the language, which always gave them all a chuckle. But he'd also witnessed how much Monet loved the authentic Mexican dishes; he'd never seen her order the same thing twice. She was adventurous, which is why that morning, he'd woken before everyone else and cooked up some Chilaquiles, a popular breakfast dish made of fried tortilla chips topped with salsa, shredded chicken, cheese, and sour cream.

Monet was delighted and genuinely savored every bite; gratefully, so did everyone else. Even Juliet was gracious in her compliments over Brady's efforts.

Monet's birthday had started off well, and as Brady drove his open-aired Jeep through the streets of Cancun, he smiled, content. A light breeze played with his hair and clothes as he navigated through the traffic, giving him respite from the humidity.

Despite the vibrant tropical scenery around him, Brady was particularly pleased that the day was shaping up to be overcast and cooler than usual.

The muted light of the cloudy day lent a dreamy, almost mystical quality to the surroundings, making everything seem a bit more magical. Brady hoped what he'd planned for the day would provide a bit of magical healing for Monet as well.

"I'm just itchin' to see what you've planned for today," Juliet said from where she sat next to Josh in the backseat. "I'm still a little miffed that you all wouldn't tell me; I wanted to be in on the surprise, too!"

"There is no way we were going to tell you," Josh chuckled. "You can't keep a secret to save your life, darlin'."

"That is not true!" Juliet spat. "I didn't breathe one word about us coming here."

"Alright." Josh's tone was still light. "I'll give you that." Brady's eyes flashed through the rearview mirror, and he witnessed Josh place a soft kiss on the top of Juliet's nose. The gesture seemed to pacify his fiery fiancé, who quickly smiled and kissed him.

"I'm right there with you, Jewels." Monet's sweet voice caused Brady to glance at her sitting next to him in the passenger's seat. "I could hardly sleep a wink last night, wondering what the surprise is."

Monet's smile was enchanting, and the excitement behind her eyes caused a moment's doubt to flitter through Brady's mind, causing his stomach to tighten at the thought of his plan disappointing her.

He'd cling to what his gut had told him, though: Monet would love it. If nothing else, she would be content spending the day with her best friends and Evan.

Cole was driving the other Jeep with Ashley, Evan, and Jesse. Brady knew Monet would want to include the Grand Jewel contractor in her birthday plans, and he was right. The way Monet's face lit up when Jesse had arrived at the villa after breakfast told Brady he'd made the right choice.

Monet had gone out of her way to include Jesse in everything the four of them did, both inside and outside of work. Although Jesse had lightened up a bit since Monet's arrival in Cancun, he'd still kept everyone at arm's length—until the day Monet fainted at Señor Frog's.

For the past couple of days, Jesse's protective walls had begun to drop, especially around Monet. You'd have thought Brady would be jealous over the fact, but it wasn't like that.

On Monet's first night in Cancun, she'd shown compassion toward Jesse, telling everyone he probably just needed more time to get over his divorce and that she understood needing time to move on from life-changing events. Brady was certain Monet had made it her personal challenge to befriend Jesse because she sympathized with him in a way, and to Brady, it seemed like Jesse was grateful for the friend.

Brady turned off the main street they had been traveling on and headed inland, away from the ocean and resorts. Gradually, the surrounding buildings became more run-down and worn, and the streets turned entirely to dirt.

Brady glanced at Monet, whose attention was focused outside the Jeep. She wore a slight frown on her brow.

"What town is this?" she asked.

"Mar Azul," Brady said. "It's a place that has become very special to Cole and me."

"How so?" Juliet asked from the backseat.

Brady's smile was wide. "You're about to find out," he said with an impish glimmer in his eyes.

Monet twisted in her seat and exchanged a curious glance with Juliet as both women's eyebrows raised, causing Josh to chuckle.

As the Jeep rumbled deeper into the small town, the neighborhood unfolded before them like a tapestry of resilience. Vibrant murals adorned crumbling walls, telling stories of hope and perseverance. It was one of the reasons Brady loved Mar Azul so much; the neighborhood, though worn and dilapidated, exuded a sense of hope amidst the adversity. He and Cole both hoped their efforts over the time they'd been there helped add to that optimism.

"Wait!" Monet gasped and turned to Brady. "Your project."

Brady simply grinned as both Jeeps rolled to a stop in front of a modest plot of land where a foundation for a small house had been laid.

"It'll be a birthday you'll never forget," he said. "I promise."

One by one, the friends climbed out of the Jeeps and greeted each other. Josh explained to Juliet about Brady and Cole's side project of helping to build and restore homes for the people of Mar Azul. Brady was a bit taken aback by Juliet's squeal of enthusiasm over the chore before them, but he didn't know why it surprised him. Monet held Juliet in the highest esteem; she was obviously a very cool person.

Cole opened the back of his Jeep, pulled out a mixture of old clothing and sturdy work boots, and passed some to the guys.

"I brought some things for us, too," Ashley said to Monet and Juliet. "I think these should fit okay." She handed them each a worn t-shirt and pants.

"Thank you," Monet said.

"Are you surprised?" Brady heard Ashley ask Monet.

Monet puffed out a giggle. "Pleasantly, yes."

"Good!" Ashley said. "It's hard work, but at the end of the day, it is so worth it."

A young boy with sun-kissed skin and tattered clothing bounced up to the group; his face was lit with delight.

"*Hola*, Luis," Brady greeted. "*¿Quién ganó el juego la semana pasada?*"

The boy's eyes sparkled, and a smile spread across his face.

"*¡Mi equipo!*"

"This is Luis," Brady said to Monet. "He plays on a small soccer team and was just telling me that his team won last weekend."

"Oh, that's exciting!" Monet said to the boy as she knelt in front of him. "It's nice to meet you, Luis, *Mi nombre es* Monet." She pointed to herself.

Luis nodded bashfully as he dropped his eyes and kicked the dirt with his foot before he whispered, "*Eres bonita*, Monet," and dashed off down the street.

Monet laughed as she stood. "What a little heartbreaker that one will be."

"They have games every Saturday," Brady said. "Maybe we can all sneak over and watch later."

"They have a soccer field here?" Juliet asked.

"It's more like a makeshift soccer field," Ashley jumped in. "The kids used to run around in tattered jerseys, chasing a worn-out ball, until Brady and Cole had jerseys made for them and donated new soccer balls."

"Wow," Juliet said. "Good for you guys!"

Brady was watching Monet, and her already wide smile broadened as she looked at him. Man! She was beautiful... and tempting. He had to hand it to himself. He'd managed to keep it together ever since Monet had kissed him in her bedroom two days prior.

As was always the case with Monet, he deserved a medal for his ability to keep his physical attraction in check with her, but his strength was waning. As far as he could tell, Monet was the whole package, and she had managed to burrow under his skin something fierce.

"Well," Monet broke into his thoughts, "I, for one, would love to watch Luis play."

"Okay, Brady, let's fire up this party," Evan said. "Where do we start?"

Before Brady could answer, the sound of several approaching vehicles drew their attention to the road.

"Right on time," Jesse said. "On top of your regular crew, I rallied up some extra help today."

"We can certainly use it; this is a new build," Brady said. "Thanks, Jesse."

Jesse nodded before turning to greet the incoming crew.

"Alright, everyone," Cole spoke up. "Let's get these trucks unloaded and get to work."

*

Once the trucks were unloaded and the group had everything in place, Brady and his friends worked with the crew to set their plan into motion. The air was filled with a symphony of sounds—a chorus of hammers striking nails, the whirring of saws, and shared laughter and stories.

Each member of the group took on a specific task, working in harmony to bring the vision to life.

Monet, Juliet, and Ashley swung hammers, nailing wooden beams together, while Brady, Cole, Evan, and Jesse lifted them into place as the crew worked to secure them.

The process was a labor of love, demanding both physical strength and careful attention to detail. Walls began to rise, supported by frames carefully secured. The roof followed, piece by piece, as sweat trickled down determined faces. Time seemed to blur as they all worked together; their focus was unwavering, knowing that every nail driven and every wall raised would bring hope and shelter to a well-deserving family.

Several times throughout the day, Brady's heart would swell over the look of selfless happiness fixed across Monet's features. It further assured him that his intentions behind a day of volunteering were the right ones.

Even Josh and Juliet, as well as Evan and Jesse, all appeared to be benefiting from the day. They, too, had a sense of lightheartedness about them, despite the hard labor. Brady smiled as he thought of his sweet Grandma Nash.

"Lose yourself in service, and you'll find yourself again..."

He knew she was right. Warmth filled Brady's chest over the thought that maybe today would be another step toward Monet's ultimate healing.

*

As midday approached, Brady called for a lunch break, which also coincided with Luis' soccer game. The crew brought their own meals, and each found a nice shady spot to enjoy their break, while others opted to eat in their vehicles where they could enjoy the air conditioning.

Brady had put Ashley and Cole in charge of their group's lunch, and they delivered! They had packed a cooler full of sandwiches, pasta salad, chips, and drinks. Brady led Monet and the others to a spot beneath a tall, majestic tree with a generous canopy, where they watched with enthusiastic encouragement as a group of young boys kicked a soccer ball back and forth in the nearby field. Wide grins lit up everyone's faces as they witnessed the pure joy and unbridled passion of the boys' game. For Brady, it was a reminder of the simple pleasures of life.

Just as the game was winding down and Brady and his friends were finishing their lunch, two women accompanied by three small children made their way toward them.

"Ah," Brady said as he quickly stood to greet them. "*Hola*, Maria," he addressed the older of the two women.

"*Hola*." Maria bowed her head as a way of greeting the group, who were now all on their feet.

Brady turned to his friends. "This is Maria and her daughter Rosa," he said. "This is the family whose home we are building today."

Monet's face brightened. "It is so nice to meet you both."

"They don't speak much English," Brady explained. "But Rosa's children know a little."

"Is that right?" Monet focused her attention on the three young children, who wore big smiles and nodded.

"And what are your names?" Juliet asked, coming to stand next to Monet.

"*Mi nombre es* Mia," said the oldest child. Brady guessed she was probably ten years old. "This is Camila." Mia pointed to her little sister.

"And I am Lucas!" the youngest sibling blurted.

Monet and Juliet both giggled. "My, your English is very good, Lucas," Monet said to the boy.

Mia giggled, too. "We learn English at school."

"That's wonderful," Monet said. "In a tourist town like Cancun, I'm sure it will be very helpful."

Mia nodded. "*Sí*—yes."

While Monet and Juliet continued to talk with the children, Maria and Rosa confirmed with Brady that the plans for Monet's surprise birthday celebration that evening were underway. Brady was grateful that Monet didn't understand much Spanish and that his secret was still safe. Everyone else was in on the surprise, too, except for Juliet. Josh wasn't confident she wouldn't let it slip. But as Brady's attention drifted to her, she was watching him with raised brows, bright eyes, and a broad grin. Clearly, Juliet understood Spanish.

Brady mimicked her rounded eyes and shook his head firmly. He hoped Monet's spunky best friend would keep the surprise to herself for a few more hours.

The group spent the next several minutes talking to the humble family. Brady explained how Rosa's husband had passed away a year prior due to illness, and Rosa and her mother, Maria, supported themselves and the children alone. They had been living in cramped conditions with Maria's sister and were deeply grateful that they had been given the opportunity to have a home of their own to raise the children.

Although Maria and Rosa couldn't convey their appreciation through English words, the moisture in their matching brown eyes and the way they placed their hands over their hearts as they gestured to the group muttering, "*muchas gracias a ti, eres una bendición*," spoke volumes.

With renewed vigor, Brady and his friends rejoined the crew, determined to make as much progress on Maria and Rosa's house as possible before sunset. At one point during the afternoon, Monet, Ashley, and Juliet approached Brady and Cole, asking if they could be part of the completion of the project over the next couple of weeks. Even though Juliet lived in New York, she offered to help remotely, coordinating supplies or managing communications. The three women were tenderhearted, and after meeting Mia, Camila, and Lucas, they wanted to contribute to those small but essential details that would make the house a home. The gesture brought renewed warmth to Brady's heart. The day had been good so far, but little did Monet know it was just getting started.

Monet

As the sun began its descent, casting a golden glow over the surroundings, Monet stood at the edge of the small piece of land and stared at the half-constructed house they'd been working on all day. Her weary body throbbed with exhaustion, with every muscle reminding her of the day's labor, yet her lungs filled with deep, satisfied breaths over what they had accomplished in one short day.

"It's a pretty incredible feeling, isn't it?" Brady asked as he walked up.

Monet exhaled a gratifying sigh. "It is," she said. "The thought that soon that sweet family will live here makes me so happy." A tender smile crossed her lips as her gaze shifted to meet Brady's. "You've given me such a rewarding gift. This experience is something I will carry with me forever," she said. "You were right. This has been a birthday I'll never forget. Thank you, Brady."

Brady's face softened, and he reached out and gently brushed the side of Monet's face, sending a warm tingle over her body. They hadn't been alone since their intimate exchange in her bedroom two days prior, and they'd been so busy with her birthday visitors that there hadn't been any stolen kisses or touches, which made the feeling of his fingers tracing her cheek all the more tantalizing.

"I'm glad that you've enjoyed helping and that this day has been meaningful for you, Monet." His voice was warm and soothing. "But your birthday isn't over yet. I've still got a surprise or two planned."

The way Brady winked at her caused Monet's belly to flutter. "More surprises?" she asked, smiling. "You've already done so much for me," she said. "Bringing Juliet and Josh, and even Evan to Cancun." She puffed an astonished breath and tossed her head. "I couldn't ask for anything more."

Brady chuckled as he placed one hand on Monet's back and pulled her closer, causing her heart to skip. "And that, right there, is why it makes it so easy for me to do nice things for you," he said as his head slowly descended. "You appreciate what's important."

Monet could feel his breath on her face as he spoke, causing her heartbeat to quicken even more, but at the first brush of his lips on hers, voices pierced the bliss-filled bubble she was in.

"That's enough, you two," Ashley hollered.

Juliet giggled. "Plenty of time for that later."

Monet heard Brady groan before pulling back. "You're all mine tonight," he said.

Monet's breath hitched, and she dropped her gaze as a delighted smile played on her lips before she peeked back at him. The word *Promise?* was on the tip of her tongue, but she wasn't brave enough to say it.

"Excuse us, will you?" Ashley said to Brady as she linked one arm through Monet's, and Juliet linked her arm through the other.

"We get the birthday girl first," Juliet said as they laughed.

"We'll see you in a bit, Brady." Ashley tossed a wave over her shoulder, and Monet's two friends guided her away from him and where the half-built home stood.

"Where are we going?" Monet was giddy.

"It's a surprise," Ashley said. "But we have to change first."

"Change?" Monet asked. "I already changed out of my work clothes."

"Yes," Juliet said. "But where we're going this evening requires a bit more *Monet*."

Monet's pulse spiked, and it wasn't due to the pace her friends were pulling her along. "What does that even mean?" She chuckled, furrowing her brow slightly.

"You'll see." Juliet tightened her squeeze on Monet's arm. "But trust us," she glanced at Ashley, "it's a good thing."

Monet's heart felt light as she questioned her friends about what they had planned and wondered if it had anything to do with the surprises Brady had in store. Juliet and Ashley were both mum on the subject, but their delighted faces and the bounce in their step told Monet that much like the day had been, this would be a night to remember.

*

"Okay, we're almost there!" Juliet's excited voice sang out as Monet's best friend guided her down the small dirt street. Monet had a red silk sash tied around her head, covering her eyes, and given the sun had already set, she couldn't see a thing.

"This is so exciting!" Ashley squealed from where she held Monet's hand.

"You can't see anything, right?" Juliet asked.

Monet laughed. "No. But I'm afraid I'm going to trip on my dress."

"Don't worry," Ashley said. "We've got you."

Juliet and Ashley had surprised Monet with a birthday present of their own. When they'd taken her to "change" earlier, they had led her to the humble home of Maria's sister. The house was home to nine people, and Monet better understood Maria and Rosa's desire to have a place of their own.

The entire family was lovely and incredibly gracious, and although Ashley knew more Spanish than Monet, they were grateful Juliet—who was fluent in Spanish—could translate.

The family had offered their home as a place for the women to change their clothes in preparation for whatever Brady's next surprise was.

When Monet and her friends had entered one of the small bedrooms, Monet's breath almost abandoned her, and swirls of adrenaline brushed over her belly and limbs.

On the opposite side of the room stood a blue wooden folding screen with three of the most exquisite dresses Monet had ever seen draped over its top.

"They're called Chiapaneca dresses," Juliet had said. She and Ashley had spent the previous day in search of one for Monet but couldn't resist and bought themselves one, too.

"This one is for you." Juliet removed one of the dresses and laid it on the bed. *"Happy birthday."*

Monet had been so captivated by the dress that she hadn't known what to say. The dress that her friends had given her couldn't have been more perfect.

The black satin bodice possessed an air of charm and seduction. Its semi-circular neckline tempted to expose her shoulders, adding an alluring touch to its enchantment. But it was the top layer of the dress where the real magic unfolded. Delicate tulle gracefully unfurled with an ethereal flourish with a profusion of meticulously hand-embroidered flowers blooming upon it, their vibrant colors intertwining perfectly. Silk threads, radiant in hues of yellow, pink, and blue, weaved a tapestry of passion. On the underside, the dress whispered of mystery and allure. The black satin swirled in a circular cut that cascaded gracefully to the floor with even more vibrant hand-embroidered flowers. It was breathtaking.

Once Monet had changed into the Chiapaneca dress, she felt both a transformation and a connection to the rich heritage and romantic essence it embodied. It was another perfect gift that helped set the tone for the evening ahead. Monet hoped Juliet knew how much it had meant to her.

"Just a little further," Ashley said.

Monet couldn't keep the smile off her face. Even though she couldn't see anything with the sash over her eyes, she could feel the air crackling with excitement.

Suddenly, she heard the soft hum of voices in the distance, but not just a few voices; there was a sea of them.

Monet could tell Ashley and Juliet were mouthing something to each other or to someone else; she couldn't tell, but gradually, the distant crowd Monet had heard fell silent.

She laughed softly as a thrilling sense of anticipation began to build. Her heartbeat increased while butterflies took flight in her belly. "Are we almost there?" she asked.

"Yes, just about," Juliet said. "But first..."

They stopped walking, and Monet felt Juliet's hand pulling Monet's hair around from her back and smoothing it over one bare shoulder.

"You look like a Mexican princess, Monet," Juliet said. "Brady won't know what to do with himself."

Ashley chuckled. "I can't wait to see his face."

At the mention of Brady, the butterflies in her stomach swirled faster, their delicate wings fluttering in sync with her excitement. Monet inhaled a deep breath and savored the mixture of nervousness and thrill that coursed through her veins.

Juliet and Ashley were always generous with their compliments about Monet, and although calling her a

Mexican princess might be a bit of an exaggeration, the dress she was wearing helped her feel elegant and bolstered her confidence.

"Are you ready?" Ashley asked as she took Monet's hand again.

Monet giggled. "I think so."

Monet felt Juliet take her other hand and smiled as her best friend whispered in her ear, "Happy birthday, beautiful."

Juliet and Ashley led Monet a few more steps, and Monet felt the gravely road beneath her feet change to smooth ground. They stopped walking, and one of her friend's fingers began to untie the sash around her head, causing Monet's heart to pound with such fierce exhilaration that it almost stole her breath.

"*Feliz cumpleaños!*" Rang out from a chorus of voices, followed by, "Happy birthday!"

A gasp stuck in Monet's throat, and her eyes widened as the sash was lifted, revealing a sight that left her stunned and frozen.

Before her, under the twinkling starry night sky, the same open lot where they had worked all day had transformed into a Mexican-infused fairyland. Delicate string lights adorned temporary posts, casting a soft, romantic glow upon the vibrant outdoor decorations. Colorful papel picado fluttered in the night breeze, their intricate designs dancing above the heads of the guests. Vibrant paper flowers adorned every table and post, their petals blooming with hues of red, orange, and yellow. The ambiance was enchanting, as if the very essence of Mexico had woven itself into the party.

As the crowd began to mingle, the enchanting atmosphere filled with laughter and animated conversations, all accompanied by the melodic strains of Spanish music. Meanwhile, the tantalizing aroma of corn and spices permeated the air, tempting Monet's taste buds and whetting her appetite.

As she took in the breathtaking scene before her, her eyes wandered, finding familiar faces among the crowd. Evan, Josh, Cole, Jesse, and the crew of workers were all cleaned up and ready to celebrate. Her gaze settled on Maria, who was standing beside Rosa and her children, while Luis and his soccer friends mingled with many others. It seemed the entire town had come.

Yet, amidst the joyous crowd, Monet's eyes sought only one person. Her attention landed on the half-built home, where romantic white fairy lights were draped around the wooden frames, and there, standing in the open-aired house, was Brady, looking so unbearably handsome Monet's breath nearly abandoned her again. He was dressed in a baby blue button-down shirt and white linen pants. His skin was freshly sunkissed from their outdoor labor that day, leaving it with a golden hue, while his unruly hair fell charmingly across his forehead, and a seductive smile played upon his lips, making him utterly irresistible.

As the shock of it all began to wear off, a cascading warmth of joy and absolute happiness washed over Monet, filling her with the knowledge that Brady cared for her. He'd shown it in so many ways, but seeing him there staring back at her with such a look of awe and admiration in his eyes touched her heart with such force that her throat grew thick and tears welled.

Monet was so focused on Brady that she didn't realize Juliet and Ashley had left her side and joined the others in the crowd.

Brady stepped off the platform of the unfinished house, his eyes never leaving hers, as he made his way toward her, step by deliberate step. The world around them blurred as he moved closer, and everything else ceased to exist at that moment. It was just Monet and Brady, their connection palpable and unbreakable.

"Brady—"

"Monet—"

They both said in unison, cutting each other off.

Monet giggled. "Sorry. You first."

"Monet... you..." he stammered. "You look absolutely stunning. I don't even know what to say." His mouth fell slightly open as his gaze remained fixed on her. "You're... breathtaking."

Brady's words caused warmth to spread through her limbs and brought a pink blush to her cheeks. She had to fight the urge to drop her eyes, and instead, Monet's focus lingered on Brady's face, captivated by his striking features and the sincerity behind his eyes.

"Thank you, Brady," she said softly. "I can say the same thing. When I first saw you, I found it hard to breathe."

Their words faltered in that moment as their eyes spoke volumes, and they shared a moment of wordless connection. There was something deeper going on between Brady and Monet. She knew she had fallen for him, and the air between them sizzled with far more than the physical attraction they shared. It felt to Monet like a comforting embrace; a gentle warmth enveloped her, and she wondered if maybe Brady was feeling the same.

"Did," Monet stuttered, "Did you do all of this?" She motioned to the party going on in front of them.

Brady grinned and winked. "I had a little help."

"It's incredible," Monet said. "You've completely transformed it. I can't believe this is the same place we worked in just a couple of hours ago."

Brady turned his gaze to the romantically lit celebration and chuckled. "Everyone was eager to help, especially after meeting you today."

Monet's eyes sparkled, and she dropped them for a moment. "Well," she said as she looked back at him. "It's beautiful. Thank you."

"You are most welcome, Monet." He smiled and held his hand out to her. "Shall we join the party?"

Monet's face lit up, and more excited swirls brushed her belly as she nodded. "Yeah," she said, slipping her hand into Brady's open one and following as he led her to her surprise party, where a crowd of anxious people was eager to wish her a happy birthday.

*

The night had been magical, filled with laughter, music, and the warmth of new friendships. Brady and the others had poured so much thought and effort into the night that Monet found herself nearly overcome with emotion a time or two during the evening.

The romantic sounds from the live music serenaded the gathering with its passionate melodies. The lively strumming of guitars and the rhythmic beat of well-worn drums intertwined with the guests' laughter and conversation, setting the perfect tone for dancing.

A group of skilled local cooks prepared homemade tamales in one corner of the outdoor area, their hands deftly crafting each delicate package of flavorful delight. The tantalizing aroma of corn husks and savory fillings wafted through the air, heightening the senses and making mouths water in anticipation.

Meanwhile, at a separate table, a birthday cake stood as the centerpiece, a work of art meticulously crafted for Monet. Adorned with delicate sugar flowers in vibrant hues, it had seemed almost too beautiful to cut—the cake, a culinary masterpiece, held within its layers passion fruit and dulce de leche. Even Juliet was in awe and enjoyed learning the secrets to what made the food so delicious.

As the sounds from the music and laughter began to fade, Monet's spirits remained high. Her heart was not just full of joy but brimming with confidence. The self-doubts that once resided in her thoughts were becoming less frequent, and although John Wessler's unexpected appearance was a jolt to her calm, Brady's overwhelming gestures continued to steady her heart.

Amidst her inner musings and lingering enchantment from the evening, Brady gently took Monet's hand and led her away from the remnants of the celebration. The stars sparkled brightly above, casting a soft glow on their path.

"I told you, you were all mine later," Brady said as he continued to guide her away from the dwindling party.

Monet smiled. "Another surprise?"

Brady's eyebrows arched, and his head tipped. "Of course," he said. "I haven't given you your real birthday present yet."

Monet giggled. "My real present?" she said. "Brady, you've given me so much. Today—and tonight—it's been like a dream for me."

Brady's eyes softened, crinkling at the corners as his lips curved softly. "You deserve it, Monet," he said. "And I do have one more gift for you."

They continued down the gravel street a short way before Brady turned them down a small stone path. The scent of jasmine and hibiscus permeated the air, creating an intoxicating fragrance that mingled with the warm Mexican breeze. The only lights were from the moon and stars, but suddenly, Monet saw soft light flickering a short way ahead, and as they got closer, she gasped.

A magnificent old gazebo stood proudly amidst a secluded garden. Draped in ivy and adorned with delicate vines and fragrant flowers, it seemed as if nature itself had embraced this enchanting structure.

"It's beautiful," Monet whispered.

Dangling from the ceiling of the gazebo, lanterns in various shapes and sizes added a whimsical touch to the scene. Soft, flickering candlelight spilled through intricate patterns carved into the metalwork, casting mesmerizing patterns on the wooden floor below. The lanterns, painted in hues of gold and turquoise, mirrored the vibrant spirit of the Mexican coast.

Brady and Monet stepped inside the gazebo, and their eyes locked. The world around them, even the charming gazebo, faded. Without a word, Brady reached into his pocket and pulled out a delicate pink box with a small white bow securing the top. At the sight of it, Monet's heart leapt, and her breath hitched.

"Happy birthday, Monet." His voice was soft and seductive.

With trembling hands, she gingerly untied the delicate ribbon and lifted the small lid.

"Oh my gosh," she breathed. "Brady."

A sterling silver necklace, attached to a silver heart pendant and adorned with three shimmering birthstones—pearl, moonstone, and alexandrite—glistened under the night sky.

"I never knew June had three birthstones," Brady said as he reached for the necklace. "But they suit you perfectly," he said. "The pearl signifies purity; the moonstone symbolizes intuition and healing; and the alexandrite represents luck and transformation. Just like you, Monet."

Monet was speechless, her heart swelling with such emotion that she feared whatever she said would come out as one gigantic sob.

"I know I already gave you a necklace," Brady said as he undid the clasp. "But I figured this one is a bit more practical."

She smoothed her hair out of the way as Brady clasped the necklace around her neck. The feel of his fingers brushing over her skin sprinkled goosebumps over Monet's body.

"Brady." Her voice was thick with emotion. "This is the most beautiful gift I've ever received," she whispered. "But it's not just the necklace; it's everything. Tonight, this place, and most of all, you. You've shown me a side of life I didn't know existed," she said. "Outside of my family and Juliet, I never imagined I'd be worthy of any of this from a man... especially a man like you."

"You're worthy of a lot more than what I've given you today, Monet." His fingers took hold of the heart pendant resting on her chest and straightened it. "You are the strongest person I have ever met. You lived through and overcame an extraordinarily difficult and challenging situation, and yet you're still so kind and caring to everyone. You're talented, open to new experiences, and so much fun to be with—not to mention breathtakingly beautiful. I admire everything about you, and I find myself falling for you deeper with each passing day."

The words Brady spoke caused Monet's heart to beat with such force that it caused her voice to tremble. "You are?"

"I am, Monet," he said as his hand moved to the small of her back, pulling her closer. "And I hope you're falling with me."

Monet's eyes lingered on Brady's lips, and her breath quickened. "You know I am."

One side of his mouth curved in a flirty smile. "I hoped so."

Their lips lingered temptingly close to each other, and Monet's mouth became moist, wanting to taste him again.

"Can I ask for one last birthday present?" Her voice was barely above a whisper.

"You don't have to ask."

Monet's entire world tilted as Brady's head dipped, and she felt his lips on her bare shoulder. She was left breathless, and her heart raced as his mouth slowly left a trail of moist kisses up her neck and below her ear. Instinctively, Monet's head fell back as he placed a soft, lingering kiss in the hollow of her throat and another over the heart-shaped pendant he'd given her. He was driving her crazy, and she loved it. His mouth on her skin wove a spell of passion over Monet, and she couldn't get enough.

"You are intoxicating," he nearly growled before his mouth locked with hers in a sincere and powerful exchange. Monet heard nothing but the beat of her own heart and the comforting rhythm of Brady's breathing. She could feel his arms as they held her next to his strong, solid body—his mouth moist, warm, and demanding.

Monet sighed, and her body surrendered and weakened against his as Brady kissed her. Her mind swirled. To be held and cared for by a man like Brady was both overwhelming and wonderful.

Monet's hands went to his face in a desperate attempt to deepen the kiss even more. Brady responded, his lips parted further, and he kissed her with such power and potency she wondered if they would ever draw breath again. Over and over again, he kissed her, and Monet returned each heated kiss with equal passion and wanting.

Just when she didn't think Brady's kiss could get any better or more blissful, he began to slow the exchange, and it became touchingly tender.

"I could kiss you all night," he whispered in that deep, raspy voice she adored.

"Then why don't you?"

Brady tipped his head as a deep groan rumbled in the back of his throat.

"Be careful what you wish for."

Monet bit her lip, secretly delighted by his words, before Brady pulled her close and drew one last kiss from her mouth, which left her breathless.

Gently, Brady entwined his fingers with Monet's and guided her away from the enchanting gazebo as they ventured down the moonlit path. Monet felt as if she were floating, her body weightless and her heart soaring.

As they made their way back to the open lot where her party had unfolded, Monet couldn't help but feel that this magical night was just the beginning—the start of something extraordinary between Monet and Brady. Monet pushed away any last doubts; *maybe*, she thought, her own love story was beginning to unfold.

Brady

The warm evening breeze swept through the open windows of the Jeep as Brady drove his friends back to the villa after Monet's birthday celebration.

Monet was snuggled in the passenger seat and slept soundly, her face serene and peaceful. Brady couldn't help stealing glances at her, captivated by the way her eyelashes gently brushed against her cheeks as she dreamt.

Juliet sat in the back seat, gently stroking Josh's hair as his head rested in her lap. A soft smile graced her lips, and she seemed peaceful and content.

Juliet's eyes locked with Brady's in the rearview mirror. "She's been through so much." Juliet kept her voice soft. "The past few years have been tough on her."

Brady nodded. He understood the weight of Juliet's words.

"She told me," he whispered, glancing at Monet, "When I think about what that man put her through..." He tossed his head, and his heart spiked at the thought of John Wessler.

"I know," Juliet said. "But she's strong. When I think about how far she's come since the first day we met." Juliet hesitated with a smile. "She's a fighter, for sure."

"How did you meet?" Brady asked.

Juliet's lips stayed curled in a tender smile. "Monet and I met at this enchanting little restaurant nestled in the heart of New York City, Peggy Ann's Cafe." Her voice held a tone of fondness.

Brady's smile mirrored Juliet's.

"I had stopped in there one day for my to-go breakfast order," she said, "when I spotted this beautiful young woman sitting alone in a corner booth. She was staring out the window." Juliet paused, and Brady's eyes flashed to her and saw her slowly shake her head. "I remember how my heart ached, not only because she seemed so alone and sad but also because of her appearance."

Brady's forehead creased. "How so?"

"Her hair was unkempt; she wore no make-up and clothes that were easily three sizes too big." Juliet sighed. "For some reason, I saw through all that; somehow, I knew it was all intentional," she said. "It's not easy for someone who looks like Monet to blend in and disappear... And it was clear to me that's what she was trying to do."

The image of Monet sitting alone, trying her best to camouflage herself to disappear from the peering eyes of the world, brought a heaviness to his chest. A flush of heat ran through his limbs, fueled by the knowledge that one man had caused her pain.

"It breaks my heart to think of her that way." Brady kept his voice low. "When I first met Monet, she was innocent and brave... her whole life ahead of her."

Juliet nodded. "I'm sure she was."

"And it was all because of one man's obsession..." He trailed off, hearing his own voice getting louder.

"Monet was lost and broken for a while, but she has worked hard on herself to overcome those demons, Brady."

"I know," he said. "And from what Monet has told me, your friendship has a lot to do with that."

"Yeah," Juliet whispered. "I hope so. But more recently, it's also because of you. Since you came back into her life, she's been different. Happier, more alive."

A flutter brushed Brady's stomach. From the moment he met Monet five years prior, he knew she was special, and he felt an inexplicable pull toward her. He knew she carried scars from her past, but he was determined to help her heal and find happiness again.

"It's not just me," Brady said humbly. "It's her too. She's allowing herself to be open to the prospect of love and trust again, and that's a courageous thing to do after everything she's been through."

Juliet reached forward and placed a comforting hand on his shoulder. "Thank you, Brady," she said. "You're so good to Monet, and I can see how much you care about her."

Brady reached up and gently squeezed Juliet's hand before she rested back against the seat and closed her eyes.

Brady's gaze once again lingered on the woman beside him; a cascade of emotions swirled within his heart. The serenity on her face ignited a profound tenderness in him, and he felt an unyielding desire to safeguard her happiness. In that moment, he knew with unwavering certainty that he was falling in love.

As the Jeep navigated the familiar route back to the villa, Brady made a silent promise to himself that he would be there for her, to continue mending the wounds of the past and help her rediscover the beauty of trust. She was a precious gift, and he was determined to cherish her like a rare treasure.

*

The days following Monet's birthday were busy, as usual. The Grand Jewel was coming together magnificently but kept everyone hard at work. There was also Rosa and Maria's house; the weekday crew was making quick progress, and Juliet was working remotely from New York on the finishing touches that she, Monet, and Ashley had talked about. On top of it all, Bethany Hawk was requesting a revamp on the design of her master bedroom.

The weekend after Monet had surprised them all by showing up at the firm in Arizona as Ashley's new assistant, Brady and Cole had finalized plans for Bethany's luxury home. The project had been underway for a couple of months, so they hoped the revisions wouldn't bring about too many complications or delays.

Unfortunately, this meant that Brady and Cole needed to fly back to Phoenix to meet with Bethany and the contractor, which was why Brady and his friend found themselves comfortably settled in plush armchairs inside the airport lounge, staring out the window at rows of airplanes resting under the early evening sunset.

Although the trip wouldn't exceed a week, Brady couldn't help but feel a pang of sadness at the thought of being away from Monet. In the past few weeks, he had grown accustomed to seeing her every day, and ever since admitting to himself that he was falling in love with her, the idea of being separated from her for even just a few days unsettled him.

As he watched their airplane roll up to the gate, Brady could sense Cole's stare boring into the side of his head. "What?" he asked as he turned to his friend.

Cole wore a slight frown. "You seem like you're somewhere else. Everything okay?"

Brady inhaled and blew out his breath. "Yeah, just thinking about Monet," Brady said. "She's become such a part of my daily life. The thought of not seeing her for a few days…" He shrugged one shoulder. "Kind of has me a little… bummed, I guess."

Cole's eyes instantly lit up, and that mischievous smile appeared.

Brady sighed. *Here it comes.*

"A little bummed?" He chuckled. "Could it actually have happened? Has Brady Nash finally been bitten by the *love bug*?" He emphasized the words in a teasing tone.

Brady dropped his swinging head and let out his own chuckle before looking back at Cole, whose eyes were wide and who wore a far too satisfied expression.

Brady's pulse quickened. Was he really ready to admit it to his best friend?

"Yeah, man," Brady said, "I have."

Cole's teasing grin instantly curved wider into a more genuine smile, and his features relaxed. "Brady, that's great," he said. "Ash and I suspected it, but hearing you admit it... it's awesome."

Brady's racing heartbeat gradually slowed, and he felt the tension in his body loosen. "She's amazing, Cole," Brady admitted. "These past few weeks of working on the resort with her have been... incredible. I never thought I could have such strong feelings for someone."

Cole nodded. "I remember feeling the same way when I first met Ashley. After a few weeks of dating, I was a goner." He chuckled. "And it only kept getting better."

Brady's eyebrows raised. "Oh yeah. It keeps getting better with Monet," he said. "It may sound corny, but since she came back into my life, everything is better." He laughed softly. "She just brings happiness into my life."

Cole's smile never left his face. "Does Monet know how you feel?"

"On her birthday, I confessed I was falling for her."

"Ah." Cole tilted his head. "That's not quite the same thing."

Confusion flickered across Brady's face. "What do you mean?"

"That's a start, but women need to hear the words, my friend," Cole explained. "You need to tell her that you love her."

Brady inhaled deeply, contemplating Cole's advice. "Monet admitted that she's falling for me too," he said. "And I know you're right; I should tell her. It's just... I don't want to overwhelm or pressure her. She still carries insecurities from her past."

"I totally get your concerns," Cole said. "But trust me when I say that Monet admitting her feelings for you is only the tip of it for her as well. You both bring out the best in each other." He chuckled. "Ashley and I talk about it all the time. You say how happy Monet makes you, but Brady, you make Monet happy, too.

"We've all seen it. She rarely looks away from you when you're in the same room, and a simple glance from you makes her blush." He reached over and firmly grasped Brady's shoulder. "Take the chance, buddy. Tell her."

Brady nodded. He would do it; Brady would take the risk and tell Monet the true depths of his feelings for her. As soon as he returned from Phoenix, he was determined to find the perfect moment to confess his love to Monet.

Lost in his reflections, he was jolted back to the present when, somewhere in the distance, an angry voice abruptly interrupted his thoughts.

"Have you lost your mind?" the voice snapped.

Brady's gaze shifted towards a man standing a few feet away in the airport lounge.

"Listen to me. Leave it alone," the man commanded as he paced.

Suddenly, the man turned, and Brady's buoyant heart plummeted into his stomach with a resounding thud.

"Cole," Brady spoke firmly.

"Yeah?"

"That man over there." He nodded in the direction of where his eyes were locked. "He was with Wessler at Señor Frog's."

"Are you serious?" Cole said. "The lawyer?"

"Yep." Brady scanned the lounge. "I bet Wessler's around here somewhere."

"Oh boy." Cole released a deep breath. "Brady, take it easy."

"If you go through with this, I'm not bailing you out again!"

"He sounds pretty ticked off at someone," Cole said.

Brady's pulse was on fire as it raced through his veins. The mere thought of seeing John Wessler filled him with fury, and for both their sakes, he hoped their paths wouldn't cross. Brady wasn't sure if he could control his anger toward the creep.

"Good evening, passengers. We are now pre-boarding flight 505 to Phoenix at gate A-10. We invite those passengers with small children and any passengers requiring special assistance to begin boarding at this time."

"That's us." Cole stood and grabbed his carry-on. "Just in time."

Brady followed suit, slinging his workbag over his shoulder. He scanned the area one last time for Wessler, but as his attention returned to Wessler's lawyer, the man briefly locked eyes with Brady before doing a double take.

Brady held his gaze momentarily before breaking eye contact and turning to join Cole.

"Hey, wait!" the lawyer called out.

Cole and Brady stopped and turned back to the man who hurriedly approached them. Brady narrowed his eyes, and a knot formed in his belly as he watched the man draw nearer.

"You!" He pointed at Brady. "You're Monet Everly's boyfriend, right?"

Brady shot a quick glance at Cole, whose frown mirrored his own.

"What do you want?" Brady's tone was harsh and unfriendly.

"I need to talk to you." His jaw tensed. "Now."

Monet

Monet stood on the villa's back deck, gazing at the ocean. The late afternoon light cast a warm, amber glow on the sparkling water. A heavy sensation was settled in her chest; it had only been a couple of hours, and she was already missing Brady. She knew it was healthy to have time apart, but she'd grown used to the comfort his presence brought to her life.

Ashley was wrapping up a few things at the Grand Jewel. Later, the two friends had planned to order in and discuss the final touches for Rosa and Maria's house. Monet hoped it would provide the distraction she needed to keep her mind off missing Brady, but based on how things were going, it looked to be a long week.

Lost in a whirlwind of thoughts, Monet was jolted by a knock at the door. She made her way to the front of the villa and could see a delivery woman standing outside through the glass. The sight of the flowers in the woman's hands caused Monet's heart to leap, and a swarm of butterflies tickled her stomach over the possibility of them being for her.

"*Hola*," Monet greeted as she opened the door.

"*Buenas Tardes*," the young woman said. "I have a delivery for Monet Everly."

Monet grinned. "*Si*, that's me." She pointed to herself.

The woman smiled and handed the flowers to Monet. The vibrant colors and delicate fragrance filled the air as Monet brought them to her nose. "They're beautiful! *Muchas gracias*."

"You're welcome," she said in her thick Spanish accent. "Have a good evening, miss."

Monet returned the woman's smile and thanked her one last time before returning inside and closing the door. She immediately went to the kitchen in search of a vase when she spotted a card nestled among the petals.

Change of plans. I missed you too much so I'm staying in Cancun. Meet me at the Marina Azul slip #5 at 8:00. I've got a special surprise planned. xo Brady

Monet's heart skipped as she read Brady's words. He'd stayed for her! A momentary thought flittered through her mind, wondering what would happen with Bethany Hawk, but she quickly dismissed her concern when she realized Cole was probably soloing the meeting.

She grabbed her cell phone and dialed Ashley, but it went directly to voicemail. Leaving a quick message, Monet explained the change of plans and promised to text her later.

Clutching the beautiful flowers, Monet made her way to her bedroom.

"A sunset cruise!" she whispered to herself. Monet quickened her footsteps, breathless, as she imagined the magical evening that awaited her.

*

Monet stepped out of the taxi, her heart aflutter as she arrived at the Marina Azul harbor. The setting sun had disappeared, giving way to the enchanting night sky that sparkled with countless stars.

As she approached the waterfront, a mesmerizing display of lights greeted her, casting a gentle glow on the surrounding area. Her eyes widened as she took in the sight before her. The harbor was elegant and sophisticated, illuminated by the soft radiance of luxurious yachts that stood like sentinels along the water's edge. Monet was captivated by the stunning array of vessels that adorned the harbor. From opulent motor yachts to graceful sailing yachts, each one seemed to possess its own unique charm.

As she strolled along the harbor, the soft melodies of music reached her ears, drawing her toward the waterfront bars and restaurants. Monet couldn't help but smile, her heart brimming with anticipation for the enchanting evening that lay ahead.

She'd chosen to wear an elegant tangerine-colored dress that flowed with every step. Her choice of strappy sandals added to the ensemble's charm, perfectly complementing the vibrant hue of her dress. Monet had artfully styled her hair into a long side braid, allowing it to cascade gracefully over her shoulder. The braid added an extra layer of allure, enhancing her overall appearance with its elegant simplicity.

Once she neared the end of the dock, her eyes fixed upon the vessel that stood out among the sea of dimly lit boats. The yacht, bathed in a gentle glow of soft lights, emanated a romantic ambiance. The sight evoked a sudden mixture of emotions within her. A spark of thrill torched her veins as an uneasy knot tightened in her belly, but Monet dismissed any flicker of unease, attributing it to the unfamiliarity of being on a boat at night—an experience she had never encountered.

As Monet stepped onto the boat's deck, the warm lights accentuated the vessel's elegant features, revealing polished wooden finishes and shimmering chrome accents that sparkled in the night.

"Brady?" she called out. Her voice echoed through the silence, but there was no response. Monet's heart fluttered between anticipation and uncertainty as she cautiously took a few more steps onto the boat.

"Brady?" she called out again, her voice trembled ever so slightly.

A moment of doubt danced in her mind as Monet glanced around, her eyes scanning the surroundings. Had she mistakenly boarded the wrong yacht?

Monet's heartbeat began to quicken when a flickering light at the back of the boat caught her attention. Her pulse began to race as she made her way around the wide cabin; her steps were measured and cautious.

As she stepped onto the back deck of the boat, she came upon an enchanting table illuminated by the flickering glow of candlelight. At that moment, she believed she had stumbled upon the surprise Brady had meticulously orchestrated. But as Monet drew closer to the table, her heart jolted.

Monet's eyes widened as her breath hitched in her throat. The table was adorned with photographs of—her. Monet's hands trembled involuntarily as her fingertips grazed the edges of the images that captured *The Look* finalist photo shoot five years prior.

How did Brady get these? Monet's mind raced, her thoughts colliding in a whirlwind of bewilderment. Her gaze shifted, searching for answers—for an explanation—but instead, her ears were met with a chilling chuckle that cut through the air, shattering the fragile bubble of confusion that had surrounded her.

As Monet's gaze flickered toward the cabin, movement caught her attention. Time seemed to freeze as a figure emerged from the shadows. The air grew heavy with an eerie stillness as her eyes widened, and an uncontrollable shudder swept her body.

Before her, once again, stood John Wessler.

Fear clawed at her insides, sending icy tendrils coursing through her veins. Her breath stuck in her throat, suffocating her as panic threatened to consume her every fiber.

Wessler approached her slowly, a sinister smile playing on his lips.

"I thought we'd finish what we started all those years ago," he said with an icy tone. "Do you remember that, Monet? The night you snuck away and left me humiliated?"

Monet's throat tightened, and her breath caught in her chest. But suddenly, the ringing of her cell phone broke through the thick fog of shock. She quickly dug into her purse hanging from her shoulder and only had time to glance at the name, *Brady*, before Wessler lunged and slapped it from her hand, sending it skidding across the deck.

With every limb trembling, Monet fought to find her voice amidst the whirlwind of emotions. Fear gripped her, but a burning determination swelled within.

"What do you want from me?" she managed to utter.

"I already told you," Wessler sneered, taking a step closer. Monet instinctively stepped back. "We're going to pick up where we left off. Different location... different yacht." His wicked gaze locked onto hers. "Same intentions."

Monet's eyes bulged as nausea churned in her stomach. This man was deranged!

"That will never happen," she spat before she turned to run.

Wessler's laughter pierced the air, a chilling sound that echoed in Monet's ears as she felt his cold, clammy hand grab her arm.

"Oh, Monet," he clicked his tongue. "You may have escaped me once," he said, his voice dripping with menace, "but tonight, there's nowhere to run. No one to protect you. Tonight, you're mine."

Monet's heart pounded with brutal force; each beat a resounding testament to her fear. Her mind raced, desperately searching for a plan amidst the chaos. As Wessler tightened his grip, she twisted her arm, fighting against his hold.

"Settle down!" he hissed, grabbing her other arm and pulling Monet sickeningly close to his body. "Don't fight me." His breath was hot on her face and held the stench of alcohol.

Wessler spun her around, holding both of Monet's hands behind her back as he pushed her toward the cabin.

"Help me!" she screamed, but Wessler's hand quickly clamped over her mouth.

"I gave you the chance of a lifetime, and you made a fool out of me," he growled in her ear. "Nobody does that." He pushed her forward again.

No! A sudden fire ignited from the depths of Monet's soul. The strength she had gathered over the years surged, fueling her resolve. She refused to be a victim again.

Summoning her inner strength and drawing upon the healing she had undergone, Monet pushed past the fear as she remembered the unwavering support of Juliet, the love and protection of her brother Evan, and her parents' unconditional love. Above all, she thought of Brady—his belief in her worth, in her strength; he had shown her what true love was, and even though he hadn't spoken the words, she knew he loved her.

Monet planted her feet firmly on the boat's deck and struggled with all her might. Wessler dropped his hand from her mouth in an attempt to regain control over her.

"You may have broken me once, but you will never break me again!"

With adrenaline aiding her, Monet freed her hands and spun around.

Determined to escape, she pushed past him, but Wessler grabbed her arm again. Monet was not the weak girl he'd once made her believe she was. Her newfound confidence and self-worth surged within her, giving her the strength to fight back against her tormentor.

"Leave me alone!" she yelled, pounding her fists against his chest in a desperate attempt to break free.

"Not until I get what I came for!" he growled, his grip unyielding as he grabbed her by her long braid.

Monet screamed, but his actions only fueled her determination. Amidst the agony, she glanced behind Wessler and realized they were near the side of the yacht. Gathering every ounce of physical strength she had left, Monet mustered one final surge of power, giving a forceful shove to Wessler's chest. The unexpected movement sent him tumbling over the side.

Wessler screeched before an enormous splash rang out. Monet, breathless and stunned, grabbed the railing and looked down into the dark ocean water in time to see Wessler resurface. Their eyes locked for a split second as he drew in air.

He coughed, then spluttered, "This isn't over!"

Monet paid no heed to his threat; she turned and fled.

Her footsteps pounded against the dock in a desperate escape from the nightmare she had endured. As Monet raced forward, she caught sight of a figure emerging from the shadows, sprinting towards her. Hope flared, and her heart leapt to a near-painful height when she recognized the familiar silhouette—*Brady!*

Tears welled behind Monet's eyelids as relief washed away some of her lingering fear. She pushed herself harder, her legs carrying her with newfound strength, desperate to reach him. As the gap between them closed, Monet fixated on Brady's face; his features were a tapestry of emotions— the lines of his brow etched with anger, his eyes ablaze with determination, and yet beneath the storm of intensity, worry radiated from his gaze.

"Monet!"

In the next instant, they collided, their bodies embracing as if seeking refuge in one another's arms. Monet felt the strength of his embrace enveloping her, anchoring her to the present and grounding her in a love that felt tangible and real. Tears spilled from her eyes, releasing the pent-up emotions she had carried, mingling with the remnants of fear that still clung to her.

Brady held her away from him. "Did he hurt you?" He scanned her from head to toe.

Monet shook her head. "Nothing permanent."

Brady's eyes bulged, and his face turned red. "What did he do?" His words were tight.

"No, he didn't hurt me," she said, stuttering. "He tried to, but... I fought back."

Brady's face tightened, and his chest rose and fell harshly. "Where is he?"

"I..." she glanced over her shoulder down the dock, "pushed him over the side of the boat."

Brady's head jerked back, and his eyes popped again. "What?"

The memory of it all was too much. Monet's body tensed, and her stomach began to twist. "I—" Monet threw herself into Brady's arms again and cried.

"Shh," Brady soothed as he tightened his arms around her. "I'm sorry."

Monet shook her head. She didn't want him to feel sorry; she loved that he was so protective of her. She just needed to be held by him, by the man she loved.

Monet felt Brady's breathing slow, and her body warmed at the feel of his lips on her head. "You're safe now," he whispered.

"Brady! Monet!" Monet turned to see Cole waving them over to the beach where he stood. "Hamlin's got him!"

The calm that had begun to settle over Monet since being in Brady's arms evaporated, and her body tensed. "Hamlin?"

"Come on. You don't need to see him; I'll get you home and explain," Brady said.

Enough was enough, Monet thought to herself. She'd stood up to him and fought for herself, but it wasn't over yet; she still had something to say.

"Not yet," Monet said as she stepped out of Brady's embrace. "I need to talk to him."

"Monet." Brady's head tipped, and his worried brow appeared.

"It's okay. I need to do this," she said, taking hold of his hand. "I want him to know he no longer has control over me."

Brady exhaled and tightened his fingers around hers. "Are you sure?"

She gave a firm nod before they turned and made their way toward Cole.

Monet's body was still trembling from the adrenaline rush of her daring escape from Wessler's clutches. However, the scene became even more surreal as Hamlin emerged from the darkness, dragging a coughing and drenched Wessler out of the ocean. Hamlin's face contorted with anger and disappointment, mirroring the depth of his friend's reprehensible actions.

"You fool!" Hamlin shouted, his sharp tone slicing through the night. "Do you have any idea what you've done?"

Wessler coughed, attempting to regain his composure. He glanced at Monet; his small eyes smoldered with an insidious spark. Finally, he sneered, "You think you've won, don't you?"

Monet stepped forward, her voice firm and resolute. "I am going to do everything I can to ensure you never hurt another woman again." She held her head high.

Hamlin's eyes widened, his gaze shifting between Monet and his disheveled friend. "And she will win this time because she will have me representing her."

Wessler laughed, a harsh, cruel sound. "You? Defending her? After everything?"

Hamlin puffed in disgust. "Yes, because what you've done is indefensible!"

Monet's attention shifted quickly to Hamlin, whose face fell. "I am so sorry," he said.

Monet nodded. Her feelings were conflicted where Robert Hamlin was concerned.

After all, he'd been the one who fought against Monet that first year. But he seemed genuinely disgusted by Wessler, so maybe he would be an ally now. Monet hoped so.

With a determined push, Hamlin propelled Wessler toward two approaching security officers. "Get moving."

Wessler begrudgingly complied, as Hamlin's grip, firm on one arm, and Cole's on the other, guided him up the beach into the hands of one of the officers.

The other approached Monet. "Miss Everly," the officer said. "My name is Officer Morales. Are you hurt?"

Monet shook her head. "No, sir."

"I'll need to take a statement from you if you're feeling up to it," he said. "Or we can take it later."

"It's okay," she said. "I can give you my statement now."

*

After Monet provided her statement, Hamlin and Cole followed the officers as they escorted Wessler toward a waiting vehicle. The entire time, Monet could hear Wessler's desperate pleas, urging his friend to reconsider. For his part, Hamlin remained resolute, steadfastly reiterating his commitment to represent her.

Monet watched Wessler's departure with a mix of relief and also lingering unease.

Was it really over now?

Just as that nagging insecurity started to build in her mind, Brady wrapped his arms around her and pulled her into his arms, where she willingly went.

Monet gazed at him. "How did you know where to find me?"

"Hamlin told us," Brady said.

Monet drew back as her eyebrows furrowed. Since Brady had given his statement separately, this was the first time she had heard it.

Brady explained how they had run into Robert Hamlin at the airport, and he'd let Brady and Cole in on Wessler's plan to lure Monet to the yacht.

"But," Brady said as he pulled her close again. "You didn't need me this time." He smiled softly and ran his fingers down the side of her face. "You are the bravest woman I've ever met."

Exhilarating tingles spread from where his fingers touched her cheek, down her arm, and through her body. "I will always need you," she said softly.

"I love you, Monet," Brady whispered, his voice filled with a depth of emotion that resonated through the night air. "So much."

A new set of tears began to flow, a mixture of release and overwhelming happiness. Despite the traumatic encounter Monet had just endured, her heart soared.

Monet's voice trembled. "I love you too, Brady," she managed to say through her emotions. "A part of me fell for that hot bellhop all those years ago, and I don't think I ever got over it."

A soft chuckle, filled with a warmth that mirrored his love for her, escaped Brady's lips. "Well, a part of me fell for that humble hottie all those years ago, and I *know* I never got over it."

Monet's smile radiated joy, and her heart fluttered like a kaleidoscope of butterflies taking flight in her belly. She felt safe and loved, and no matter what life had in store for her, Monet would be okay.

"Then kiss me," she whispered, her eyes fixating on his tempting lips, a magnetic pull drawing her closer.

Brady's mouth curved into a playful yet irresistible grin. "I thought you'd never ask." With a tender confidence, he closed the remaining distance between them, his lips meeting hers in a kiss that spoke of love and passion.

Monet's heart brimmed with a sense of contentment and wonder. Cancun had gifted her more than she had ever imagined—an unwavering love, a second chance at happiness, and the affirmation that even amid obstacles and hardships, dreams could indeed come true.

FIVE MONTHS LATER

Monet stood on the sidelines, captivated by the tender exchange between Juliet and Josh. The warm, mellow flicker of light cast a romantic glow on their faces as they playfully bantered.

The wedding cake, a masterpiece in its own right, stood tall and proud on a gilded table. Its ivory tiers were flawlessly adorned with delicate white fondant flowers, each petal painstakingly crafted by a skilled pastry chef. Ribbons of luscious buttercream frosting cascaded down the sides, creating an enticing texture that begged to be tasted.

As Josh held the knife, the room buzzed with anticipation. The scent of the freshly cut cake wafted through the air, a tantalizing blend of vanilla and almond. Juliet's eyes sparkled with excitement and a hint of trepidation, knowing the mischievous nature of her new husband all too well.

"Don't even think about it!" Juliet playfully threatened, her smile as radiant as the Mexican sun. Her white dress, adorned with embroidered flowers, hugged her figure gracefully, accentuating her every move.

With a mischievous twinkle in his eyes, Josh held up a small slice of the cake, teasingly inching it closer to Juliet's lips. Her laughter bubbled up, filling the courtyard with a melody of joy. Monet couldn't help but be swept away by the infectious sound, her heart soaring at the sight of her best friend so deeply in love.

"I am not kidding!" Juliet's playful protest echoed through the warm evening air. "We talked about this, and you promised!"

Josh's rich, melodic laughter intertwined with the sound of the Spanish guitar. "Darlin'," he chuckled, his voice laced with affection. "Do you trust me?"

Juliet's gaze softened, her eyes locking with Josh's. Monet felt the weight of their love in that single look, as if the entire world had faded away, leaving only the two of them.

"Of course, I trust you," Juliet whispered, her voice carrying a depth of emotion that made Monet's heart swell.

"Then open up, sweetheart," Josh taunted.

A radiant smile illuminated Juliet's face as she obediently parted her lips, allowing Josh to place the morsel of cake between them. The enchanted guests erupted in cheers and applause.

The wedding had turned out more beautiful than Monet had ever imagined. Every detail she had meticulously planned and coordinated had fallen into place seamlessly, and a sense of satisfaction washed over her.

The inner courtyard of the Grand Jewel had been transformed into a breathtaking space that evoked the essence of a Mexican-inspired celebration. The whitewashed walls were adorned with delicate lace and vibrant bougainvillea vines, transporting guests to a picturesque villa. The courtyard was aglow with the warm, romantic ambiance of string lights and lanterns, casting enchanting shadows that danced upon the stone floor.

The tables, covered in crisp white linens, were elegantly set with gold-rimmed plates and sparkling crystal glassware. Delicate lace runners adorned each table, adding a touch of intricate elegance. At the center of each table, exquisite floral arrangements burst forth from hand-painted ceramic vases, showcasing an array of vibrant blooms that mirrored the natural beauty of the Mexican landscape.

A contented smile graced Monet's lips as she watched Juliet's mother, Camilla, who had been notoriously hard to please throughout the wedding planning process. Yet, at that moment, even Camilla seemed enchanted.

Monet's gaze floated around the courtyard, her heart filled with warmth as she took in the sight of friends and family gathered to celebrate the joyous occasion.

Juliet, in her usual thoughtful manner, had surprised Monet by flying in her parents, Evan, and Lily, for the wedding. The gesture had touched Monet deeply, and she couldn't help but marvel at the incredible bond she shared with Juliet. It was a friendship that felt like magic, as if some mystical force had brought them together.

Lily's presence had brought a bittersweet mix of emotions. While their friendship had changed since their high school days, Monet felt a glimmer of hope that they were on the path to rebuilding what they had lost. It seemed to Monet that Lily had finally forgiven herself for persuading Monet into entering the contest that brought John Wessler into her life. Evan had been the one to remind Lily that the same contest had also brought Brady into Monet's life, and for that reason alone, Monet would go through it all again; well, most of it, anyway.

As her mind dwelled on the past, Monet let out her one-hundredth sigh of relief that her tumultuous journey involving John Wessler had finally come to an end. Along with obtaining a permanent restraining order to keep him away from Monet, Wessler had also received a sentence of probation, with the condition that he regularly undergo therapy for his mental health. Some individuals in Monet's inner circle felt that the punishment was too lenient, but for Monet, it was at least something to bring her a sense of closure.

Monet shifted her thoughts back to the present, turning her attention to Juliet's brother, Sawyer, and his wife, Violet, who stood in a corner of the courtyard.

The love between them was palpable, as strong and passionate as the day they had exchanged vows a year and a half prior. A smile graced Monet's lips as she watched Sawyer's tender touch on Violet's belly, a silent gesture of their shared secret. Juliet confided in Monet that Violet and Sawyer were expecting their first child, a precious secret waiting to be unveiled once the excitement of the wedding had passed.

Lost in her thoughts, Monet's gaze landed on a tall, enigmatic figure leaning against the courtyard wall. Beau Nash, Brady's brother, exuded an aura of brooding intensity that both intrigued and intimidated her. She'd immediately understood Ashley's opinion of the man. His piercing blue eyes seemed to smolder with irritation, casting an air of mystery around him.

Monet had caught glimpses of Beau's protective side, particularly when Brady was present, and she couldn't help but sense a flicker of compassion beneath his rugged exterior. For that reason, she had decided to give him the benefit of the doubt, hoping she could someday break through his walls and understand the man behind the aloof facade.

With quiet resolve, Monet silently vowed to herself that she would find a way to bridge the gap between her and Beau Nash, uncovering the layers of complexity hidden within him. She believed that deep down, there was a story yearning to be told and a pain longing to be healed.

Suddenly, Monet's breath hitched, and her heart leapt at the familiar spice-infused scent that filled the air. An instant later, strong arms wrapped around her waist from behind, pulling her close to his body.

"Hey." Monet's voice was barely audible as she leaned into his embrace.

"You've truly outdone yourself," Brady whispered. "The night has been nothing short of magical."

A soft smile curved Monet's lips, and her heart swelled with warmth.

"Well, the venue is half the charm," she said, turning her head slightly to meet his gaze. "You might have had a little something to do with that."

Brady grinned as he leaned in and placed a tender kiss on the tip of her nose.

"Can I steal you away yet?" he asked in the seductive tone she'd come to crave.

Monet couldn't help but giggle. "Not quite yet, but soon, I promise."

A soft groan escaped Brady's lips, vibrating against her ear. "Okay," he said. "Carry on with your maid of honor duties, but after that, I get you all to myself."

With a mischievous glint in her eyes, Monet spun around so that their bodies were now face to face. She wrapped her arms around Brady's neck, drawing him closer.

"Deal," she whispered.

Brady pressed a tender kiss to her lips, a fleeting taste of the passion that always awaited them.

*

The vibrant colors of the Mexican sunset painted the sky as the wedding reception began to wind down. Monet watched as Juliet and Josh swirled on the dance floor, their smiles radiating pure happiness.

As the music floated through the air, Monet's attention was diverted by the sight of Ashley approaching her, a knowing smile on her lips. During the time they had spent together, working tirelessly to bring the Grand Jewel to life, Ashley had become a dear friend to Monet.

"Hey," Monet greeted. "What's in the bag?" She gestured to the large pool bag Ashley held.

"There's been a slight change of plans," Ashley whispered as she glanced around. "Brady has a surprise for you, and you'll need this."

A nervous excitement built inside Monet, her breath catching slightly as she peeked inside the bag and quickly looked back at Ashley, who winked.

"Where is he?" Monet asked. The fluttering in her chest now tickled her belly.

Ashley grinned and pointed in the direction of the resort's newly completed infinity pool. "Go find out for yourself."

Without hesitation, Monet said goodnight to the newlyweds and quickly made her way through the courtyard, unable to keep the silly smile from her lips as her pulse quickened.

Once outside, Monet ducked into a nearby cabana and quickly changed from her vibrantly colored maid of honor gown into the sleek black swimming suit Ashley had smuggled in for her. As she emerged from the cabana, a gentle breeze kissed her cheeks as she made her way around the dimly lit pathway.

Monet rounded the last corner leading her to the infinity pool and was instantly grateful for the cover of night to hide the way her eyes widened and her jaw dropped. Standing next to the shimmering pool was Brady.

Over the past six months, Monet had grown used to seeing him in a swimming suit, yet his striking form never ceased to take her breath away.

Dressed casually yet stylishly, he wore tailored swim trunks, emphasizing his sculpted thighs and powerful calves. A subtle sheen of water droplets glistened on his skin, a testament to his recent dip in the pool.

Monet swallowed and gave a slight shake of her head as she made her way toward him. The closer she got, the more she could see his eyes gleaming with a secret and a smile tugging at the corners of his lips.

Monet's heart gave a little leap as she approached him, her eyes never leaving his face.

"Finally," Brady said as he took a step closer. "Alone at last."

Brady reached for her dress that she had folded over one arm and, without another word, took it from her and laid it gently on a nearby lounge chair. Monet followed suit and dropped the bag Ashley had given her next to the dress.

Brady held his hand out to her, and she took hold without hesitation, feeling the warmth and strength of his touch. Brady guided her to the pool's edge, and together, they stepped into the shimmering water.

The sensation of weightlessness enveloped Monet as they swam side by side, their laughter and joy mingling with the gentle sounds of the evening. The infinity pool stretched out before them, appearing to merge with the horizon—a symbol, in Monet's mind, of infinite possibilities and boundless love.

"I can't believe you remembered," Monet whispered as Brady gathered her effortlessly in his arms. "My first day here, I told you I'd never swum in an infinity pool before."

"But you've always wanted to," Brady finished for her.

Monet nodded as Brady gently swirled them around in the water.

"I remember every wish you've ever told me," he whispered. "And I'm going to spend my life making each one of them come true."

A rapid flutter began deep within her chest, and every nerve tingled over his words.

"Your *whole* life?" Her voice was breathy as she smiled playfully.

One side of Brady's mouth twitched, but he didn't answer. Instead, as their bodies gently drifted around the pool, Brady's hand slipped beneath the water, his fingers toying with something in his pocket.

Monet's hand went to her parted lips, and her heart quickened almost painfully as Brady withdrew his hand. There, glistening in the moonlight, was a breathtaking pink and platinum engagement ring.

"Monet," Brady said. "You have enchanted me from the first moment I saw you standing in the lobby of the White Rainbow Hotel five years ago. You blew me away with your bravery and strength then, and you have blown me away with the same strength and bravery now. Your kindness and compassion, talents, and the way you love to immerse yourself in everything around you have transformed my life. You possess a beauty that transcends appearances, and you have captured my entire heart. I cannot imagine a single moment without you by my side."

The tears that welled in her eyes cascaded down Monet's cheeks, and she clutched her hands to her chest, feeling her heart swell with so much love she thought it might burst. At that moment, Monet knew that Brady was her forever, the missing piece she had been searching for.

"Will you be mine?" he asked.

"Yes," Monet's voice trembled, and she nodded. "Forever."

The world around them seemed to fade as Brady slipped the ring onto Monet's finger.

"I love you," Brady said as he took Monet's face in his hands.

"I love you," she breathed an instant before Brady pulled her lips to his. Brady's taste, his scent, and the warmth and power of his body flooded her senses. Monet basked in the knowledge that Brady was hers, and she was his.

In that magical moment, Monet knew her journey had led her to the grandest jewel of all—Brady's love. And together, they would embark on a lifetime of love, passion, and memories to be woven and cherished forever.

From The Author

Much like my first book, *New York In Love*, *Sun, Sand, and Second Chances* was a joy for me to write because it was inspired by an actual event in my life. It seems like a lifetime ago—probably because it was—that I was selected as the winner of a modeling contest hosted by an agency in Costa Mesa, California. The prologue, set in Costa Mesa, recounts factual events that I experienced, except for the addition of a smartphone, which wasn't around in the early '90s. After my dinner with the kind and charming bellhop that night, I returned home with no expectation of ever seeing him again. Yet, life had other plans, and I bumped into him two years later. Although the story of Monet and Brady unfolds much differently than ours did, the whole experience taught me a lot about myself and left me with an incredible story to tell.

If you enjoyed the story, please help spread the word and rate or review it on Amazon and Goodreads.

Thank you!